Valdez turned to face
the Wolf Girl of the

She stood as near
fondly imagined he h
would never do to l
than stand, stooped,

As she stood and h
she caught sight of a man who towered over the others
and had apparently worked his way down the side of
the tent until he now stood near the front. His height
and breadth blocked the view of those behind, who
protested vigorously that they were missing the climax.
It was an impression she gleaned, not details—of size,
of dark hair and light eyes, unusual in a largely Mexican
and Indian population, of the tanned skin of a
frontiersman.

Those strange eyes held hers for a moment, the eyes
of a man who was hard and ruthless. There was no
sympathy in them, but neither was there condemnation—nor vicarious lust. She found herself hypnotised
by those eyes, the first she had seen since her capture
that held no hint of the accustomed salaciousness. The
expression that flitted briefly across his face was one of
disgust, yet she sensed that that disgust was not directed
at her but at his fellow spectators, and she was oddly
comforted by that knowledge . . .

Janet Edmonds was born in Portsmouth and educated at Portsmouth High School. She now lives in the Cotswolds where she taught English and History in a large comprehensive school before deciding that writing was more fun. A breeder, exhibitor and judge of dogs, her house is run for the benefit of the Alaskan Malamutes and German Spitz that are her speciality. She has one son and three cats and avoids any form of domestic activity if she possibly can.

Janet Edmonds has written three other Masquerade Historical Romances, *The Polish Wolf*, *The Happenstance Witch* and *Count Sergei's Pride*.

WOLF GIRL

BY
JANET EDMONDS

MILLS & BOON LIMITED
15-16 BROOK'S MEWS
LONDON W1A 1DR

First published in Great Britain 1987
by Mills & Boon Limited

© Janet Edmonds 1987

Australian copyright 1987
Philippine copyright 1987

ISBN 0 263 75787 0

Set in Monotype Times 10 on 10 pt.
04-0787-81607

Typeset in Great Britain by
Associated Publishing Services
Printed and bound in Great Britain by
Cox & Wyman Ltd, Reading

HISTORICAL NOTE

LEGENDS of children brought up by wolves have occurred throughout history and in most countries where wolves are found. There is a strong tradition in Texas of a girl who was brought up by wolves and when, at the age of about eleven, she was discovered and removed from them, her wolf 'family' rescued her. The last known sighting of her was about six years later when she was seen bathing in the Rio Grande.

I have not been able to discover whether there is any evidence other than an oral tradition to support this particular story, so I have had no qualms about moving the last sighting and subsequent imaginary events a few hundred miles up the Rio Grande into the neighbouring and much more interesting Territory of New Mexico. I have based descriptions of her behaviour immediately after her capture on the well-documented twentieth-century evidence relating to two sisters in India who were brought up by wolves and who, sadly, did not long survive their later 'rescue'.

New Mexico is a vast and beautiful land made the more fascinating by the interplay of three cultures—Indian, Mexican and Anglo—which have not always been mutually compatible.

All the places mentioned exist. Cerrillos was once considered as a possible State capital. In the 1800s it boasted twenty-one saloons and four hotels. Now it is a ghost town on the so-called Turquoise Trail, just beginning to come back to life with two antique shops, a general store and a 'petting zoo'. In the 1850s Albuquerque had a population of only 1,700. Now it is the largest city in the state. Santa Fe was the capital of New Mexico under the Spanish conquistadors and is the State capital still. All these towns developed round a central plaza, or square, and all buildings were made of adobe: sun-dried bricks made of mud and straw, a form of construction necessitating very thick walls, so that old adobe houses are cool inside no matter what the outside temperature.

The larger houses were built round a quadrangle called a *patio* or a *placita* (small plaza) in the largest ones. The arrangement ensured some shade throughout the day and enabled the house to be easily fortified. The Vigils' house and store is based on the historic Huning house and store in Los Lunas, south of Albuquerque, and, while the convent is entirely fictitious—as is, to the best of my knowledge, the order it houses (I took the name from the Sangre de Cristo Mountains near Taos)— it is physically based on the fascinating Martinez house built in 1804 near Taos, which is now open to the public. The Governor's palace—the oldest fortified building in the USA—is open to the public, and the Indians still sell their craftware under the arcade. The cave dwellings and the ruined pueblos beneath them are part of Bandelier National Park, and the inhabited one is based on Taos pueblo in the north of the state.

With the possible exception of Tezzie, all the characters are fictitious and I tender my apologies to the ghosts of the ladies of Cerrillos, who were almost certainly predominantly Mexican and who therefore would have taken a more pragmatic view of their husbands' little weaknesses!

My thanks to all those New Mexicans, Indian, Mexican and Anglo, who showed me their houses, explained their traditions and patiently answered my questions, but particularly to Jeri Lea Hooks, who enabled me to see everything in this book and quite a lot more besides.

Janet Edmonds

CHAPTER ONE

Two MEN drew rein on a bluff overlooking a bend of
the Rio Grande. Below them the old Indian trail clawed
its narrow way between the juniper bushes, hugging the
line of the river as closely as the sandstone rocks
permitted. A sure-footed horse could manage the trail
without difficulty, but its restricted confines allowed no
room to manoeuvre—and these riders were taking no
chances. New Mexico had been a Territory of the
United States for two years now, but there was still a
festering resentment among some of the Mexican citizens
whose ancestors had come to this northern outpost of
New Spain two hundred years earlier, and who saw no
reason to welcome the Yanqui newcomers.

Not that these two men were likely to be welcomed
by the more respectable of their own sort. In a land
where water was more precious than gold, no one
condemned a traveller for being unwashed and unshaven,
but these men belonged to a ruthless breed instantly
recognisable to those who hacked out a tenuous living
in the forests and deserts of the frontier. Always on the
move, keeping ahead of any civilising institutions, they
kept alive in part by hunting and trapping, but found
an easier living plundering outlying homesteads,
murdering isolated miners—for these hills were rich in
gold, silver and turquoise—and waylaying legitimate
travellers who were unwise enough to journey alone.
The Territory was not yet sufficiently organised to track
this kind down and bring them to justice, and when
they figured that that day was close, they would move
out of New Mexico as they had already moved out of
Texas, and on into Arizona or Utah.

'I don't see nothing moving,' one of them said tersely, shading his eyes with his hand and staring down at the river.

'By that outcrop there. Same colour as the rocks, almost.'

Both men studied the river with the far-seeing keen eyesight of the professional hunter.

'Got it! What is it, for God's sake?'

The figure below them crouched, bear-like, in the water, but it was too small for a bear. From time to time it stopped as if scenting the wind, like a coyote, but it was too big for a coyote. It seemed to be splashing the water.

'What's it doing? Fishing?'

'Dunno. Could be. Bears catch fish with their paws.'

'They don't splash, though. Know what? I reckon it's bathing.'

They stared in silence.

'Know what I reckon?' the first one said at last, and his friend shook his head. 'I reckon it's human.'

His companion went on watching, and finally nodded agreement. 'Only thing it can be, and yet . . . It doesn't move right, somehow. Has to be Indian, I reckon.'

'Not likely for one Tesuque to leave himself open to attack.' The first man paused and studied the hills opposite. 'No sign of anyone else.'

His friend was still studying the figure in the river. 'It's no Indian! Look at that hair.'

The first man looked and nodded. 'That hair's never black. Must be Anglo.' They continued their scrutiny in silence, and then a grin stretched slowly across the first man's face and he laid a scarred and grimy hand on his companion's sleeve. 'I'll tell you something else, Mick, my friend. That there's a woman!'

Mick narrowed his eyes and kept staring. 'What would an Anglo woman be doing in a place like this? And why does she walk like that? It ain't normal.'

'I don't know.' The first man began quietly backing his horse away from the edge of the bluff. 'Get back,

Mick. If she looks up and back, she'll see us. At least we're upwind of her.'

When they judged their horses to be out of sight from the river, the men dismounted and, after fastening the reins to a handy juniper, crept forward until they could lie unsilhouetted and try to assess what they were seeing.

'Remember that story we heard in El Paso?' the first one said at last.

His friend nodded. 'El Paso's a long way off, though.'

'But it's on the Rio Grande. Safest way to move would be upstream, avoiding the settlements but staying near water.'

'Thought you didn't believe that yarn?'

'I didn't, not entirely, but this makes you think. It's the way she moves—that's what clinches it.'

'What are we going to do, Red? She won't stay there all day.'

Red was already wriggling backwards towards the horses. 'We catch her first,' he said. 'Then we decide what to do with her.'

They remounted and then retraced their path for a few yards until they came to a narrow, steep *arroyo* that led straight down to the river. They turned their horses into the stream-bed, and gave them a loose rein to find their own way down the precipitous path.

No horse, however sure-footed, can descend a steep incline without dislodging fragments of rock and sand, and it was the faint sound of these that caught the bather's ear. She hesitated and turned, sniffing the air like a scenthound. It told her nothing. She glanced up for other signs of intruders, but there was only a red-tailed hawk cruising on the thermals, searching for lizards. Whatever had caused the noise had not disturbed that hunter. Nevertheless, she had heard something, and she had no intention of staying here long enough to find out what it was. She must make for the narrow trail and vanish among the rocks. If it proved dangerous, she would be safely hidden. If not—well, she had spent too long in the river as it was, and needed to be on her way.

She proceeded among the rocks at the river's edge cautiously enough to eliminate any splashing, and was hauling herself up on to the bank when she heard the noise again, but closer. Looking round, she was horrified to see two horsemen appear, momentarily checking their horses for fear they should overshoot into the river. Whatever happened, they must not catch sight of her! She slipped, crouching, in among the junipers and ran swiftly and silently between their dark green shapes, almost invisible unless a watcher had known where to look.

These watchers did, and had the added advantage of being mounted and therefore able to look down over the low scrubby bushes. The crouching, swiftly moving, figure which blended so well with the ochreous coral of the sandstone was not so well camouflaged while it moved. The two men kept to the trail but their eyes were fixed to the point above and ahead, waiting for the moment when their prey either broke cover or went to ground among an outcrop of rocks.

The girl dared not move uphill to find refuge because the incline would make her moving shape easier for the riders below to spot and she could achieve nothing by breaking on to the trail: they would assuredly see her then, and she could not outrun a horse. She must lie low somewhere here. She glanced quickly around. There were plenty of rocks, but none large enough to hide behind. There was only one alternative. If she lay prostrate against the sand and rocks between the junipers, she should attract no more notice than any other irregular hump in the ground. Unaware that the two riders had seen her long since and were not just idly passing along the trail below, the girl flattened herself into the sand and waited for the hooves to pass by beneath her.

They did not do so. Her keen ears, their hearing sharpened by necessity, caught the moment when they split, one horse carrying on along the trail, the other turning up the incline at an angle that must bring it dangerously close. Her instinct was to flee once more, but if she did so, she could not fail to be spotted. No, hard though it was, she must stay where she was and trust to chance that he would pass by and not select the space between these particular junipers for his passage.

So intent was she on reading the vibrations from the horse that had first left the trail that she missed entirely the fact that the other rider, having passed by below her, was now approaching from the front. As soon as he was downwind of her she had caught the scent, but she had failed to notice its gradual strengthening.

She knew she was trapped when her eyes, the only part of her body she dared move, saw the hooves stationary before her. A quick glance behind told her the other rider was there. Only one choice remained. She sprang to her feet and ran in that strange crouching posture up the sloping hillside, scrambling to reach rocks that a horse could not tackle.

She failed. A rope sang through the air and caught her ankle, flinging her to the ground before dragging her back towards the horses. Her naked body slid easily through the sand. Easily—but painfully, for the sand was abrasive and stones and small rocks lay hidden in it. She was eventually brought up short when her body lodged against an intervening juniper.

Red Carlisle wound the lariat end round the saddle-horn and dismounted. He stared down, grinning, at the prostrate body before him and then, grabbing one of its arms, flipped it over on its back. He whistled.

'Look what we've caught ourselves, Mick,' he whispered, amazement at their unexpected good fortune subduing his voice.

His partner joined him, and his eyes widened. They had known the figure in the river was female; they had guessed it was neither Mexican nor Indian; they had not bargained for its being young and shapely! It was impossible to tell if the girl was beautiful: her face was now so covered in dirt and sand that her features were almost indistinguishable, but that was not what took their attention. Her body was another matter.

That, too, was grimed with sand, and blood was now beginning to ooze from the superficial cuts and scratches inflicted a few moments before at the rope's end. But no amount of dirt could disguise the girl's shape. She could have been no more than seventeen or eighteen. Her breasts rose round and firm, their nipples now hardening with fear, from a slender body that led her eyes down to the unconsciously inviting swell of her hips, an invitation accentuated by the fact that, one ankle being held firm by the lariat, her legs were necessarily splayed as if their owner sought but one thing, an impression enhanced by her breathless panting.

The second man whistled, an echo of the first. 'Ain't she something!' he breathed.

'Maybe that tale we heard was true, after all,' said Red. 'She's about the right age.'

Mick nodded. 'There was that old man in the saloon, remember? He said as how history was full of children brought up by wolves, so it wouldn't do to scoff too much. Wonder if we can find out? Ask her.'

His partner looked at him scornfully. 'Which language do you reckon wolves will have taught her? English? Spanish? Or maybe Tiwa or Keres?'

The other man looked disappointed. 'Reckon you're right. I guess we'll never know for sure!'

Red looked back down at the girl before them, his eyes raking her naked body. 'There's a lot to be said for a woman who can't speak!' he said. 'Let's get her to somewhere more sheltered. Then we can set about teaching her the ways of her own kind.'

He bent down then, intending to haul her to her feet, but as his fingers closed round her wrist, the girl sank her teeth into his hand until she drew blood. The man leapt back, cursing, and wound his bandana round the injured hand, tying it with his teeth.

His partner grinned. 'Let's hope she's not rabid!' he said.

'Don't stand there grinning like a death's-head!' Red snarled. 'Give me your bandana and hold her still. I'll be damned if she's biting again!'

Mick dutifully removed his neckerchief and handed it over silently. Then, while Mick held her arms down, the other man gagged her with the sweat-and dust-impregnated bandana. When the girl had been efficiently gagged, Red took the lariat from his partner's saddle and between them they secured her hands behind her. Even with two of them, this was no easy task as she writhed and struggled, fear giving her an almost super-human strength; but she had an impossible task and, though she left them panting for breath, the outcome was inevitable.

'Right,' Mick said at last as they stood up. 'Where to?'

'Nowhere,' Red replied savagely, nursing his bandaged hand. 'Not yet, at any rate. No woman bites me and gets away with it!' He put out a boot and kicked the girl over on to her back again.

The girl stared up, fear dilating her pupils. She understood nothing of what the man said except the tone, and that was sufficient to tell her they meant her no good. Her bound wrists bit into the small of her back and, with one ankle still secured, she was helpless. If death was to come, she hoped it would be swift.

The man who had gagged her unbuckled his gun-belt and threw it to one side. Then he unfastened the leather chaps that protected his trousers from the acacias and mesquites of the desert, and they followed the belt. He stepped over the rope holding her ankle and stood between her legs. There was that in his face, in the way his gaze slowly travelled from her eyes to her breasts and on down in speculative anticipation, which told her something of his intent, and she swiftly brought up her only remaining weapon—her free leg.

She was not swift enough, for he anticipated her, and

caught the ankle before she could slam her foot home.

'Hold it!' he commanded without removing his eyes from her body. The other man wrenched the leg to one side and held it down hard.

There was no scream. The gag saw to that. It was the girl's eyes and the sudden rigidity of the body she no longer commanded that told the men how intense was the pain she experienced, and both took a sadistic satisfaction in the knowledge. She felt as if a spear had pierced her vitals, and wondered that with so much thrusting agony, she should still live. Death should be swift, her mind cried.

When the second man took her, she was unconscious.

CHAPTER TWO

IMPORTANT A TOWN as Cerrillos was, the circus came there rarely. It was welcomed by young and old alike for its entertainment, for the dash of barbaric, glittering splendour it brought to lives spent wresting a living from the desert and the mines, and for the news that came with it from town and territories that were just names to most of the population.

There was the circus itself, all colour and spangles and thrills, with exotic animals—this year there was a real elephant!—and oriental tumblers who, it had to be admitted, looked marginally less oriental if one happened to meet them in their everyday clothes. Then there were the side-shows.

It could not be denied that there was a frisson of delighted revulsion to be had from observing such unnatural occurrences as a bearded woman, a two-headed calf or a real live cannibal. (Could those possibly be human bones he was gnawing?) Sometimes the side-shows were rather disappointing. The Fattest Man in the World, for instance, was certainly very fat, but several Cerrillos citizens expressed the view that Onofre Armijo, over in Trujillo, was fatter, and *he* had never made such grandiosely cosmic claims. Strangely enough, the owner of the Fattest Man seemed not at all enthusiastic at the idea of someone fetching Onofre for comparison on the spot. Some of the Mexicans had already laid bets on the outcome when it was realised that, by the time Onofre could be brought to Cerrillos, the circus would be miles away, a discovery at which the Fattest Man's owner tried hard to look disappointed.

The most exciting side-show of all this year was a

new one which was—tantalisingly—open only to men.
Someone had succeeded in capturing the Wolf Girl of
the Rio Grande! Her owner rolled his drum and
reminded his audience of the story—a story of which
many rumours had been heard over the years and which
therefore could only be true.

No one knew who the Wolf Girl was or who her
parents had been, but, as they would see, she was of
Anglo birth. Some said she had been lost as a toddler
in the confusion of the Alamo and adopted by wolves.
Others maintained that wolves had stolen her from her
cradle on a remote Texan homestead, though why her
parents had apparently made no attempt to get her back
was somewhat puzzling, and was generally held to lend
strength to the Alamo version. Whatever the truth of
that might be, at the age of about eleven her existence
in a wolf pack had been discovered and she had been
rescued by outraged and, it must be said, compassionate
settlers with the intention of turning the little animal
back into a human being.

Her owner advised his listeners to recall how she had
been said to be unable to stand upright and only capable
of growls and snarls. Her domestication proved short
lived, for her wolf 'family' rescued her and she had
never been seen again—until two men came upon her
bathing in the Rio Grande and reluctantly allowed
Pedro Valdez (and here the gentleman indicated with
touching modesty that he was that very same lucky
man) to buy her from them. The cost had been phenom-
enal, but if what the gentleman saw impressed upon
them the importance of taking care of their infant
daughters, then he, Pedro Valdez, had not spent his
money in vain. It was a noble sentiment which went
down well with his audience, and if any were churlish
enough to wonder whether Mr Valdez might not already
ave recouped his investment several times, they were
wise enough to keep their doubts to themselves.

And why was this splendid example of the need for

parental watchfulness to be viewed only by the gentlemen?

Mr Valdez sighed, and shook his head. He had no wish to shock the ladies present, but it was the sad fact that a girl brought up by wolves was not accustomed to wearing any sort of clothing, and had proved quite dangerously violent when he had tried to indicate to her that she might, like Eve, cover her nakedness.

The audience gasped delightedly and one gentleman thanked Mr Valdez for his consideration. It occurred to no one, man or woman, that, in the circumstances, it might have been more fitting to allow her to be seen only by the ladies.

There were exclamations of dismay when the good citizens of Cerrillos learnt that it would cost a whole dime to see this timely warning, but most of the men persuaded themselves that it was a small price to pay for a lesson so graphically illustrated. They paid over their little silver coins and trooped into the tent.

It was not a large tent—Mr Valdez had no intention of satisfying everyone's curiosity at once—and half of its space was taken up with a large cage of the sort in which performing bears were usually housed. Filthy straw covered the floor, and there was a small pile of filthier blankets in one corner, among which crouched an equally filthy figure.

The girl peered out with lack-lustre eyes at the sightseers who had trooped in. They looked the same as the sightseers at every other place they had stopped, and the rank smell of her cage was supplemented by the equally unpleasant smell of too many people in too small a space. She knew what she had to do. She must stay where she was until the tent-flap had been dropped and secured. No one outside must catch a free glimpse.

She had been here for a long time, though how long she had no idea, and she yearned to breathe fresh, clean air again. Not once since the two men had sold her to Valdez had she been in the open: when they were stationary, she was in the tent; when they were travel-

ling, her cage was boarded up to prevent her being seen.
She had no idea where they were or where they had
been. She had had no opportunity to escape, though
she never ceased to be on the alert in case such a chance
should arise. Valdez left nothing to luck, boarding up
her cage at night, even when she was hidden by the tent
from possible view. Perhaps he was afraid someone
would sneak in under cover of darkness without paying
their dime.

Her only interest was in listening to the people who
came to gawp at her. She did not always understand
what they said, which was probably just as well, since
what she did understand indicated that they thought
her incapable of such comprehension. Gradually, over
the weeks and months, echoes—faint at first but then
stronger—of words she had heard before in long-
forgotten times came to her, and as she recognised the
words, she recalled their meanings, just as she had been
beginning to do when the wolves reclaimed her. She
had been so happy with the wolves, the only family she
knew, but perhaps if she had been able to foresee the
destruction of her family, she might have been wiser to
stay with those strange, if well-meaning, people who
had taken her in.

She remembered with horrifying vividness the pleasure
with which the pack had fallen upon that sheep's carcass.
She had been slower than they to reach it, having
injured her foot, and in the few minutes it took to catch
them up, three youngsters, having gobbled down huge
chunks of the sheep's offal, were writhing in agony on
the ground until the final convulsions of death. The
carcass was unfit to eat, and she now realised it must
have been laid as poison bait by wolvers. For more
than two winters she had roamed alone and lonely until
that day, that ghastly day which she preferred to forget,
when she had bathed in the Rio Grande.

She shuddered, and realised Valdez was beginning to
glower and the spectators seemed restless. She must give
them what they wanted, or there would be no food. So

she snarled and came forward on all fours.

'Will you look at that?' one man exclaimed. 'She don't even walk normal!'

Someone always said that, and what satisfaction there would be in disproving it! At night, when she was alone and unobserved, she practised repeating softly to herself the things she heard; sometimes she held little conversations with herself, though the subject matter was necessarily limited and there was far more in her head than she knew how to express. She practised standing upright, too, for it was perfectly obvious she was made the same way as these people, just as it had been perfectly obvious she had not been made the same way as her wolf family. Once her muscles had accustomed themselves to the unaccustomed posture, she found it was easier to sustain than the crouch she was used to, and she then practised moving about in this new position as the spectators seemed to do, and Valdez, too.

Instinct told her that it would do her no good if Valdez learnt that she could speak, stand and move like a human. Once, in the early days, she had sensed that her nakedness had something to do with people paying to see her. The look in the eye of even the most respectable onlooker was not dissimilar to the look she had seen in the face of the man by the Rio Grande just before . . . Anyway, she had tried to wrap herself in one of the filthy blankets, and found that Valdez could wield a bull-whip with skill and accuracy through the bars. Now she tried to divorce herself from the salacious stares, and sometimes she was successful.

She prowled round her cage snarling and growling, and then began the pacing up and down which she had originally done naturally, out of boredom, and which she had later gathered from comments overheard was behaviour generally expected from caged wolves.

Valdez appeared from behind the cage. If she sat on her haunches now and howled, she would be fed. She got a little food at each performance and none at all in between, even if they were on the road for two or three

days. She loathed the need to go through this ritual,
just as she loathed having to eat in full view of all these
people,but she did it or starved—and starvation was a
slow death. She sat back and howled.

A couple of sheep's ribs with some meat attached
were tossed through the bars. She grovelled in the filthy
straw and picked them up. They were none too fresh,
but that was nothing new. She began to gnaw.

'That meat's raw!' one man exclaimed, as someone
always did.

'What would you expect a wolf to eat?' someone else
replied. 'Enchiladas?'

A wave of laughter rippled across the small crowd.
She had heard it all before in one variation or another.
She concentrated on her bones. The intensity with which
she gnawed them had nothing to do with the need to
give a performance.

This particular performance was nearly over, in any
case. The last part, the part that seemed to delight the
men most, was totally unnecessary. She must move well
away from the small heap of blankets on which she
slept. They stank, but they were dry.

She threw the bones to one side, her eye on Valdez
and his bucket. Then she stood as nearly upright as she
dared. Valdez fondly imagined he had trained her to do
this, but it would never do to let him know she could
do more than stand, stooped, for longer than a few
seconds.

As she stood and heard the inevitable, salacious, gasp,
she caught sight of a man who towered over the others
and had apparently worked his way down the side of
the tent until he now stood near the front. His height
and breadth blocked the view of those behind, who
protested vigorously that they were missing the climax.
It was an impression she gleaned, not details—of size,
of dark hair and light eyes, unusual in a largely Mexican
and Indian population, of the tanned skin of a
frontiersman.

Those strange eyes held hers for a moment, the eyes

of a man who was hard and ruthless. There was no sympathy in them, but neither was there condemnation—nor vicarious lust. She found herself hypnotised by those eyes, the first she had seen since her capture that held no hint of the accustomed salaciousness.

Suddenly, inexplicably, it mattered to her that he should not see her like this. For the first time she felt that her nakedness mattered. She longed to snatch up one of the filthy, tattered blankets, but dared not. Instead, she tried to cover herself with her hands, and the audience, who thought this was all part of the performance, laughed raucously. She noticed that the tall man with the strange eyes did not laugh. The expression that flitted briefly across his face was one of disgust, yet she sensed that that disgust was not directed at her but at his fellow spectators, and she was oddly comforted by that knowledge.

Any modesty she might have achieved was short lived. The force with which Valdez doused her with a bucketful of cold water caused her to stagger backwards, gasping, as it always did.

Valdez turned to face the audience. 'Thank you, gentlemen. That concludes this afternoon's exhibition. The Wolf Girl of the Rio Grande will be on exhibition again this evening for those of you who wish to confirm your original impression—or to check the accuracy of your recollection of her!'

This sally was greeted with appreciative laughter as the men filed out and the girl crouched among her blankets, not daring to cover herself with them until Valdez had seen the last spectator off.

The tall man was one of the last to go, not because he lingered but because he had been one of the furthest from the entrance. He seemed to be with another man, and when he spoke to his companion, his deep voice carried quite clearly over the murmur of the many satisfied customers.

'You mean you've been taken in by all this hogwash, Pete? You're a fool! The whole thing's a fraud—well done and certainly titillating to some, I grant you, but a fraud for all that. I'll lay you any odds you like that, as much as he's taken this afternoon, he'll take a whole lot more by selling her favours tonight. Some of those worthy citizens can hardly wait!'

Joel Kanturk would have lost his bet. When Valdez had bought the bruised and battered wolf girl from the two unsavoury characters who had captured her, the possibility of a more lucrative use for her than just putting her on exhibition certainly come into his calculations, and was fuelled by the discreet enquiries that were made on the subject by some spectators. There were problems: her sellers had warned him that if he gave her so much as an inch, she would be gone, and that the listlessness she exhibited was deliberately deceptive. One of them showed him the very nasty marks of a bite she had given him when he had done nothing more than try to help her to her feet.

Valdez did not entirely believe that this was all the man had been doing, but he was not himself remotely courageous and it did not escape his notice that the girl sometimes had a far from listless glint in her eyes that put him very much on his guard. He never risked going into her cage in case she tried to overpower him, as he rather suspected she might be desperate enough and savage enough to do. Consequently, when approaches for her services were first made to him, he declined them regretfully even though satisfying such a market had been part of his original intention. Then, about three months after she had come into his possession, he had been made an offer he simply could not bring himself to refuse. He explained to the man that it had never been tried and she was hardly likely to co-operate, but this was dismissed. The creature's co-operation was unnecessary: the cage had bars, and presumably Mr Valdez owned ropes? Valdez wondered that he had never thought of that himself.

It had proved more difficult than he had anticipated to catch her and tie her wrists to the bars, and it didn't occur to him that it might be unwise to leave her feet free. Both men had assumed that the girl would be quite unaware of her intended fate, but they mistook the matter rather badly and found that captivity had done nothing to blunt the creature's reflexes or the unerring aim and unexpected force with which she could use her knee. The customer picked himself up out of the sodden, stinking straw, doubled over with pain but angry enough to disregard it long enough to strike the girl. As his hands descended across her mouth, her teeth closed on it, and a second man would bear the marks for the rest of his life. So angry was the customer then that he drew his gun, and it was only the hurried intervention of Valdez, who could see his livelihood vanishing, that stayed his aim.

That little incident cost Valdez not only the return of the customer's money—regrettable, but fair—but also a new suit of clothes and a doctor's bill. Valdez did not like losing money. He retrieved a little of it by cutting down on her food though he knew it would be counter-productive to exhibit her in any noticeable degree of emaciation. He was, however, disinclined to repeat the experiment, even though it would be perfectly possible to prevent both kicking and biting. Better, he decided, to look to the longer term. She was a very popular side-show, and it would be years before they had covered the country.

CHAPTER THREE

THE GOOD LADIES of Cerrillos had accepted without question the showman's explanations of his side-show, but when they asked their husbands about it they received very unsatisfactory answers. The creature—it was putting it too strongly to say 'girl'—was certainly female, and naked. Of course, she was so filthy that it was difficult to form any clear impression of what she was like. Their wives had not missed much, they said dismissively.

Which made it all the more perplexing that their husbands should go so often to see that particular exhibit.

The husbands did not exactly volunteer that piece of information to their wives, but Cerrillos was not so large that one woman would not recognise another's husband, especially if he were coming out of the wolf girl's tent. Few husbands when challenged denied their return visits, and fewer still—perhaps wisely—attempted to explain them. There were times when it was extremely useful to be able to retreat behind the lofty dignity of being master of the house.

Over coffee-cups and tea-cups the ladies put their heads together. What actually went on in the showman's tent none of them knew. One or two husbands had said the girl just snarled and paced about on all fours and gnawed some bones, but if that were all, why did so many of them go back again and again for another look?

'You mark my words,' Hannah Barton told her friends. 'There's more to it than that!'

They nodded agreement. All sorts of guesses were

made as to what the 'more' might be, ranging from the possible to the wildly improbable, but there were some things that were unarguable.

First, everyone knew—because that dreadful Valdez had admitted as much—that the girl was an Anglo and was exhibiting herself nude. Indians might well do all sorts of strange things and even some Mexicans had unusual customs, but no Anglo girl would exhibit herself in that way unless she were morally beyond redemption.

Hannah Barton was emphatic. 'We've managed to keep that sort of female out of this town so far—and it hasn't been easy with so many miners in the area—and I, for one, don't want to see their sort creeping in by the back door, so to speak.'

Second, although their husbands insisted the girl was filthy dirty and singularly unattractive, that was obviously quite untrue. No one would pay twice to see an unattractive, filthy female. In short, it was not very long before the ladies of Cerrillos had convinced themselves that a veritable siren lurked in their midst, seducing their husbands by means unspecified from their previously unblemished paths.

Their husbands must be saved from themselves. This was a conclusion which received unanimous agreement. How their laudable aim should be achieved was less easy to see, especially since they were determined it should be done in a way sufficiently public to deter any future emulation of the offence.

No one was surprised that it should be Hannah Barton who thought of the perfect solution. The creature was to be tarred, feathered and ridden on a rail out of town, a punishment more commonly seen in Mrs Barton's native Missouri than out here, but none the less effective for that. The blacksmith had tar, everyone had feather pillows, and as for a rail, well, there were plenty of pine *vigas* waiting to be put into the Boarstalls' new adobe—one of those would be just fine.

They got to work on their husbands that evening, and those whose husbands had unexpected business

meetings that took them in the direction of the circus
were tackled on their return.

Just as Hannah Barton was the most determined, so
was her husband Abel the most reluctant to support
her plan.

'Oh, come on, Hannah,' he said, trying to sound
reasonable. 'Even if your suspicions were right, what
would it matter? The circus'll be gone in a couple of
days.'

'It's the principle of the thing,' she told him with self-
righteous dignity. 'It's not right that decent women
should have to mix with the likes of her!'

'But you don't have to,' her husband pointed out. 'In
fact, you can't! Valdez won't let women near the place.'

'Exactly—and why? Because it ain't decent, that's
why! Besides, who knows what it could lead to?'

'If the circus is moving on, it can't lead to much, can
it?'

'The devil works in mysterious ways,' Hannah
reminded him, and he forbore, for the sake of peace
and quiet, from reminding her that this characteristic
was more generally attributed to what he supposed one
might regard as the other side.

When the men in desperation sought refuge in the
saloon and compared notes, they realised they were the
victims of a concerted and co-ordinated effort. The wolf
girl was a vicarious and short-lived pleasure. Their wives
they had to live with for the foreseeable future. Besides,
when you thought about it, the novelty was beginning
to wear off, and the tarring and feathering might be
quite entertaining.

Among the many people in the saloon listening with
avid interest to the plans being laid was an old man
whose sister's husband's cousin was married to the
brother of the wife of one of the tumblers. It was
therefore only to be expected that old Chavez should
feel obliged to pass on to his distant relative by three
marriages any information that affected the circus and
its satellite side-shows. Word accordingly reached Valdez

before the men in the saloon had finished talking about it.

He wasted no time wondering whether the men of Cerrillos meant it or whether they would carry their intentions out. It was their town. They could—and would—do precisely what they liked. It only remained for Valdez to salvage what he could out of a potentially disastrous situation. Accordingly, he spruced himself up—but not enough to make himself look prosperous— and made his way to the saloon. He knew the accuracy of his information was confirmed when a sudden silence greeted his appearance. He ignored it, and went over to the bar. Valdez downed the first shot of whisky in one gulp, but lingered over the next as if he were there for the night. A murmur of conversation rose again, and he noticed that the worthy citizens of Cerrillos avoided his eye. He waited until it seemed they were about to drift away in ones and twos, and then he laid his hand on the arm of one of them who, by chance, happened to be Abel Barton.

'Hold on, my friend,' Valdez said in his most ingratiating tone. 'Let me buy you a drink. This town has been good to me. I'd like to show my gratitude.'

Abel shifted uneasily. 'No need to,' he said. 'Besides, Hannah'll murder me if I'm not home soon . . . You know what wives are!'

Regretfully Valdez confessed that he had not been as lucky as Mr Barton. 'Let me buy you a drink to celebrate your better fortune,' he concluded.

The tension that had greeted his appearance was diminishing. It looked as if the little Mexican had been drinking before he reached this particular saloon and he was very nearly maudlin; why not humour him? So the citizens relaxed, Abel Barton accepted the offered drink, and Valdez congratulated himself on a promising start.

Maudlin or not, the whisky certainly made him loquacious and confiding, and the citizens soon learned how bad luck had dogged him until the wolf girl came into his possession, and how he hoped that, by exhibiting her with as much success as here in Cerrillos, he would not only make a passable living but also—who knows?— be able to get the poor girl some sort of civilising education.

Not every listener was entirely taken in by this touching prospect, but whether they were or not, they could not help being made to feel rather guilty at their own plans.

'I don't deny she's a savage,' Valdez almost sobbed into his glass. 'She's quite a responsibility, in fact. But what livelihood would either of us have if I lost her? It doesn't bear thinking about.'

Unease reasserted itself among his listeners. Abel Barton coughed uneasily. 'You've put your finger on it, Mr Valdez,' he said. 'She *is* a savage, and the ladies . . . Well, they've got it into their heads that to have such a female around is a corrupting influence, and I can't deny they may be right. The thing is, they want her gone.'

He paused, and Valdez stared at him in well-feigned surprise tinged with a hint of fear. 'You mean I have to move on with her before the circus strikes camp? I've got to get that lumbering cage across the territory without the protection of being part of a larger group?' Anxiety oozed from every pore.

'That wasn't quite what we had in mind,' one man said, and then coughed awkwardly.

'Why? What do you mean? What else *can* you mean?' Valdez looked from one to the other with every appearance of bewilderment.

'The ladies want a lesson taught—an example made,' Abel Barton told him. 'Not to put too fine a point on it, they want her tarred and feathered and ridden out of town.'

Valdez sank his head in his hands. 'And me?' he asked.

'No one wishes you any harm,' another listener assured him. 'You'll be left alone, unless you interfere.'

Valdez shook his head. 'I wouldn't dare,' he admitted. 'But this is my livelihood. What do I do when she's gone?'

The citizens looked at each other. They were no more compassionate than the next man, but the truth was that they were not the ones who wanted the girl gone—and the man did have a point. They had been happy enough to pay to see her. No doubt others would be equally willing, in other towns. They had to live with their wives, though, and there was the undeniable fact that the planned expulsion would be hugely entertaining.

Barton turned to his fellow citizens. 'What say you we have a whip-round to compensate this man—a fairly substantial whip-round?'

'What guarantee do we have that he won't pocket it and then pack up and go in the night?' one of them asked.

'In this territory?' Valdez interjected. 'Not at night, my friend. But it's a fair question.' He took a bunch of keys out of his pocket. 'I'll give you the key to the cage. Will that satisfy you?'

'How do we know that's the right key?' one of them asked suspiciously.

'Take the bunch,' Valdez replied.

'He may have duplicates,' a voice at the back volunteered.

'I haven't,' Valdez lied. 'What's to stop you putting a watch on the cage to make sure?'

It was a fair offer, and the men conceded that they would not get a better one. Someone removed Valdez' hat from his head, and it was passed round. When it returned it was gratifyingly heavy, and Valdez was pleased to note the occasional glint of a gold nugget and the odd piece of turquoise. One or two men had cut off a silver concho from their belts. All in all, it looked as if he would do better out of this deal than he had expected. Thank goodness this incident had chosen to happen in a prosperous town! He handed over the keys, and there was a hasty conference to appoint the sentries to see that Valdez did not make off with both the money and the girl.

To do him justice, Valdez had no intention of reneging on the deal. Why should he? Once the girl was safely out of town, she would be in no condition to go anywhere. All he had to do was to re-capture her and lie low until the circus left. There were plenty of people with the circus who would bring his wagon and the cage along for him. His plan had worked. This was turning into quite a profitable little venture!

The deal with Valdez concluded, the citizens of Cerrillos drifted back to their homes. Their wives would receive a satisfactory account of the night's events, and they would sleep soundly in the happy expectation of a good day's sport on the morrow.

Most of the miners drifted off, too, also determined to return next day and get their money's worth. They did not all leave, however. A little group of some half-dozen or so remained in one of the drinking-booths, unaware that the adjoining booth was also occupied by two strangers in town, one of them quite remarkably tall, whose arrival they couldn't help noticing but whose presence had been so unobtrusive that they had forgotten about it. The miners kept their voices down, or thought they did, but all had been drinking, and while they were by no means drunk, they were not so much in control of their voices as they thought they were.

'Did you ever see a tarring and feathering?' one of them asked the group at large. They shook their heads. 'Well, I have—in Mississippi one time, it was. A preacher-man with an eye for the wealthy widder-women. Not a pretty sight, he wasn't—and they let him keep his clothes on. Now, I don't reckon this wolf girl's going to be going far when they've finished with her— it'll be uncomfortable to move, and if they give her a bumpy ride, it'll make it worse. She's not going to be able to get the tar and feathers off, either, so she's going to have to lie low—and do it fairly close to wherever they put her down.'

His cronies nodded. This all made sense, but what of it?

'Seems to me,' the first man went on, 'that we'd be doing her a favour by rescuing her—give her somewhere to live till the tar and feathers has wore off.'

'Are you out of your mind?' one of the others demanded. 'Why should we do a thing like that? She'd have to be fed, for one thing.'

'She eats raw meat, so where's the problem? There's plenty of jack-rabbit about. You're missing the point, my friend. She would naturally be suitably grateful.'

His companions smiled knowingly and nodded, but one of them refused to be convinced.

'She's wild!' he protested. 'She won't understand things like gratitude, and you sure as hell can't explain.'

The others grinned at his naïvety. 'She'll understand soon enough,' the first man said. He looked round at the group. 'I don't think we'll have much trouble explaining! Are you game?'

They unanimously agreed that they were, and it was the general feeling that the next day's events would become even more exciting once the official entertainment was over. It was a good half-hour later before they left the saloon to sleep off the effects of rough whisky and to prepare themselves for the next day.

Joel Kanturk and Pete Lingstrom did not leave the adjacent booth until they were gone.

'Nasty!' the latter remarked.

'Very,' his friend agreed. 'The whole thing's a fraud, of course, but the girl doesn't deserve what's coming to her, no matter what she is. It's not a way I'd want to see a sister of mine earning a living, but that's all she's doing, after all—earning a living.'

'Some living—raw meat and filth!' Pete paused on the steps outside the saloon. 'Are you going to watch?'

A harsh, humourless grin broke briefly across Joel's face. 'Fancy it, do you? Don't blame you—if you've never seen one before. One thing I'm sure of, that little bunch of miners will be there. Think you'll recognise them?'

Pete nodded. 'Fairly sure. I noticed them when we came in—and watched them leave.'

'Fine. Then you go and watch tomorrow. Only watch them as well as the rail-riding. Don't lose them.'

'What'll you be doing?'

'Not sure. I'll be around, but I'll be damned if I want to watch tomorrow's spectacle.' And with that, Pete had to be satisfied.

The girl knew that today was not a normal day. The sounds from outside her shuttered cage told her that activities around the circus were already well advanced, yet Valdez had not come to open up. The small round ventilation-holes at the top of the shutters told her that it had been daylight for some hours. Perhaps he had died! If that were so, it was to be hoped that someone remembered to feed and water her, and if they did, perhaps they would prove to be less vigilant and less cautious than Valdez in his dealings with her. Perhaps she might at last get the opportunity she had hoped for all these months—the opportunity to escape.

She heard the rope that laced up the tent-flap being pulled through its eyelets. Someone was coming. No, her ears told her, several people were coming. She tensed in her corner, clutching a skimpy piece of worn blanket to her. The shutter padlocks were undone, and clumsily inexperienced hands lifted the shutters off. Because the tent-flap had been left open, more light than she had seen for months came into the cage and, with it, a breath of clean air.

Four or five men stood outside the cage. None of them was Valdez. One of them held Valdez' keys, though. Did that mean he *was* dead? They stared at her and she stared back, her mind working rapidly to analyse what she saw. Two of them held ropes, and one had a gun. The one with the keys also held a whip. None of these items betokened either charity or lack of caution. There were quite a number of people outside the tent, too: apart from those she could see through the open flap, there were the silhouettes of others against the canvas walls. It seemed to add up to a considerable crowd, and it was a crowd tense with excited anticipation.

The key was inserted in the cage-door, and turned. The man with the gun and one of the two men with a rope came in. Her eyes flickered to the door, but it was locked behind them. Reluctantly, she got to her feet. Whatever they wanted—and she thought she knew— she would make it as difficult as possible.

It was the rifle that brought her up short. Pushed, crouching, into a corner, she felt the barrel at her throat. She tried quickly to assess how likely the man was to squeeze the trigger, but she thought too slowly, and before she could come to any conclusion, the other man had the rope round her wrist with a jerk which obliged her to drop the blanket. The other rope was passed through the bars and tied to her other wrist, and then the signal was given to open the cage.

She was dragged, half crouching, half stumbling, out of the cage and the tent, and she stood there, dazzled and partly blinded by the unaccustomed light. She was given no time to get her bearings but was dragged through the waiting crowd to where a bucket stood over a fire and, by it, men with brooms and a pine trunk.

Tar was a precious commodity, chiefly used to seal damaged hooves on any of the variety of animals whose soundness and good health was an essential priority to farmers, merchants and travellers. Cerrillos boasted a blacksmith, the only person with sufficient tar for the present purpose, and he had not been over-generous in the bucketful he reluctantly sold the citizens for a very inflated price.

'You won't thank me when I've run out and your mule splits his foot,' he told them.

Someone stirred the bucket, and removed it from the

fire. It was nicely liquid now, and probably not too hot.

The girl was dragged to the centre of a ring formed by the spectators, and her arms were pulled out at right-angles so that she was held too taut to evade what was in store. The first broom went in the bucket and came out dripping with hot tar. Fortunately its passage through the cold air cooled it down to less than a scalding heat, but the girl was entirely unprepared for the hot, harsh bristles with their black load being raked down her body, nor was she prepared for the gladiatorial cheer that went up at the sight of the successfully applied ribbon of black that stretched from her neck to her thighs.

The other men who had drawn the lucky lots to apply the tar could not linger over their task as they might have wished, for the tar must not be allowed to dry before they had finished or the feathers would not stick; and though there was not enough to put a thick coating on the girl, they made sure that she was as thoroughly coated as they could manage. Then, when she was sure it must be over because they held up the bucket upside-down to demonstrate that it was empty, the crowd joined in, the children with handfuls of feathers, the adults with pillows, until she was unrecognisable as a human being and the ground round her was a sea of feathers.

Long before they man-handled her astride the *viga* and tied her on, Pete Lingstrom felt nauseated by what he was seeing. Had it not been for his undertaking to watch the miners, he would have left the scene, as one or two others had quietly done. He took a little comfort from the fact that, if he kept his eye on his targets, he would catch no more than accidental glimpses of the girl. He found it frightening, too, the way that, as their treatment of her made her look less and less human, so the crowd's behaviour became less and less humane.

Two men at either end of the *viga* took it on their shoulders and marched with it out of town towards the surrounding sagebrush and juniper and away from the little stream that watered the town. An excited crowd of cheering onlookers accompanied them, the children dancing up and down and pelting their unfortunate victim with anything that came to hand. Not all the audience was shouting and cheering, however: a small group of miners joined the procession but kept themselves a shade apart, and Pedro Valdez followed it at a discreet distance. The miners were probably the only people to see him, and they nudged each other and a nod of the head advised each to look in his direction. The miners also spotted a rider some way off. He seemed to be travelling parallel with the cavalcade, but perhaps that was a coincidence. One of them thought he recognised him and then decided he was mistaken: the man he thought he recognised had only ever been seen with a friend.

The procession went a long way. The *viga* with its load was no light weight, but there were plenty of willing shoulders. Nevertheless, influenced by the fact that, no matter how far out they went, they must return over the same distance in far less exciting circumstances, it was felt that five miles was far enough, especially since the land here was singularly inhospitable and there was no water for a long way. So they finally set down the *viga* and warned the spectators to stand back.

'This is a wild animal,' one of the men reminded the crowd. 'We're going to cut it free. If it thinks it's cornered, it could attack. Keep back!'

The crowd did, and an expectant silence fell. The speaker took his hunting-knife out of his belt.

Only pain and discomfort had kept the girl conscious, and now that the agonising ride had stopped it could only be because something else was in store for her. When the man took out his knife and the sun caught the blade in a mirror-flash, she thought that now, at last, she would die. It was a welcome thought. She could hardly believe it was true when the knife slashed through the ropes that bound her, and the men stood back.

What now?

What would they do if she ran?

Did she really have a choice?

Slowly she stood up. Every muscle ached. She doubted if she could run at all, much less at the sort of speed she used to attain. She rubbed her wrists and stared round at the waiting spectators, her eyes white in an unevenly black face. The crowd backed. They're frightened! she thought suddenly, and the realisation gave her a flash of hope. They don't know what to expect! She turned round, apparently staring back at her observers, but in reality surveying the land behind them. If she was to escape, if she was to find water to wash this stuff off, she must first get well away to a terrain where they would have difficulty following, either on foot or on horseback. Over there—that was the direction. She wondered fleetingly if she would be shot as she ran. Perhaps. It couldn't be worse than what had already happened to her, and she must take the chance. She was unlikely to get another.

When she took to her heels, desperation lent her a speed beyond her expectations. The crowd backed hastily away, letting her through, and there was no crack of a rifle. She was free!

As if the speed of her flight released them from an evil *bruja's* spell, the crowd dissolved into individuals once more. The man who had warned them to keep back became suddenly human enough to recognise once more their victim's humanity.

'Let her go,' he called out. 'She's earned her freedom. Let's get back, all of us. It's a long walk.' And he remained at the back of the retreating townsfolk, herding them all—even the miners who had tried unobtrusively to evade his watchful care—back to Cerrillos. No one noticed Valdez, who sat down near a juniper, cursing because he had come along with no water-bottle and wondering how he could possibly hope to catch up something with the turn of speed the wolf girl displayed. He had an unpleasant feeling that one part of his plan had just misfired.

Pete returned with the herd. His instructions had been to follow the miners, and he did not think they had given up yet. Joel could be anywhere, but not far off: he had caught a brief glimpse of him earlier. They both knew this Territory well enough to be able to find each other with a reasonably degree of certainty when they needed to. He was already estimating the most likely places to offer shelter within a thirty-mile radius, come nightfall or a sudden storm. Meanwhile, what would those miners do? There was only one way to find out.

CHAPTER FOUR

THE GIRL kept running for longer than she believed
herself capable, straining her ears for the sounds of
pursuit. The citizens of Cerrillos had taken her northwards, away from the river, and although she knew she
could not keep going indefinitely without water, she
nevertheless continued to head north in order to put as
much distance between them as possible. When she
finally paused it was as much to establish some bearings
as to rest muscles unaccustomed since her captivity to
so much exertion.

It did not surprise her that the landscape was of
sandstone mesas and covered in sagebrush, junipers and
cholla cactus. She had never seen any other landscape,
and did not know of the existence of the green pastures
of Kentucky or the neat fields of New England, and the
softly rolling tree-covered mountains of Tennessee would
have seemed strange indeed to one accustomed to the
high snow-clad peaks that rose behind every mesa. She
did not realise how fortunate she was that her release
had occurred in a terrain in which she knew how to
survive. Far, far to the left, further than she could walk
in a day, she could see the Jemez Mountains. She did
not know their name, but she knew their outline. In
that direction, then. There should be a river to cross,
and then perhaps she could find the cliff-face pock-
marked with old abandoned caves. There was a stream
at its foot, where game both large and small drank. It
was a perfect place to lie hidden until this stuff—and
she absent-mindedly started plucking off one or two of
the looser feathers—wore or could be washed off.

She set off again at a steadier pace, one which, in the

old days, would have allowed her to cover the ground effortlessly and relentlessly. The effort to sustain it was far greater now, and the only thing that forced her to keep going was the knowledge that Cerrillos was still too close, and a man on horseback, once he picked up her trail, would have no difficulty in overtaking her.

That one such had never lost sight of her, she did not know. Perhaps captivity had dulled her senses more than she realised; perhaps in her anxiety to put distance between her and Cerrillos she was less observant than was advisable. Whatever the reason, she remained quite ignorant of Joel Kanturk's presence. He was not close, but he did not find it hard to keep abreast of her steady, crouching lope. Only when she used the dry bed of an *arroyo* did he hold back: he must use it, too, and was therefore obliged to keep out of sight, sound and smell.

When, after several hours of alternately running and resting, she came to the Rio Grande, she knew the river at once, and heaved a sigh of relief. She knew every inch of this river, at least as far south as that family who had separated her from her real family for a brief while before the wolves took her back. It was also the river that had led to her more recent capture. This was no place to stay, then—she needed more seclusion.

She stayed long enough to drink deeply and rest in the shelter of some rocks, and then she crossed the river and loped back down the old Indian trail for a short distance before scrambling up a narrow canyon that turned back again and led north towards the distant mountains.

Still on the Cerrillos side of the river, Joel watched her every action. There was now a decisiveness in her movements that told him she knew where she was—and where she was going. If she maintained her present route, it would bring her to the Frijoles falls and then to the shelter of the caves. He could think of no more natural place for someone in her situation to go to. The route she had taken was not a good one for a horse. Better to head up the Rio Grande on the Indian trail and turn straight into Frijoles canyon. He would be there before her.

In Cerrillos, the miners were huddled together at one end of the saloon's bar, arguing. At the other end stood Pete, gazing down into his beer, listening. Some of them were of the opinion that they should go straight after the girl before she got too far away. Others thought that they had lost enough time already and should be back at work. The discussion was prolonged, and seemed, despite the need to keep their voices down, heated. Finally it looked as if a decision had been reached. The miners would return to their claims. Pete finished his beer in one swallow and went out.

The miners watched him go, and one of them became very thoughtful. 'Recognise that man?' he asked.

His friends shook their heads, though one of them admitted cautiously that he had thought there was something familiar about him.

'He's only been around a few days. Mostly hangs about with that very tall man. Know who I mean?'

They nodded.

'I saw that tall man—or I thought I did—and dismissed it because he was alone. Now I'm not so sure. This one—the one that's just left—he came along this morning with everyone else. But there was someone riding some distance from the rest of us, but in the same direction.'

'So?'

'So maybe they've got the same idea as us. Maybe the other one is following her right now.'

'Then why was this one with the rest of the crowd?' someone asked. 'Why wasn't he with his friend?'

The first man shrugged. 'Who knows? Perhaps they were hedging their bets: if another group—like us, say—went after her and were likely to get there first, maybe they'd have joined up with it.'

'And now they're separated,' another miner objected. 'If the tall one has the girl, he's got her to himself.

Lucky devil!' he added resentfully.

'Use your brain, man! They'll have fixed up some place to meet. All we've got to do is to follow this one. My guess is he'll lead us straight to his friend—and the girl.'

'What then?'

'There's more of us than of them. Think it out for yourself.'

They thought, and could find no flaw. They would have to be exceptionally careful. As miners, they had few other frontier skills and it would not be easy to follow their guide unobserved, but it was worth the try.

A few enquiries elicited the information that the stranger had left Cerrillos some several minutes ago, heading broadly north. It was no good trying to follow him on foot, and by the time they had caught their mules, corralled outside the town, and saddled them, Pete had had at least an hour's start. When they reached the place where the tarring and feathering had been carried out, he was nowhere to be seen, and in the confusion of tracks they could find no clue. Cursing the failure of a good plan, they returned to Cerrillos.

Once Pete had left behind the trampled, muddled tracks of the morning's crowd of sightseers, the girl's trail was not hard to follow: every so often a feather had caught on a juniper branch or a cholla spine. Within a couple of hours he had guessed where she was headed. Within three he was certain.

The girl slid and scrambled down into Frijoles canyon and, having reached the bottom, slipped unobtrusively into the underbrush before taking the risk of coming into the open. A creek, clear and cold, ran through the canyon, and because of the water there were trees and bushes in plenty. Grass, too. No wonder Indians had settled here so long ago. The adobe ruins of their pueblo were overgrown now but the outline was clear enough, especially when one was clear above them. More easily recognised for what it was, was the old adobe ruin that had been built against the cliff-face opposite.

She studied the cliff-face. How strange it looked! The sandstone face rose sheer from the canyon floor, riddled with holes so that, from this side of the creek, it looked like a huge version of the goats' cheese she had been given during that short stay with a human family. It had tasted quite pleasant, too, she remembered, once she had got used to it. It was the holes—the caves—not the old adobe, that were her destination. They did not lead to passages and vast caverns within the mesa itself, but each cave was a small room shaped in part by the people who had once lived here and whose painted wall decorations could still be seen at the back of some of them. Why they should ever have left so ideal a situation was a mystery. The girl could think of no better place to live. There was shelter, water, game and berries. What more could one ask for?

A whip-tailed lizard basked on a rock in the sunlight on her right. Further up the canyon two ravens tore at something dead. Nothing threatened. Nothing unusual stirred. This place was safe. She would drink. Then she would scramble up the barely visible footholds into one of the caves, curl up against its far wall, and sleep. When she woke, she would wash off this foul stuff and start living again.

She slid into the river wolf-fashion, drinking in great gulps as she went, and then she stood up to her knees in the crisp, cold creek, exercising, for the first time since she left her cage, her recently acquired ability to stand upright. Suddenly, to be free and to stand like this was an unexpected delight, and she turned her face to the sun and stretched up with her arms as if to clutch the life-giving force that warmed her upturned face and closed lids, in unconscious echo of all who worship the sun.

From nowhere a rope whistled through the air and settled taut round her waist, a cruel return to the world of men. She spun round, crouching again, and looked along the line of the rope. He had been concealed in the ruined adobe. Fool that she was not to have considered the possibility! She tugged experimentally on the rope, and knew at once that the man who held it was stronger than she. Despair, like a stone, dragged her spirit down. Did it all begin again? The man on the bank began to reel her in like a trout, except that she offered no resistance. What would it achieve? Escape—permanent escape—seemed impossible, and because it had been her custom for so long in the presence of the observers, she returned to her crouching posture.

'For God's sake,' the man said, exasperated, 'I've just seen you standing up. You can stop the play-acting now.'

She looked up at him then more closely, recognising the voice of what had, until then, been simply a man and a threat. He was unmistakable. Even taller than she had thought, now that she saw him with only herself for comparison, his broad shoulders tapered to slim hips above long legs straddled just now it case she made a sudden lunge to escape. His hair was as black as the pitch with which she had been covered but, unlike a Mexican's, it curled. She was totally unequipped to guess his age, but he was no boy. His face, as lean as the rest of him, had been lived in a long time. His eyes had struck her before. Now she knew why: in a land where black hair meant brown eyes, it was a shock to see grey looking out at you from skin as tanned at that of any Indian.

Joel was making a similar appraisal, but with less result. The girl was smaller—much smaller—than he had thought. The floor of the cage must have given an illusion of the height she lacked. He had seen nothing tempting, nothing attractive, in the filthy caged figure that crouched and paced and snarled. Obscenely covered as she was in tar and feather, she was even less appealing now. Only briefly, a few moments before when she had reached up to the sun, had there been any hint at all of grace of form—and that was probably false, he thought.

Keeping his eye on her, for he had no desire to be

caught off guard, he reached down behind the wall that
had hidden him and brought out a blanket, which he
held out to her.

'Put this round you,' he said tersely. 'Unless you
prefer being seen like that.'

The girl stared at the blanket in disbelief. It was old
and worn, but it was clean, and the indigo and cream
zig-zag patterns were, to her eyes, unbelievably beautiful.
It was so far a cry from the filthy rags she had had at
the circus that it seemed a crime to sully it with her
horribly mired body.

Seeing her reluctance, Joel became impatient. He
picked it up and threw it over to her. 'Wrap it round
you or go without,' he said. 'Just remember it gets cold
at night.'

She only half understood his words, but she understood the tone and the gesture and bent to pick up the
blanket and wrap it round her shoulders.

He watched her in silence and then, when she was
decently covered, he commented drily, 'So you do
understand when it suits you! Do you know a group of
miners plans to take you?'

She looked at him blankly. She had practised talking
in her cage, had practised little conversations, but when
she spoke to herself she planned what she would say—
and what she would reply—before trying it out aloud,
mouthing the words silently first. This was very different.
Some words she recognised, but not many. She dared
not put her own words together. Perhaps they would be
equally meaningless to him. Perhaps he would laugh at
her.

'Are you going on playing this wolf girl?' Joel asked.
He began to wonder if the girl was stupid, or if she
thought he was. He had seen her stand upright. She
had certainly understood what he meant about the
blanket. Surely she must realise that that meant he
knew her game? Or maybe she had been playing the
part so long that she believed it. It would be a damn
sight more convenient all round if she would come out

and admit she was a fraud! Then he could treat her
normally and explain her situation. Of course, she
would probably misjudge the reason for his assistance,
but that couldn't be helped. She would soon find she
was wrong. He might be living the life of a frontiersman,
but that didn't mean he wanted to come home to it.
Mind you, apart from those two slips, she kept it up
well. Almost convincingly. Whether she intended to go
on with the pretence or not, the fact remained that
those miners might not be too far behind, and they
would both be better off in one of the caves. He tugged
at the rope and saw the wariness return to her eyes. He
jerked his head towards the cliff behind him.

'Come on. Over here. We'll get in one of the caves.'

She did not disguise her reluctance to follow him. She
knew what he wanted. He must have realised that once
she was up there, the confined space left little room to
struggle.

Joel had to drag her over to the cave he had chosen.
Its entrance was only just large enough to clamber in,
but it opened up into a reasonably sized chamber in
which the girl, at least, might even be able to stand up
if she chose to drop this charade. It was not too high
up to be at all difficult to reach, but one person could
defend it indefinitely.

He pushed the girl in front of him to the entrance.
'Up,' he said.

She looked at him briefly, debating whether she could
take him off guard and flee, but that one look told her
he was ready to cope with any attempt she made, so,
instead, she reached up to a hand-hold and from there
to the lip of the cave. As she hung over the lip,
scrabbling to get her feet over as well, she felt his hand
grab her ankle and push it upwards and knew he was
so close behind that he would be in the cave before she
could turn and push him backwards off the cliff-face.

Once inside, it was obvious he had prepared the cave
in advance: a bed-roll, a water-bottle, saddlebags and a
rifle were stacked neatly at one end. For the first time

she wondered where his horse was. It must be somewhere near, and saddled, since there was saddle in the cave. She mentally reviewed the canyon as she had seen it from the brush. The horse must be further upstream, concealed by a bend, and probably hobbled to prevent it straying too far.

She crouched as far away from the man as she could get, knowing that even so she was still within arm's reach. She shivered. Why was he waiting? The others hadn't waited.

He untied his bed-roll and spread it out. He took a strip of dried meat from his saddlebag and cut it in half, offering one portion of the jerky to her. She took it gratefully, for it was a long time since she had eaten. They chewed in silence, and Joel sat well back but in a position from which he could command as much of the canyon downstream as was visible before it turned one of its many bends. The shivering that had started when the girl came into the cave ceased while she ate, but Joel noticed it begin again when she had finished. It was certainly cool in the cave and she must be cold, he supposed. He dared not light a fire. The only possible place for one was the entrance, and he had no intention of advertising their presence.

He picked up the blanket that was his bed-roll and placed it round her shoulders. As he did so, he felt her tense, and the face that looked up at him was rigid and staring with fear.

Comprehension dawned in a mingling of pity and disgust. He tucked the blanket securely round her, suddenly aware that beneath the filth and the tar was an unexpectedly fine-boned and very vulnerable body.

'No,' he said as gently as his feelings of revulsion for her expectations permitted. 'You've nothing to fear from me.' He laughed, and added as if to convince her with a clinching argument, 'I'm no monk, but I'm not reduced to snatching it from anything vaguely female.'

He turned away from her then and resumed his surveillance of the canyon below.

When a solitary horseman rode openly along the bank of the little stream, his interest intensified. The sun was low and would soon disappear behind the hills, but the rider was unmistakable. Joel waited only long enough to be sure his friend was not followed before hailing him.

Pete drew rein below the cave. 'Easy enough trail to follow,' he said. 'Feathers everywhere. You've got her, I suppose?'

Joel nodded, and jerked his head to indicate the cave behind him. 'What about the miners?'

'They've given up. Decided they'd wasted enough time. Might as well let her go—she's safe enough from them.'

'Are you sure? They sounded pretty determined before.'

'If everyone hadn't been herded back to town, they'd have followed her. As it was, they were divided as to what to do. The lure of gold won.'

Joel nodded thoughtfully. 'Rest your horse and come up here. I've a plan.'

The last dregs of light were draining away when Pete finally clambered up into the now very crowded cave. He could just make out the girl's shape huddled under blankets in the corner. She could see only a slightly built man whose voice suggested he was the younger of the two. He was probably the man who had been with her captor at the side-show that first afternoon.

'We can't let her go, you know,' Joel began.

'I thought your aim was to stop the miners getting hold of her,' Pete said. 'We've done that, it seems. So why keep her? Always thought you were a shade . . . fastidious,' he added.

'Don't be a fool!' Joel snapped. 'I told you before that I thought she was a fraud, and now I'm sure of it. I've seen her stand as upright as you or me and I'm dead sure she understood something I said. But that's no longer the point. It doesn't much matter whether she's genuine or not. If she is, she needs help. If she isn't, she's simpled-minded and needs protection. She's huddled in that corner, terrified.'

'You frighten a lot of people,' Pete told him. 'You even frighten me sometimes! Mind you, most women seem to like being a bit frightened.'

'That's different—they know it's not real. This is sheer terror. She's been given good cause to fear men, and it's not a fear of being killed.'

'You reckon you're the one to protect her, do you?' Pete was clearly amused. 'Turning philanthropist? No one'll believe your motives are honourable, you know.'

'To hell with what they believe! I know where she can go for protection, and we'll take her—but not like this, tarred and feathered, and wrapped only in a blanket. Go into Cerrillos and get yourself some new clothes. The moon will be up soon. Get them first thing, and come straight back here.'

'Cerrillos? Wouldn't it be wiser to get them somewhere else?'

'Why? You've been seen around Cerrillos. It won't look odd.'

'Why don't you go? I could use the rest.'

'Because clothes that fit you will be a damn sight closer to her size than clothes that fit me, that's why.'

'I'm not buying dresses,' Pete said warily.

'That *would* attract comment! She'll have to wear men's clothes. It may not be decent, but it'll be better than what she's wearing right now.'

'I still don't see why Cerrillos. There are trading-posts nearer.'

'Sure, and they don't carry the stock. You can walk into any store in Cerrillos and pick up what you want straight away, and be gone. Anywhere else there'll be a long discussion about everything under the sun and a good chance there's nothing to fit you anyway.'

'It won't matter, will it? It isn't going to be for me.'

'It's got to look as if it is. What man buys clothes for another man?'

Pete had to concede that that clinched it. Cerrillos it had to be.

The moon was full and high when he at last set out. The night stretched before him, and there was no need to risk his horse by taking short cuts over untrodden ground or by pushing the animal too hard. There should be plenty of time for a rest before dawn outside Cerrillos, and that would ensure the animal was fairly fresh for the return journey.

It was a cold, clear night and the horse was so sure-footed that only half the rider's attention needed to be on the journey, leaving the other half free to think. Pete had been riding with Joel Kanturk for something over a year, and he knew it was a partnership that struck other people as being unlikely. Pete was by nature gregarious, while Joel was the archetypal loner. Pete had left his home in Virginia because the West had sounded like an exciting place to be. He had no idea where Joel originally came from, but he knew the attraction of the frontier for the older man was that it enabled him to get away from other people. This made it all the more strange that he should tolerate himself. Joel was entirely self-sufficient. He needed no one. He was generally taciturn, and when he did speak, he was often sardonic, a characteristic that led, as Pete had mentioned that evening, to many people fearing him. Pete's experience was that when Joel had something to say it was usually to the point, and there was often a dry humour behind his comments.

Women found Joel Kanturk fascinatingly irresistible but, incredibly, he didn't seem to care. Pete sighed. What wouldn't he give to have women making up to him as they to Joel! But any interest Joel exhibited in the opposite sex was relatively superficial. He certainly enjoyed the company of attractive women, but he was very careful not to let any hint of a permanent commitment be encouraged. He was perfectly ready to indulge in a flirtation—sometimes quite a deep flirtation—but no woman was ever allowed to expect it to turn into something more.

Why he did tolerate Pete's company was a mystery to many, including Pete himself. At twenty-two he was the younger by ten years, slightly-built, ordinary-looking, and almost invariably cheerful. He had met Joel in a saloon in San Antonio. Pete—still green in those days, he thought scornfully—had allowed himself to be lured into a card-game and was being steadily fleeced. He had known it, known he should withdraw. He didn't because his youthful pride told him he would look silly, and an insidious little voice inside told him his luck was bound to change soon. It did, but not in the way he had expected.

One of the spectators in the latter stages of the game had been Joel. He had watched the steady fleecing of the young greenhorn and then, his gun cocked, had intervened, suggesting mildly that he would like to see the cards of the only remaining opposition. There had been several protestations that the game should be allowed to continue, but Joel had kept his eyes on the gambler and his gun at the ready. His silence was intimidating, and eventually other bystanders called for a display as well. When the gambler suddenly drew a small pistol, it was no sooner in his hand than it was sailing across the saloon and Joel's heavier weapon was smoking. Joel had leant forward then and removed cards from the man's sleeve and two from his boots. The pack had had an unusually large selection of aces.

The pot went to Pete, and as he put the money in his pocket, Joel had said, 'I reckon you're just about the worst card-player I've ever seen. You can buy me a drink for teaching you to stick to what you know.'

It had not taken much conversation over that drink for Joel to learn that very little of what Pete knew was of any use on the frontier. He could ride and he was a good shot. That was about it and, as Joel pointed out, it was all very well being able to hit a mule deer straight between the eyes, but first you had to find him and then you had to sneak up within range. When Joel moved on, Pete went with him. Joel didn't seem to mind, and Pete learned a lot. The older man never commented on what Pete did and only gave advice if it was asked for— and sometimes not even then, preferring to counter with a question that made Pete think things out for himself. Pete knew that if he decided to go his own way or to stay behind in any of the places through which they passed, Joel would accept his decision without comment and with no indication at all of being either pleased or sorry.

It was not only Joel's past that was a mystery, either. Pete had no idea what his mentor was seeking in the West. They lived mostly off the land. Only very rarely did they take work. They were not headed anywhere in particular. It was almost, Pete thought, as if Joel was in some sort of limbo until some day he perceived a goal. Until that day, he existed efficiently and humanely: Pete never saw him angry nor, in a cruel land, was he ever unnecessarily cruel. That was the only reason Pete could think of for Joel's determination to help the wolf girl: he might believe her to be a fraud, but her inhumane treatment was something not even that could justify. Now he had decided she was simple-minded, he would be even less likely to leave her to her fate, though what on earth Joel was going to do with her, Pete had no idea.

Pete rode into Cerrillos as early as he decently could, not wishing to look as if he had been travelling all night. He tied his horse outside the store and bought himself some new trousers and a shirt. He bought a belt, too, as the girl was likely to need one, and this raised an eyebrow or two: a travelling man might have these strange ideas about needing two sets of clothes— but two belts . . .?

One of the raised eyebrows belonged to a miner whom Pete did not even see, let alone recognise. The miner recognised him, though, and slipped quietly out

of the store to seek out his companions of the day
before.

They were very quick to make an accurate assessment
of the situation. A naked girl was the only possible
explanation for a spare set of clothes; obviously the tall
man was keeping guard on the girl. If they followed
Pete this time and took care not to lose him, they were
home and dry: six of them—seven if O'Brien could be
persuaded to come—against only two, and the girl
already caught. What could be easier? It took five
minutes to decide, another ten to throw saddles on their
mules. When Pete left Cerrillos, they were a long way
behind. The distance was deliberate, and it did not
increase.

CHAPTER FIVE

NEITHER JOEL KANTURK nor the girl slept. The girl did
not dare. She did not—could not—believe that the man
would leave her unmolested for long, and she was
determined to be ready to counter his assault when it
came. She found it odd that he had made no attempt
to secure her except by the rope that remained round
her waist, the other end of which was now attached to
his arm. It would be easy enough in theory to undo the
rope at her end, but when she had made a tentative
effort to do so, she learnt that even so slight a movement
as she had made transmitted itself along to the man
who had appeared to be dozing. All he had done then
had been to tip back the broad-brimmed hat that had
been tilted over his face and look at her. It was all he
had needed to do. It told her she was dealing with a
man who slept like a wolf: lightly and with part of his
mind still awake. Even if she succeeded in untying the
rope without waking him, she had still to step over him
and scramble down the cliff without his becoming aware
of the fact. It was probably not possible, and her
battered, exhausted body ached so much that, without
a strong likelihood of success, she was disinclined to
make the attempt. So she crouched under her blanket
and fought off the fatigue that threatened to overwhelm
her.

Joel despised himself for tethering the girl in this way,
yet how else could he ensure her safety? She would
escape if she could, and he could not blame her for
wanting to. If there had been any chance of her understanding what he said, he would have explained the
danger in which he believed she stood and his intentions

as to her future well-being. She seemed incapable of comprehension, whether through fear or feeble-mindedness, and he could see no other way of keeping her safe for the present. So he lay across the cave entrance with his stetson over his eyes and dozed. She was quick enough on the uptake, he noticed: when he had felt the rope move, he had needed only to look at her and she had abandoned that attempt.

When dawn broke, he handed her his water-flask and some more jerky, and sat down again to await Pete's return. At the thought of the younger man, he frowned. Pete was not cut out for the lonely life of a hunter on the frontier. He was a nice boy, even-tempered and cheerful, and had proved himself willing and able to learn, but his natural habitat was a town. If ever a man was cut out to settle down and raise a family, perhaps to run a store and become a pillar of the community, it was Pete Lingstrom. Yet the boy still, after all this time, saw the new Territory of New Mexico as representing some great romantic adventure and showed no signs of outgrowing that appealing but inaccurate picture. Perhaps the far from romantic way in which this girl had been treated would force him to start seeing the truth. It was certainly time!

Joel rather envied Pete his obvious suitability for domestication. Pete would find it quite easy to fall in love with some nice girl whom he would marry and with whom he would have a generally happy and unexciting life, which would suit them both. A month of such a woman would drive Joel back on the trail out of sheer boredom, yet there was even less point in his taking a serious interest in the other sort. Joel grinned sardonically to himself. There were plenty of women to be had, even in this remote Territory. Some were as compliant as a man could wish, so long as he had money in his pocket; some saw him as a welcome change from their husbands. What hope of happiness would there be with either? A woman who was unfaithful to one man would not hesitate to treat another in the same way, and a woman whose only real concern was what a man could spend would not be slow to transfer her affections if someone else offered more. He had twice thought himself in love. He supposed he should be grateful that in each case he had learnt the truth before it was too late to draw back. Of course, he had been younger then. A lot younger. Not much older than Pete. Maybe Pete's expectations were lower. He was certainly less likely to be disappointed.

The sound of an iron shoe on stone broke into his thoughts. A swift glance across the cave told him the girl had heard it, too. Joel drew back from the entrance and looked cautiously out as the lone horseman appeared round the bend of the canyon. Then he heaved a sigh of relief. Pete had made good time.

The younger man threw up into the cave a pair of trousers made of tough brown denim, a chequered shirt in red and black, and a heavy leather belt with a brass buckle shaped like a horse-shoe. Joel unrolled the garments and held them up against himself before tossing them over to the girl and untying the rope that tethered her to his arm.

'Put these on,' he said, and then gestured with his head towards the cave entrance. 'I'll be right down there, so don't try to get away.'

The girl understood perfectly well what to do with the clothes, but doing it presented problems. Untying the rope was simple, and it was easy enough to get into the trousers, but she had never handled buttons before and these were not easily accessible. The shirt was even more difficult: she could put one arm into a sleeve, but unless she put the shirt on back to front—and she knew that was not right—it was extremely difficult to contort herself into the shape necessary to get her other arm in. Eventually this, too, was accomplished and the front buttons fastened; but what was she to do with the sleeves? Like the trouser-legs, they were far too long. Unlike the trouser-legs, they had buttons—but how could you fasten them with only one hand?

The men gave her what they judged to be more than
enough time, and when Joel pulled himself once more
over the lip of the cave he was pleased to see that the
girl was at least decently covered. She stood before him
with the legs in folds over her ankles and her hands
quite hidden somewhere in her sleeves. She had not
made any attempt to tuck the shirt in. He laughed, but
not unkindly.

'Come here,' he said, reaching for an empty cuff.

The girl hesitated momentarily and then allowed him
to lift the arm. He rolled her sleeves up and was pleased
to see that the thinner layer of tar on her arms was
beginning to crack. Then he knelt down and turned up
a broad cuff at the bottom of each leg. As he did so, it
flashed through the girl's mind that he was now at a
disadvantage. Almost as quickly she realised that Pete
was outside, and that any advantage she gained would
soon be lost. When Joel reached out to tuck her shirt
in, she stiffened and pulled back, staring up at him in
wary fear.

For the first time she thought she saw understanding,
possibly even pity, in a man's eyes.

'I shan't hurt,' he said in the soft tone he would have
used to a hand-shy puppy.

The voice had its effect, and he pushed the shirt
quickly into the too-wide waist of the trousers and, as
he did so, he became aware once more how slight was
her frame. The girl was still clutching the belt, and
when he reached for it, she snatched it away and
clutched it close to her, caressing the shiny buckle as
she tried to keep it from him.

Joel pointed to his own belt and then to her waist.
'Give it to me,' he said gently. 'I'll not take it away.'

She glanced down at her waist and then at his. She
handed him the belt with an air of extreme reluctance.
Joel slotted it round her waist and fastened it. He had
to make an extra hole with his hunting-knife, and as he
pulled the belt together, it crossed his mind that his two
hands could have spanned her waist.

He stood back and looked at her dispassionately. What a sight! With her outsized clothes and a face from which she seemed to have plucked most of the feathers but which was still coated in tar, while her hair looked like a nesting-box, she was enough to terrify small boys and to make him despair. What could be made of a creature like this? Not very much, in all probability, but the alternative was to let her return to the life she had known before, and that was unthinkable. In the meantime, she must stay here a while longer. He picked up the rope that lay discarded on the floor and tied it round her again. He did not miss the look of disappointment in the eyes that gleamed unnaturally white in so black a face.

'Up here, Pete!' he called out.

Pete looked at the girl with the critical eye of one whose sartorial judgment is at stake. 'I suppose it's an improvement,' he said. 'I didn't think of boots, though,' he added, looking at her bare feet.

'Doubt if she could wear even moccasins yet,' Joel said. 'Anyway, where she's going, she'll be on horse-back, so it won't matter.'

'Where *is* she going?' Pete felt his curiosity was entirely justified.

'Let's leave that till it's sure,' Joel told him. 'Now listen carefully. I'm going now. I aim to be back a good two hours before nightfall, and we'll need to be on our way as soon as I return.' He fastened the other end of the rope to Pete's arm. 'Don't get soft-hearted, Pete. If she can take you off guard and escape, she will, believe me. Rest, but don't sleep. I'll water your horse, and hobble him further up the canyon where mine is. You'll need your rifle and your bed-roll; I'll throw them up. Keep half an eye on her and half on the canyon below. the other eye can sleep.' He looked steadily at the younger man. 'I mean it, Pete! Don't relax. I've a feeling in my bones. Stay on your guard.'

Pete nodded. Joel was seldom so vehement, and he did not think he was a man who set much store by

hunches. Perhaps the girl had gone for him in the night.
That would account for the severity of the warning.

The sound of a single horse coming back out of the
canyon carried clearly, and the miners scattered hastily
for cover. Peering out from behind a high outcrop, they
saw a tall man ride out of the canyon and turn down
the Indian trail. So they had been right! The youngster
had met his friend, and now the youngster was left
behind, presumably to watch the girl. Not much of a
problem there, then: the opposition had been halved,
and with no effort on their part. The two of them were
almost certainly holed up in the Frijoles caves, probably
with inadequate supplies of food and water, since they
might expect to use the stream and its visiting game as
victuals became necessary. There was no knowing how
long the tall man would be gone, of course, but, by and
large, things were falling out very favourably.
    When the tall man was safely out of sight and sound,
the miners resumed their cautious journey into the
canyon.

A stranger might have missed the convent of the Sisters
of the Blood of Christ. The soft ochreous orange of its
blind adobe walls melted into the soft ochreous orange
of the mesa behind it, only the dark brown protrusion
of the *viga*-ends at regular intervals a foot below the
top of the walls revealing that the structure was man-
made and not simply another strangely eroded outcrop
of rock. Between the building itself and the Santa Fe
River lay the convent fields, small patches of cultivated
ground where a system of *acequias* and the smaller
branches of *sangrias* led water from the river to irrigate
the corn, chilis and pinto beans, the crops that formed
the staple diet of the nuns as well as everyone else in
the Territory. The nuns had a small flock of sheep, too.
This provided milk, butter and cheese as well as wool
and when one died there was mutton to be enjoyed as
a special treat.

Joel Kanturk rode up to the heavy double doors and hammered on them. A shutter in the sun-bleached door was opened and a wimple-framed face peered through the lattice.

'Mother Superior,' he said tersely. 'Tell her it's Joel Kanturk.'

The door opened a few minutes later, and he led his horse through the *zaquan*, the roofed entrance that let into the shaded *placita*, a patio so large it was more like a small plaza, hence its name.

'We have a stall over here,' the nun said, her homespun habit of undyed wool gliding before him across the sand of the *placita* and past a simple shrine that probably represented Our Lord and had certainly been carved by an Indian. 'In here.'

Joel ducked his head beneath the lintel and found two small stalls, one of which was already occupied by a small, stringy, ewe-necked, roach-backed paint with a decidedly evil look in his eye. He put his own mount in the neighbouring stall and uncinched the saddle.

'If he can be fed and watered, sister, I'd be grateful. Where did this come from?' He indicated the paint.

The nun smiled. 'Reverend Mother says she has seen better, but we were given him in return for hospitality— a most generous gift! He is a true godsend when we bring fuel down from the mountains.'

'I imagine he must be, though Mother Superior must cringe whenever she looks at him. I doubt she ever saw the like in Ireland.'

'As I recall, she stared at him in total silence for several minutes and then said that the Lord's ways were mysterious indeed.'

Joel's lips twitched at the picture the nun had unwittingly painted but made no comment, and when his own horse was settled, he followed her back across the *placita* to the little room where Mother Superior received visitors.

It was a small, bare room with an earthen floor and lime-washed walls. A large table of scrubbed pine in the

middle did additional duty as a desk, a fact evidenced
by the papers with which it was now neatly stacked.
There were two heavy chairs of Mexican design, one of
them against the wall and the other behind the table. A
roughly carved crucifix hung on the wall above the
small fireplace, and a *retablo* in the Mexican style,
depicting the Nativity and framed in tin, decorated the
adjacent wall behind Mother Superior.

Mother Superior rose from her chair as her visitor
was shown in and went forward to welcome him, her
hands outstretched and a smile of pure delight on her
face.

'A surprise indeed, and none the less welcome for
that!' she said.

Joel took her hands and kissed them, and then swept
her into his arms. 'It's been a long time,' he said.

'And whose fault was that? I've been here these
twenty years, and for the last ten I've been hearing
about you, so you've not been far off. What brings you
here now? Are you visiting Mother Superior or your
old Irish auntie?'

Joel smiled ruefully. 'Both. I need help now, and I
can't think of anyone better to offer it—if you will.'

The nun returned to her chair and indicated its
companion. 'Draw that chair up, Joel, and let's get one
thing clear. The days of seeking sanctuary in a convent
are gone—if you've broken the law, you face the consequences. In any case, you could hardly come here,
among nuns.'

'What you've been hearing about me clearly hasn't
been flattering! It's nothing like that, I promise you. It
isn't really even for me.' As briefly as possible, Joel
sketched in what he knew of the wolf girl, both her
recent known past and her alleged history, adding his
own opinions as to the probability of the latter. 'You
see, Reverend Mother,' he concluded, 'she needs protection from her own weakness. What I hoped was that
she could come here initially for sanctuary, and that the
sisters would do what they could to turn her into the

semblance of a civilised human being. Perhaps they could then find her some sort of basic job within her capabilities—which are going to be limited, I feel bound to say.'

'Of course she must come here, that goes without question, but I wouldn't be too quick to discount her history. Such things have happened, you know.'

'So they say. I find it hard to believe.'

Mother Superior smiled. 'You haven't lost any of your childhood scepticism, I see! You will find, however, that when stories of a certain nature are reported from unconnected places at different times in history, it is a foolish person who discounts them. If you accept the possibility that the story is true in this particular case— and you will notice I do not say "probability"—you must also accept the possibility that her capabilities may be greater than you imagine.'

Joel shrugged. 'What difference does that make? It does not alter what the convent can offer, or what she needs.'

'That's true enough.' The old woman hesitated before deciding that a direct question might be best. 'What is your interest in her, Joel?'

'My interest? Why, none!' He laughed. 'You've been hearing strange things about me, indeed, if you think such a one could be of any interest to me—as you will realise when you see her.'

'You were never much noted for compassion, Joel Kanturk. Particularly not where women are concerned,' she said bluntly.

His tanned face darkened with an angry flush. 'That was a long time ago,' he said.

'Yes, it was. And your face tells me it still rankles.'

'Would you have had me marry a woman who had already deceived me and was carrying another man's child?'

'I wouldn't have you marry any woman you didn't love, but I wouldn't have had you put her from you quite so publicly as you did.'

'It could hardly have been managed with discretion in so small a place.'

'You think not? I remain unconvinced. At least, by coming to New Mexico, you left no one any hope you might change your mind. Why *did* you choose New Mexico?'

Joel shrugged. 'It was a long way off; and because I knew you had been sent here, I had heard of it. It didn't matter much to me where I went, just so long as it was as far from Ireland as possible.'

The old nun looked at him shrewdly. 'You couldn't have come to a more different place. Don't you sometimes long for the green fields and the mists from the sea?'

He hesitated as if reluctant to give an answer that might reveal a weakness. 'Sometimes,' he admitted at last. 'I look at the scrawny scrub cattle scratching a living among the tumbleweed and the sagebrush and think how they would flourish in lush pastures. That's when I miss Ireland. Then I remember Susannah and our respective families, and I thank God I am too far away even to hear about them, let alone run the risk of a chance encounter.'

'That sounds suspiciously as if you haven't altogether put her out of your mind,' his aunt commented.

'I'll never forget her deception,' he said bitterly. 'Never. Nor forgive it, either. My love died when I discovered how she had betrayed me, and hate replaced it, but even that has gone now. No, I have no feelings about her at all, but what she did to me I can never forget.'

'Wounded pride takes a long time to recover,' his aunt remarked, but not unkindly. 'Was escape your only goal in coming here?'

'I suppose it was the main one at first,' he admitted. 'I figured it would give me a fresh start where no one knew me or was likely to find out.'

'Is that what you call this life you live now? A fresh start? This drifting from one place to another? Forgive me if I speak frankly, Joel, but as a start it strikes me as being more like an ending. It certainly hasn't led to much.

Joel stood up, anger clouding his face. He tossed two silver dollars on the table. 'That will pay for my horse's feed,' he said. 'What I choose to do with my life is no one's business but my own. Just take this girl in.'

Mother Superior was quite unperturbed. She picked up the coins and dropped them into the small purse that hung from her belt. 'I'm sure the horse hasn't eaten that much, but the contribution is very welcome.' She stood up and smiled. 'When will you be back with her?'

'By nightfall. Sooner, perhaps.'

'Then you will eat with us.' She paused and put a hand on his arm. 'What you're doing is a good thing, Joel. It's just that I don't understand why.'

He bent down and kissed her briefly. 'Maybe I've developed a taste for helping the underdog,' he said. 'Believe it or not, it isn't the first time,' he added, thinking of Pete.

'There's hope for you yet, Joel Kanturk. Be gone now—and may God go with you.'

The sound of sporadic gunfire greeted Joel as he approached Frijoles canyon. Dismounting, he tethered his horse among the bushes and small trees that covered the canyon on this side and drew his rifle from the saddle-holster before advancing cautiously. His progress was necessarily slow, but he finally discovered that his bones had not been misleading him. He hoped Pete had not been taken by surprise.

From a position well back from the little creek and safely hidden behind a boulder, he was able to assess the situation. He could see the entrance to the cave quite clearly. Every so often a rifle fired out. Pete was there, then, keeping out of sight. Presumably the girl was somewhere behind him. At the foot of the cliff below the cave entrance a body sprawled. Pete had got one of them, it seemed. The question was, how many more were there?

Joel was in no hurry to enter the fray until he knew the number and position of the enemy. So far as he could ascertain, there were six of them, all using long-guns, but that didn't mean they had no hand-guns—on the contrary, it would be wise to assume they had. They were not very cleverly disposed, all six being placed in a rough semicircle in front of the cave where, from the safety of the old adobe walls and the occasional large boulder, they could fire at the cave entrance. Joel judged that Pete's ammunition was running low by the infrequency of his return fire and the investors clearly knew it, too. So confident were they of their eventual success that they had not set any sort of guard against an approach from the rear.

Joel narrowed his eyes, seeking closer identification of the attackers. Miners? Quite possibly. His eyes ranged further afield then and he made out the unmistakable shape of ears among the brush. Mules' ears. So miners it must be. He smiled grimly. There were six of them, but miners were rarely crack shots. The odds improved!

He advanced slowly. He must be careful and his shooting precise: only his first shot would have the element of surprise. Selecting a position behind a rock, he stood up and took careful aim. His rifle cracked and a miner slumped sideways.

The remaining five he could see whirled round and, although Joel could no longer be seen, they guessed the identity of the person who had so unexpectedly taken a hand in events. In their attempt to gun down their new attacker, they forgot the danger of becoming easy targets for the man in the cave, and before they could formulate a battle-plan and position themselves to deal with an assault from two sides, their number was reduced to four.

A rifle gleamed in the sunlight, and Joel fired at a point some little way below it. There was a cry, and the clatter of a gun as it fell on to rocks. From various points in the landscape, three men rose, holding their weapons in the air, while a fourth clutched his arm and stumbled towards the partly hidden mules, closely followed by his companions. Seven, not six, Joel thought. He must be more careful: that could have been a fatal mistake. He let them go, and smiled to himself as he realised that they were making no attempt to take the spare mules with them. A shot in the air hurried their egress from the canyon, and Joel made his unhurried way after them to collect his buckskin which was happily browsing among the bushes.

Pete welcomed him back with undisguised relief. 'They must have seen you leave,' he said. 'They were here within half an hour of your departure. I don't know how much longer I could have held them off.'

'As long as you stayed in the cave, indefinitely. After all, as soon as a hand appeared over the entrance, you should have been able to shoot it off.'

Pete shuddered. 'I suppose so. At least it didn't get that desperate. What now?'

'How's the girl?'

'No trouble. Don't think she was any happier to see them than I was.'

Joel cast a knowledgeable eye up at the sun. 'Buck needs a rest, and so do I. Fetch down those mules; we can use them. I reckon we can give it an hour, no more. Then we're off.'

'Where to?' Pete asked. 'Or is that still a secret?'

'No secret. Santa Fe, more or less. Any objections?'

Pete sighed. 'Not if it means a good night's sleep in a soft bed.'

'I don't vouch for a soft bed, but you'll get your sleep.'

Pete laughed. 'Right now, I'll settle for that. Does she ride with you?'

'Not now—we've got mules. We'll put her on one of them.'

'Maybe she can't ride,' Pete objected.

'Maybe she can't,' Joel agreed. 'I reckon she'll have learnt by the time we get there, don't you?'

By the time the little procession reached the convent, both the riders and their mounts were exhausted. Joel Kanturk rode in the van, leading the mule that carried the girl, the rope round her waist tied to his saddlehorn. Behind them came Pete, with the two remaining mules tied camel-fashion one behind the other.

The nun who opened the doors to them threw up her hands in dismay. 'We have only the two stalls, and one of those is occupied! What are we to do with all these?'

Joel dismounted. 'We'll put the second horse in your feed-store,' he said. 'The mules can be hobbled outside, once they've been watered—that is, unless you don't mind them wandering round the *placita* all night.'

The nun shook her head. 'I can't see Mother Superior allowing that, but bring them in for the time being.' If she felt any curiosity about the tar-encrusted girl with the rope round her waist and the bare feet, she gave no indication of it.

Mother Superior appeared at the door of her office as they came into the *placita*, and frowned. 'I don't know that we have the feed for three mules,' she said. 'It's not that I begrudge it, but it just isn't there. You said nothing about them, you know.'

'Because I didn't know I'd have them,' Joel told her. 'They'll forage well enough outside. I brought them for the convent. I suggest you keep one in place of that appalling paint, and sell the paint and the other two.'

'Did you come by them honestly, Joel Kanturk?' she asked suspiciously.

'I didn't steal them, if that's what you mean!' her nephew replied.

'Then in that case I'll accept them with gratitude— but we keep the paint. He won't fetch as much as a good mule, but he's good enough for what we need, and the sisters have a soft spot for him.'

'As you choose. You should get a good price for these—they're good Missouri mules. Don't let them go for a song.'

'Are you telling an Irishwoman how to sell horseflesh

now?' she laughed. 'Don't worry. The Lord equipped me with the right skills for that task. Now, let's have a look at your wolf girl.'

Joel tugged the girl forward into the now fading light of the *placita*, and the elderly nun looked at her in silence.

'We can do away with that,' she said at last, and unfastened the rope. She beckoned a nun over. 'It's not only hot water you'll be needing, but lard and butter, too, I'm thinking.'

The younger nun looked doubtfully at the girl. 'Do you think she's accustomed to bathing, Reverend Mother?' she asked.

'I doubt she's ever had a bath in her life,' she replied cheerfully. 'You'll need at least two more pairs of hands.' She turned to the girl and smiled. 'Now you go with Sister Maria,' she said kindly. 'She'll do you no harm, I promise you, and then we'll get you something to eat.'

The girl had realised two things. The most important was that, with the doors closed, there was no means of escape from the convent. The other was that these women in their shapeless homespun woollen habits meant her no harm. She went with Sister Maria to a room on one side of the *placita*, while Mother Superior led the two men into her office on the other side. The table had already been laid, and the two men feasted on the luxury of *burritos*—crisply-fried blue-corn tortillas wrapped round cooked ground mutton and covered with hot green chilis. There were pinto beans by way of an additional vegetable, and hunks of freshly baked corn-bread to fill any gaps. It was the best meal either of them had eaten for some time.

Their meal was punctuated by gales of laughter coming from across the *placita*. Joel looked questioningly at Mother Superior. 'Don't you feel a need to find out just what's going on?' he asked eventually.

'Not in the least,' she told him. 'I imagine there is quite a lot of splashing over there. If they need me, they'll let me know.'

Pete grinned. 'I wouldn't mind being a fly on the wall,' he said.

'That, young man, is a most improper remark!' the nun said sternly, and was inwardly amused to see him blush as he realised the implication of his comment.

The three nuns who had been set the task of cleaning up their visitor had discarded their habits, the shifts underneath being much easier garments to dry after the soaking they were likely to get. The room in which they set about their task was their laundry, and a huge half-hogshead was the bath. They were relieved to find that the girl had no false modesty about removing her clothes and seemed quite willing to step into the tub, though she drew back momentarily when she found the water was very warm.

'Come on,' Sister Maria said encouragingly. 'It's not hot, and cold water would only set the tar more firmly.'

The girl was glad of the chance to bathe, for this had been denied her since her original capture, but when she was handed a rough bar of yellow soap—a precious commodity the nuns made themselves—she had no idea what to do with it. It was the demonstration of this skill that began the laughter, and then the girl recalled that the human family with whom she had briefly lived had used a similar substance on her. Where the tar coating was thin, a vigorous soaping was enough to remove it, but elsewhere it took the assistance of the nuns to rub in the purer fats that gradually lifted and dissolved the foul coating. The water was continually emptied and renewed, bucketful by bucketful until, after a couple of hours' work, the water was clean save for a soapy cloudiness, and the girl stood before them, thoroughly clean except for fragments of tar still clinging to a few strands of hair. The earthen floor of the laundry was fast returning to the mud whence it came, but Sister Maria expressed the opinion that that was a small price to pay for so spectacular a success.

They dressed the girl in a novice's habit, the only

female garment they had to hand, and tied her golden hair back with a piece of ribbon that had been intended to decorate a statue of a saint later in the year. The nuns had folded the girl's unsuitable male clothes into a neat pile, and were alarmed when she went over to them.

'You can't wear those!' Sister Josepha exclaimed. 'Not now, not when there's something more suitable available.'

But all the girl wanted was the belt with its beautiful shiny buckle, and when the nuns realised this, they agreed that it would look very well, in addition to transforming the habit into a dress. Sister Josepha showed her how it fastened and then handed it to her. Mother Superior had said the girl might be simple-minded, but she showed no sign of it now.

When the nuns had discarded their soaked shifts and replaced their heavy habits, they stood back to admire their handiwork.

'You look quite different,' Sister Maria told the girl. 'Reverend Mother won't recognise you.'

Reverend Mother had less difficulty than her guests. When Sister Maria led the girl over to Mother Superior's office, where her visitors were drinking coffee and relaxing in the room's almost meditative calm, they automatically stood up at the entrance of the nun and the young woman she pushed, not unkindly, over the threshold in front of her.

'Here you are, Reverend Mother,' she said. 'It wasn't easy, but at least our victim co-operated.'

Pete gasped openly, and even Joel, who rarely betrayed his feelings, caught his breath as the girl came into the lamplight. She was small and slight and almost as drowned in the habit as she had been in the outfit in which she had arrived. But the belt cinching her waist revealed unexpectedly delectable curves on that slight frame, and they could see that the face, which they had never before seen cleansed, was one of considerable beauty. The eyes were large and long-lashed, set wide apart above a straight, slim nose. Below that, her lips were full and betokened a promise of which she was quite ignorant. The whole was framed by the loosely-restrained halo of golden hair, several curling tendrils of which had already escaped the ribbon and hung, temptingly vulnerable, on either side of her face.

Mother Superior smiled with satisfaction. 'You've done well, Sister Maria. Did you have any problems?'

'Only getting the tar off—there is still some in her hair, I'm afraid. We used a sinful amount of water, and the soap is almost gone, but at least she's clean.'

'I hope she realises that she's to stay here,' Mother Superior commented. 'And that means she needs a name.' She turned to the two men. 'You found her. What name would you like to give her?'

The girl reached out a tentative hand towards the elderly nun, and touched her sleeve.

'What is it, my dear?' Mother Superior asked with an encouraging smile.

The girl pointed to herself. 'Tezzie,' she whispered. 'Tezzie.'

'Tezzie?' Mother Superior repeated. 'Is that your name? Tezzie?'

The girl nodded.

'Hm. Tezzie. Probably short for Theresa—and a good Catholic name it is, too! Then Tezzie you remain. I hope you gentlemen have no objections?'

Pete shook his head. Joel frowned. 'None at all. It reinforces my suspicions, though: she understood what you said, and she has a name. That rather disposes of the unlikely story that she was brought up by wolves. Be careful, Reverend Mother. You may have a very skilful deceiver on your hands.'

'Not so very long ago you expressed the opinion that she was simple-minded,' his aunt reminded him. 'You can't have it both ways! Nor does it entirely disprove the story, you know: the girl you mention spent a little time in human company. Certainly long enough to have acquired a name and an understanding of simple words.'

'You've been out of the world too long, Aunt,' Joel said harshly. 'You've become gullible!'

'Nuns are rarely gullible! We see too much of human frailty in all its guises to be under any illusions. No, Joel, I am not gullible merely because I leave my mind open to possibilities that, though unlikely, may prove to be the case. Sister, take Tezzie away and feed her. She will sleep in the dormitory with you and the other sisters. Joel, you and your friend will sleep in the barn. We will see you on your way after breakfast.'

Tezzie's night on a pallet of straw was inevitably restless. For one thing, she was not alone. For another, so much had happened in the last two days that it was almost impossible to stop her mind from going over and over recent events and trying to decide whether they were for good or ill. Of only one thing was she certain: the nuns seemed kind and friendly and, since her life since the destruction of her wolf 'family' had been lonely and ultimately disastrous, it made sense to stay here, at least until she had learnt enough to attract no undue attention outside. Then perhaps she would decide whether to remain among people or to return to her lonely independence.

Her mind turned to the two men who had brought her here. She still did not quite understand their motives. The tall one had not used any conspicuous kindness in his manner of capturing her or keeping her, and she had dreaded the moment when he, like those others . . . But he had not done so. Instead, she had been brought here, a place she did not understand, but where she felt safe in a way she could not define. Perhaps she had cause to be grateful. She saw no significance in the fact that, though she acknowledged a possible debt to two men, it was only one of them that she actually saw in her mind's eye. When she had first seen that tall man watching her in Valdez' side-show, her instinct had been to cover herself. Now she had clothes—proper clothes like anyone else—she had no need of that particular modesty. She knew how to stand up. She could do so now in front of him and perhaps not see that scathing look.

A nun called the two men to breakfast, and they joined Mother Superior in her office once more. She watched them dispose of fried tortillas topped with eggs and red chilis and washed down by several mugfuls of coffee, and when that had gone and she expressed concern, they promised her that there was no danger of their starving to death that day, even if they ate nothing more till next morning.

'You've done us proud!' Pete assured her. 'We've eaten better last night and this morning than we have done for weeks past. My only fear is that you've left yourselves short.'

Mother Superior shrugged. 'The chickens will go on laying, and the sale of the mules—for which we are truly thankful, I promise you—will ensure that my nuns go short of very little.' She stood up. 'Now, if you're ready to go, get your horses saddled while I find the girl you brought here. Whatever you believe her to be, Joel, that was a kind act which I hope may be the forerunner of many more.'

'I don't aim to go round looking for girls with spurious origins,' he said drily.

'You know perfectly well I meant no such thing! Just don't belittle the importance of the occasional disinterested good deed.'

When they led their horses out into the blazing sunlight of the *placita*, Mother Superior was waiting to bid them farewell, and by her side, flanked by the protective form of Sister Maria, stood Tezzie. There was no lamplight to soften a face into beauty out here, and the men stood in silent astonishment that, under this clear unequivocal light, she was even more beautiful than she had seemed the night before. It was Joel who broke the silence.

'I know you'll look after her,' he said, unable to take his eyes from the girl. 'But I beg you, Reverend Mother, don't turn her into a nun.'

'I shall turn her into nothing she does not wish. Will that satisfy you?'

'It must, since I have no choice in the matter.'

'So you are learning resignation too! There is hope for you yet, Joel Kanturk! Do you expect to be back this way soon?'

'Not soon, but some time it is inevitable, and when I come I shall look for an accounting.'

'I do not make myself accountable to you, Joel,' his aunt said quietly. 'If, however, you mean you will request me to let you know how Tezzie goes on, then of course I shall.'

'That is what I meant.' He bent down and kissed her. 'Goodbye, Aunt—and thank you.'

Pete, who also had not taken his eyes off Tezzie during this exchange, reached forward and took one of her hands, kissing it lightly. 'Goodbye, Tezzie,' he said, and was rewarded with a shy smile before her glance moved to his companion.

'Never let it be said I lack Pete's gallantry,' Joel laughed, and possessed himself of the hand Pete had just relinquished. He, too, kissed her fingers and as he raised his head, found himself looking into eyes so heavily flecked with green that they could have been so described, and which carried an expression he could not recall ever having seen before. There was shyness there, but there was also an appeal under those heavy golden lashes that he did not quite understand—and neither, he suspected, did she. On an impulse, he tipped up her chin and kissed her lightly on the lips, and was surprised that her hand fluttered momentarily to his sleeve before she dropped both her hand and her eyes.

'I think you had best be on your way,' Mother Superior said firmly, leading the way across the *placita* to the heavy doors.

Joel looked back over his shoulder as his horse moved off. Mother Superior stood there waving, and beside her stood the slight, golden-haired girl he was leaving. He was suddenly reluctant to go, and the image that inexplicably remained with him over the next few months, to fade away at last under the heavy necessity of staying alive in an inhospitable country, was not the image of the old nun.

CHAPTER SIX

TEZZIE SOON proved herself to be very far from simple-minded. Her inability to understand more than a few simple sentences was initially her main handicap, but once her vocabulary increased—as it did very rapidly—it became clear that it was only necessary to tell her something once for it to be remembered. She learnt to spin, weave and sew, to make butter and cheese, and to milk the cow the sisters bought with some of the money the mules fetched. She learnt to grind corn and to make tortillas. She learnt how to dry the red chilis that hung from the outside ends of the *vigas* in the *placita* until they were needed for flavouring. Mother Superior taught her to eat gracefully, with tools, and to read and write. She learnt how to fire the *horno*—the beehive-shaped clay oven that sat in the *placita*—how to rake out the hot ash and replace it with the risen dough so that, within the hour, crisp, fresh bread stood waiting for the hungry nuns when their day's work was done.

The months Tezzie spent at the convent were very happy ones. She was keen to learn, and there was plenty to be learnt. She disliked inactivity, and there was plenty to be done. She enjoyed a good argument, and Mother Superior played devil's advocate well. If her thoughts sometimes strayed in a rare moment to the tall, harsh-featured man who had brought her there, it was only to be expected. She had once asked Mother Superior if he was likely to return—she would like to thank him, she said—but Mother Superior was unhopeful. All things were possible. Some were very unlikely.

She had told Mother Superior enough of her story to convince the nun that she had indeed been brought up

by wolves, and the nun was further of the opinion that
the name 'Tezzie' went back earlier in the girl's memory
than the family that had looked after her so briefly.

Anxious to determine whether it would be possible to
identify Tezzie's real family, Mother Superior probed
tactfully and skilfully, but could find no hint of what
her surname might originally have been. So, since the
girl's survival at all was nothing short of miraculous,
the nuns decided she might as well be called Theresa
Milagro, despite the fact that she clearly had no Mexican
blood in her veins. It was not a choice that pleased the
bishop when the time came for the girl to be baptised.
He said he was not at all sure it wasn't sacrilegious, but
Mother Superior was more than capable of dealing with
a mere bishop, and Theresa Milagro she became.

Only one thing occurred to mar the even, busy tenor
of those days. As Tezzie squatted one day on her stool
beside the cow, hidden behind the adobe walls from the
sight of anyone outside, she heard a voice that froze the
blood in her veins. She felt herself blanch with fear, and
was barely able to command herself sufficiently to get
up from her seat and take stool and pail over to the
wall not far from the door, where there was no likelihood of the speaker catching a glimpse of her, but from
which position she could most easily overhear any
converse outside.

The voice belonged to Valdez, and it brought horren-
dous memories flooding back, memories she had never
thought to have forced to the front of her mind again.

He was being indignant. Tezzie knew the scene well:
she could picture him drawing himself up to the full
extent of his limited height and thrusting out his chest
as he demanded to see Mother Superior to 'right a
wrong'.

The nun to whom he spoke had no idea who he was,
but she knew he was not the sort of person Mother
Superior would wish to be left unattended and free to
poke and pry and peer into the rooms of the convent.

She called over a novice, and told her to fetch Reverend Mother.

One glance at Mother Superior's shrewd face told Valdez that she was not someone who would automatically believe every word he said. Ingratiation would be necessary to convince her. He had come prepared for the extended courtesies that, to a Mexican, were an expected preparation to any business discussion. Mother Superior was not a Mexican, and was therefore able deliberately to disconcert him by coming straight to the point.

'You wish me to right a wrong. I believe, Mr . . .?'

'Valdez, Reverend Mother. Yes, indeed, I have been grievously wronged, and I come here for justice.'

'The Governor's Palace would be a more fitting place, don't you think? One of my sisters will direct you if you are unfamiliar with Santa Fe.'

'You misunderstand, Reverend Mother. It is within your power to help, to restore my livelihood.

'Explain, Mr Valdez—and be brief: we have work to do here.'

It was not a promising start, Valdez thought. It was not the sort of situation that could be dealt with briefly, not if he was to enlist her sympathy—an attribute that did not seem to loom large in her manner. 'A few months ago I was robbed,' he began, glancing hopefully at her face.

'I commiserate,' the nun said brusquely, 'but what has that to do with me? I presume you are not accusing one of the sisters of theft?'

'No, no, nothing like that!' he hastened to assure her. 'The thing is, I had a girl—I had rescued the poor thing, you understand—who had been brought up by wolves. Yes, I know it is an improbable story, but I swear on my mother's grave it's true, Reverend Mother. I loved that girl like a daughter, but she could not adapt to a normal life, and one has to live. So we joined a circus and people paid to see her, thus enabling me to feed and clothe her, but she was stolen from me, and

I learnt she had been brought here. I am grateful for your care of her, Reverend Mother, but I am here to take her back.'

Mother Superior's lips were compressed into a straight line, and Valdez had the uncomfortable feeling that she had not believed him.

'I have heard about this girl,' Mother Superior told him. 'For what it is worth, I believe the story of her origins.'

A beam suffused Valdez' unshaven face. 'I knew I could get justice here!' he said.

'Indeed, I think you will. As I have just said, I believe the girl may well have been brought up by wolves, but then my information differs subtly from yours, Mr Valdez. All sorts of stories get back to us, you know, and the one I heard was that you bought her, that you kept her in appalling conditions, feeding her only on raw meat, and that, finally, you had sold her for a considerable sum to provide the townspeople of Cerrillos with the great entertainment of tarring and feathering her.'

Valdez paled. How had this old woman living away from the world heard all this? The girl certainly could not have told her. Or had the nuns taught her to speak? He rushed to his own defence.

'Lies, Reverend Mother! All lies! A gross distortion— and even if it was true, the girl still belongs to me.'

'Not if you sold her,' Mother Superior pointed out. 'If she belongs to anyone, it is the citizens of Cerrillos; and they, having had their fun, turned her loose.'

'And now she is in need of my protection again,' he protested.

'No one is in need of the sort of protection you offer, Mr Valdez,' the nun told him.

It was quite clear he was not going to be able to convince her with soft words. Valdez narrowed his eyes, and his voice changed its ingratiating whine and became unpleasantly menacing.

'I want that girl, Reverend Mother, and I intend to

take her! It will be easier for everyone if you just hand
her over.'

'I cannot hand over what is not mine to give. It is
true the girl was brought here, but where she is now, I
am not prepared to say.'

'Are you telling me you haven't got her? I don't
believe it!'

'You may believe what you wish, Mr Valdez! I think
it has been made perfectly clear that you have no
business with us. I am sorry so much of your time has
been inadvertently wasted. Good day, Mr Valdez.' She
moved slowly but inexorably towards the doors as she
spoke, and Valdez found himself being obliged to go
ignominiously backwards in the same direction. As the
doors closed behind him, he had the uncomfortable
feeling that he had been completely out-manouevred,
yet he could not quite decide how it happened nor the
precise point at which he had lost control of the
exchange.

Mother Superior's air of aloof disinterest vanished as
soon as the door was safely bolted, and she hurried
over to the little cowshed to find Tezzie cowering behind
the wall.

'I take it that *was* the man who held you so long?'
she asked.

Tezzie nodded miserably. 'I knew his voice at once,'
she whispered.

The nun put her arms round the girl and raised her.
'Leave the cow for the moment,' she said. 'I think you
need something a little stronger than milk. I have some
brandy—for purely medicinal purposes, you understand—and this seems an appropriate time to break
into the bottle.' She paused and looked down at the
girl. 'You didn't think I'd let him take you, did you?'

Tezzie smiled diffidently. 'He is not a pleasant man. I
thought he would frighten you into it.'

Mother Superior laughed. 'It would take more than
our very unpleasant Mr Valdez to frighten me into
anything! Come, the brandy will do you good.'

As Tezzie sipped the burning liquid obediently, disliking its taste but bowing to Mother Superior's opinion of its effects, she ventured to question her mentor.

'You know I was listening behind the cowshed wall,' she began.

'I should have been surprised had you not been.'

'Reverend Mother, you lied to that man.'

'How so?'

'You told him I wasn't here.'

'Not at all. I told him that I was not prepared to say where you were.'

'You had told him I had been brought here. Then you told him you wouldn't say where I'd gone. Won't that make him think I *have* gone?'

'I have no control how he chooses to interpret my words.'

Tezzie looked at her shrewdly. 'Did you choose your words to make him think just that?' The nun's calm face told her nothing, and Tezzie drew her own conclusions. 'You did, didn't you?' she said. 'Even if the actual words were true, doesn't using them like that make it a lie?'

Mother Superior smiled blandly. 'Now you venture into the realm of semantics, my dear, and a simple Irish nun cannot be expected to understand such fine points.'

Tezzie smiled. 'Dear Reverend Mother, you are not at all simple, as you very well know, but whatever it was you told him, I am grateful for it.'

'Don't imagine you have got rid of Mr Valdez so simply, Tezzie. He is likely to be in the general area for a long time—after all, he does not seem to have left it in the months since he lost you—and he may not give up all that easily. It would be wise to stay on your guard.'

This frightening episode was the only event to mar Tezzie's time at the convent and, although in the days immediately following it she had been reluctant to venture outside the strong adobe walls, the fear that

Valdez might be lying in wait somewhere among the sagebrush and the chamiso gradually wore off, and her life returned to normal.

Eventually Mother Superior decided that Tezzie had become as civilised as she was likely to be and it was time to fulfil the other part of her promise to Joel: namely, to find the girl suitable employment.

This was not as easy as it might have been. There was absolutely no question of Tezzie's becoming a nun: not only had she expressed no interest, but Mother Superior was of the opinion that she was far from suitable. Tezzie was always very prettily behaved and did as she was told, but she had a disconcerting habit of always finding the weak spot in any argument and ruthlessly uncovering it. Mother Superior did not consider this a fault, but whether it was desirable in a nun was another matter, especially in one so young. Joel's fears on that score were unfounded.

The only feasible alternative was some form of domestic service. There were many army households in the Santa Fe garrison that would jump at the chance of a convent-trained girl, but Mother Superior was of the opinion that it would be better for Tezzie if she were not plunged into a society so predominantly male.

The girl's beauty raised problems with domestic service in any household, and Mother Superior felt a great deal of responsibility towards the girl's welfare. If the head of the household were elderly, there was a strong likelihood of his having susceptible sons, and if the employers had only young children, then the husband might well take too strong an interest in his maidservant. The situation looked uncomfortably like an impasse.

Until Mother Superior bethought herself of the Vigils. Hernando Vigil was a member of a prosperous Cundiyo family who had married Luz Ortega and had set up a business on the Santa Fe Trail, just outside the limits of the capital, where his wife had been born. They had built themselves a large adobe that enclosed a particularly fine patio, and at the front had added a general store. There were many such stores in the capital, but it was generally held that Vigils' had the widest selection as well as stocking items that others had barely heard of. The Vigils were approaching middle age—and middle-aged husbands were something to be avoided in the usual course of events, Mother Superior considered— but they had a large and happy family of boisterous children, and the nun could think of no other family more likely to treat Tezzie as one of their own or to safeguard her interests.

Accordingly, Mother Superior, accompanied by Sister Josepha, trudged into Santa Fe and on out to the Vigils' store. The Vigils' hospitality was legendary, and they insisted that the nuns should eat with them while they considered Reverend Mother's suggestion. The *burritos*, Sister Josepha noted with delight, were filled with that unbelievable luxury, beef, the honey was served in a huge clay pot and, just in case they needed more sustenance, there was fresh bread and a mound of butter. When the nuns returned to the convent, it was with the news that the Vigils were to take Tezzie under their wing and, as a demonstration of their intent, they gave Mother Superior enough good, serviceable calico to make the girl two dresses to replace the novice's habit she customarily wore.

The fabric was brown, plain and unexciting, but to Tezzie it represented unimaginable luxury after the rough homespun of the habit. She must depend on the nuns' judgment of a suitable style, and begged but one thing: that the dresses should be so designed that she could wear her belt with them.

Sister Maria sighed. 'It isn't customary for a lady to wear a belt at all, Tezzie,' she said. 'Especially a belt like yours—that's a man's belt.'

'I don't care what's customary—nor that it's a man's belt. I love that belt and I intend to wear it! You must agree that it will go well with the colour of the material.'

When Mother Superior saw the finished garments on their proud owner, she had misgivings, though she

wisely kept them to herself. Now that Tezzie was dressed
in a way more usual among young women, she realised
that the slight form under the voluminous habit had
been misleading. The girl was more of a woman that
she had allowed herself to realise. She had told the
Vigils she thought her to be eighteen or nineteen. Now
she reckoned she must be at least twenty, and quite
possibly more. The long skirt which fell from a gathered
waist was not so full as to interfere with the girl's work,
and the bodice above it was plain, modest and adorned
only by a plain white detachable collar. But, modest as
the bodice was, it fitted Tezzie with a precision that
revealed every curve. Even the colour, which had seemed
so suitably discreet, was as clever a foil to the girl's
golden hair as could have been devised. The straight
sleeves fastened at the wrist, but were loose-fitting
enough to roll back while she scrubbed or cooked, and
everything about the dress was designed for the sort of
life its owner would be leading. Yet it achieved a great
deal more than that, and Mother Superior could only
be glad Tezzie was going to the Vigils and not to a
family within the garrison. She noted the belt. It was
incongruous, and it unnecessarily accentuated Tezzie's
very tiny waist, which was a pity. Still, the girl was as
devoted to it as a more fortunate woman might be to a
piece of jewellery, and it would generally be hidden by
an apron, so no harm was done.

Mother Superior made her turn round. 'Very nice,
my dear. Very suitable. I'm sure the Vigils will be
pleased. Now, I have just one small thing for you.'

She took a small package from the table and handed
it to Tezzie, who took it rather gingerly, and said, 'May
I open it now?'

'If you wish.'

Mother Superior had devoted many hours to making
the linen apron that lay inside. Its basic design was
simple, but it was decorated with exquisite drawn-thread
work and, above that, an intricate design of yuccas
embroidered in self-coloured threads.

Tezzie stared at it and then ran her fingertips lightly over the surface, feeling the textures her eyes had already appreciated. 'You have been very busy, Reverend Mother.'

'Time well spent if it gives you pleasure.'

'I shan't wear it, you know. It is far too beautiful for that! Well, perhaps on Sundays,' Tezzie relented. On an impulse she reached over and kissed the nun. 'It is a generous gift indeed, from one whose sight is not as good as it once was.'

'You've noticed that, have you? You're a deal too sharp for your own good, my girl,' Mother Superior told her, but not unkindly. 'Just promise me one thing.'

'Of course.'

'Two things—don't agree to promise anything without first finding out what it is! Will you promise me that you will come back here if you are ever in need of the help we can offer?'

'You don't have to make me promise that, Reverend Mother. This is the first place I should think of coming to.'

'Good. Now, Sister Josepha and Sister Concepcion will take you to Santa Fe—I am too old to make that journey twice in so short a time and, besides, Sister Concepcion will enjoy the Vigils' hospitality. The Vigils are good people. Be guided by them, and I think you will not go far wrong.'

Tezzie made no attempt to disguise her tears as she left the convent. This was the only home she had ever known. The wolves had looked after her, in their way, as well as the nuns had done, but they had had no settled base and she now knew that she had never really belonged with them. It was frightening to be obliged to leave the safety and security of the convent, but she knew Mother Superior believed it to be for the best, and she had faith in her judgment. It was just that it was so hard to be on her own once more. Not quite on her own, of course, but it would seem like that until she was fully accepted into the Vigils' home.

The sense of being alone was much shorter lived than she anticipated. The Vigils made sure she felt she belonged with them. They included her in their discussions and generally treated her like an older daughter. Her main duty was to supervise the children, for Mrs Vigil had a very shrewd business head and preferred to help in the store, where she could exercise some restraint over her husband's tendency to succumb to a hard-luck story.

The thing that never ceased to amaze Tezzie was the extent of the Vigils' table: after her time with Valdez, she had thought the nuns lived well. Now she knew they barely scraped a living from the desert and wondered that they had been so willing to take in an extra mouth.

When, after several weeks with the family, Mrs Vigil became ill, she implored Tezzie not to nurse her.

'Tell Estefana to look after the children in the kitchen and ask Juana to keep an eye on me,' she said. 'I want you in the store. Hernando is a good man, but he believes every tale he's told, and the less likely the story, the more gullible he becomes.'

'But I don't know anything about the store,' Tezzie protested.

'You're a bright girl—you'll pick it up soon enough. The important thing is that as soon as you see Hernando being taken in, you interrupt and tell the customer he pays good specie or goes elsewhere.' Mrs Vigil had little faith in paper money.

With considerable reservations, Tezzie did as she was told. The store proved an interesting place to be and, as Mrs Vigil had predicted, she picked the work up very quickly. She had thought it would be embarrassing trying to explain her presence to Mr Vigil, but he had taken one look at her and laughed.

'I know why you're here,' he said. 'Luz doesn't trust me not to give the store away to some hard-up prospector, and you're to step in if I look like doing so. Right?'

Tezzie could only nod.

'It's only ever happened once, you know,' he went on. 'Once in twenty years! But Luz says that was once too often. She can't quite believe I learnt the lesson. I don't mind, though. She's a good business woman and an excellent book-keeper. I'd be lost without her.'

As Mother Superior had said, the Vigils were good people. Tezzie had been very anxious at the prospect of being obliged to live in close proximity once more to a man, but Hernando Vigil was a very different sort from Pedro Valdez or those other two, and it was not very long before she felt able to put her fears away from her where he was concerned. Over nearly two years now, his attitude to her was little different from his attitude to his children, and Tezzie found herself envying the stability in which the little Vigils were able to grow up.

It was a solitary trooper from the garrison who returned to barracks one evening with a scarcely credible tale of the beauty who had replaced the formidable Mrs Vigil in the store. His friends laughed at him. He had been out in the desert too long, they said, and inquired whether he had left his hat off in the heat of the day. He swore he hadn't, and that he knew a real beauty when he saw one. Since he was only eighteen, there were those who doubted this, but there was only one way to settle it, and so next day a reconnaisance party of half a dozen older soldiers found business in Vigils' store. Their verdict was inevitable: young Bud had not had too much sun or too much liquor; he might be only a young 'un, but he sure knew a beauty when he saw one.

The Vigils' business increased overnight, and when Mrs Vigil recovered, she very quickly realised why. It was the first thing about Tezzie since the girl's arrival that she discussed with her husband in the deep-feathered privacy of their bed.

'They come to see Tezzie,' she said.

'Do you blame them?'.

'No, of course not. They spend well, too, especially if

she serves them. There's no question about it. She's
good for business. That's not what worries me.'

Hernando patted her hand. 'I know. You're thinking
of what we were told of her past. It's a question of
whether we should let her remain in a position where
she meets so many soldiers—it was something Mother
Superior had sought to avoid.'

Luz nodded. 'I'm never quite sure . . . I don't think
she realises how beautiful she is. If anyone took advantage of her while she's in our care, I'd never forgive
myself. But there's no denying she's good for business.'

'Maybe we should ask her how she feels about it.
She's going to have to meet men some time.'

'Mother Superior expected that—it was one reason
for getting her out of the convent—but I don't think
she envisaged letting her meet them in quite such droves.'

Tezzie had no objection to working in the store, but
she was concerned that the Vigils should not feel she
was letting them down in some way—after all, she had
been employed to look after the children. Mrs Vigil
waved aside her objections.

'It doesn't matter, Tezzie. As long as there is someone
in the store to keep an eye on Hernando, I don't mind
who it is. I can perfectly well look after the children if
you would like to be in a position to meet more people.
It's only natural that you should wish to do so.'

In the end, since Tezzie knew Mrs Vigil herself enjoyed
being in the store more than just supervising her household, they decided to take turns, and Mrs Vigil was
amused to observe that, once the routine was established, the store's military customers were more
numerous on Tezzie's days of duty than on hers.

One soldier in particular was especially drawn to
Tezzie. Lieutenant James Garway was a tall, fair-headed,
good-looking young man some two or three years older
than she. His attentions were assiduous, and they
provoked some good-natured banter from his colleagues,
which he laughed off with a commendable lack of
concern. He was unfailingly courteous—chivalrous,

even—and Tezzie enjoyed talking to him in the relatively
rare moments when business in the store was slack. He
was a pleasant man, even though he struck her as being
rather young, and she looked forward to his visits to
the store. Mrs Vigil and her husband teased her about
her admirer and, though Tezzie blushed and disclaimed
any particular feeling for him, she was not displeased
that the assumption had been made. Her face lit up
when he came into the store, and the Vigils were not
the only ones to predict for her a life following the
drum. Tezzie herself insisted that she had no such
thoughts, but she considered it all the same, and it was
not an unattractive prospect. Nevertheless, when he
asked her if she would consent to walk with him in the
plaza on Sunday afternoon, she shook her head.

'It would not be right, Lieutenant,' she said. 'I have
no duenna, you see.'

'Wouldn't Mrs Vigil come with you?'

'Mrs Vigil is my employer—how can I ask her to
chaperon me?'

He considered this reasonable objection. 'What about
one of the Vigils' maids?'

'Why should they give up their few hours away from
work to accompany me? They have families to visit,
sweethearts to walk with. No, I'm afraid it can't be
done.'

Lieutenant Garway could think of no other solution,
and Tezzie regretted it as much as he did. She liked the
young man, and although it would be very pleasant to
stroll in the plaza with an agreeable escort, it could not
be denied that to do so would give them a far better
opportunity for quiet conversation than was offered in
a crowded store. The plaza would be busy, of course,
but busy with young couples similarly disposed, each
couple totally oblivious of the others. The assignation
could hardly be regarded as clandestine, yet its very
nature offered a high degree of privacy and Tezzie was
strongly tempted to put her scruples aside. The fact
remained that she had no duenna, and she knew that

the Vigils would be greatly shocked if she met the lieutenant without one. So she declined firmly—and noted that her decision had certainly not lowered her in his esteem.

It proved much more difficult to decline an invitation to the garrison ball. For one thing, Tezzie had never been to a ball, and the thought of all the colour and music was very tempting. But again she shook her head.

'If I can't walk with you in the plaza unchaperoned, I most certainly can't go to a ball,' she told him.

'I've already discovered that the Vigils are invited,' he replied, a hint of satisfaction in his voice. 'That means you can't possibly feel yourself unchaperoned.'

'I still can't ask my employer to be my duenna!' she exclaimed.

'Perhaps not, but I can.' The lieutenant crossed over to Hernando Vigil. 'Mr Vigil, I understand you and your wife are invited to the garrison ball,' he began.

Mr Vigil nodded.

'I would very much like to take Miss Milagro, but she feels she cannot ask your wife—her employer—to act as her duenna, so I am asking it on her behalf.'

Hernando Vigil smiled. 'It is a foolish man who speaks for his wife! Tezzie, mind the store for a few minutes.' With these words, he disappeared through the door that led to the house. When he emerged shortly afterwards, it was to tell Tezzie to go and talk to Mrs Vigil.

'Do you want to go to the ball, Tezzie, or are you giving your lack of a duenna as a reason because it is kinder than saying you don't want to go?'

'I just don't know,' Tezzie told her. 'In a way, I'd love to go: it sounds exciting and fun, and like nothing I've ever done before.'

'Then why not say "Yes"? I'm perfectly willing to be as much a duenna as your mother would be to you.' She paused, and looked at the girl shrewdly. 'Or are you afraid things may get out of hand? That Lieutenant Garway will overstep the bounds of propriety?'

'It I have a duenna, he can hardly do so, can he? No, it isn't that. Perhaps I simply don't want him to think I feel deeply for him.

'I hardly think going to a ball will make him think that, especially if your own behaviour gives him no excuse to do so—and I'm sure you will be most circumspect. Come, Tezzie, he's waiting to know whether I agree to chaperon you. What shall we tell him?'

When Mrs Vigil appeared in the shop with Tezzie close behind her, the lieutenant studied her face with some apprehension.

'I see no reason why Miss Milagro should not come to the ball,' Mrs Vigil told him. 'I am perfectly willing to chaperon her, but I don't feel it is entirely fitting that she should go at your invitation. My husband and I will bring her as part of our party—we are responsible for her in much the same way as parents would be, and I think it is better if we arrange matters like this.'

A smile of mingled relief and pleasure burst over the lieutenant's face. 'I appreciate your scruples, Mrs Vigil. I am just delighted to know that Tez—Miss Milagro will be there. You have made me very happy, ma'am.'

Mrs Vigil laughed. 'Good. May I respectfully suggest that you go now and enjoy your happiness elsewhere? Miss Milagro is going to have to spend some time making her ball-gown.'

The smile vanished, and dismay took its place. 'You mean you wish me to stay away from the store?'

'Not at all. Merely that if you do come here, you can't expect to see Tezzie quite so often in the next few weeks.'

Although Tezzie still served in the store more often than Mrs Vigil had implied would be the case, it was for the next little while on a less predictable basis. Lieutenant Garway still dropped in, but it was very much a matter of chance whether he saw Tezzie, and Tezzie admitted to herself that on those occasions when he was not there, his absence was almost a relief.

It was on one such occasion that two new customers

came in. Tezzie and Mr Vigil were very busy at the time, a group of miners from the Ortiz Mountains having come in to replenish their stocks of such staples as corn-meal, sugar and coffee. Only a fleeting glimpse of an exceptionally tall man framed in the doorway and ducking to enter caused Tezzie to look again. Her heart leapt in a way that was totally unexpected—and in a way it had never done for Lieutenant Garway. It was nearly three years since Joel Kanturk had left her at the convent. She had once expressed the hope to Mother Superior that she would have the opportunity of thanking him, and Mother Superior had effectively squashed that hope. Here he was, and with him the opportunity she had wanted. Now that it was so easily achievable, Tezzie felt unaccountably shy. It became important to her to know whether he had come here to seek her out, in order to see how she did, or by chance. There was no logical reason why the explanation should matter so much if all she wanted to do was to thank him, but it did.

It soon became evident that Joel and Pete had no idea that the girl they had rescued was at the Vigils' store. They had not been directed there by Mother Superior. They browsed idly among the goods cluttered together just inside the entrance, as people do who find they must wait to be served, and Tezzie, strangely disappointed, returned to the task of totting up the bill of one of the customers.

Joel was the first to glance up and see the golden-haired beauty behind the counter. He stared at her briefly, and frowned. The girl looked familiar. Very little reflection was needed for him to recall the shy and frightened newly-scrubbed face of the wolf girl to whose golden hair fragments of tar still clung. Could this be she? This was no timid girl, but an apparently self-confident young woman whose slight frame bore unmistakably mature curves that the close-fitting, high-cut bodice of her brown dress did nothing to conceal. Her hair, no longer dulled by a film of tar, gleamed like burnished gold in a thick, rich coil at the nape of her neck. It was perfectly possible for the nuns to have found a position for her in a place such as this. Was it also possible that such a transformation could have been achieved?

Pete, whose general interest in young women was a great deal more pronounced than that of his companion, had no doubt of her identity. He recognised the brightly polished brass horse-shoe buckle on the belt she wore.

Assuming that Joel had not seen the girl, he moved over to him. 'Guess who's here?' he said.

'I've no inclination to play games. Who?'

'Over there, behind the counter: that's our wolf girl! What did they decide her name was? Theresa?'

'Tezzie. What makes you so sure?'

'The belt I bought. Remember?'

Joel did, and a quick look confirmed the accuracy of Pete's memory.

'Let's make ourselves known,' Pete went on.

'Do you imagine she hasn't recognised us? I fancy she will have had less difficulty than we did. Leave it till these people have gone. She may not wish to be reminded, in front of witnesses, of a very unhappy past. Watch your tongue, too. We don't know how much her employer knows.'

Pete looked slightly abashed. 'I hadn't thought of that,' he admitted, and both men turned their attention to a pile of blankets, Mexican and Navajo, indiscriminately stacked together.

It seemed an age to Tezzie before the miners' needs had been met and their reckonings paid with Mrs Vigil's beloved specie. She was undecided whether to wish to hasten their departure or to prolong their business. She wanted the opportunity to talk, however briefly, to the two men to whom she owed so much, yet she dreaded the moment when she would be obliged to initiate that conversation, and then, overlying both considerations, was the fear that Joel and Pete would find nothing in the store they wanted and would leave before she had finished.

But eventually the last miner carried his last sack out to his pack-mule standing patiently at the bottom of the wooden steps in front of the store, and there was a respite for both Mr Vigil and his assistant.

Pete was the one to step into that hiatus. 'You're Tezzie, aren't you? I recognised that belt. Remember me? Pete?'

Tezzie smiled at him, almost wilfully avoiding looking at his companion. 'Of course I do,' she said. 'I have worn it every day.' She turned to her employer. 'Mr Vigil, these are the two men who took me to the convent. Pete and . . . Joel, I think.'

Joel moved forward. 'Joel Kanturk and Pete Lings- trom,' he explained. Mr Vigil must know something of her story, it seemed.

Hernando Vigil beamed. 'Then I am delighted to meet you, gentlemen. You may not realise it, but you found a treasure!'

'In what way?' Joel viewed the Mexican with a caution that bordered on hostility. To what sort of man had Mother Superior entrusted her charge?

'Tezzie came to us originally to look after the children,' Hernando told him. 'Then, when my wife was ill, she helped out here and proved just as adept at that—and of course she has been quite a lure to the Santa Fe garrison. Our business has increased considerably since she has been dealing with customers.'

'I can believe it,' Pete said, looking at her with unfeigned admiration.

Tezzie blushed and lowered her eyes, but not at the nature of the compliment—she had heard far more extravagant ones from the military, and laughed them off with no embarrassment. This time she was very aware of the presence of Joel Kanturk standing almost silently just across from her at the end of the counter.

'Have you been working here long?' Joel asked.

'Nearly two years,' Tezzie told him, 'But not all of

that time in the store.'

'Were you happy with the nuns?' he went on.

There was no mistaking the warm pleasure in her eyes. 'You can have no idea how kind they were to me—or perhaps you can, since you chose to take me there.' She hesitated briefly as if unsure whether this was the moment to press on, and then decided it was. She looked up at him, a shy smile on her lips. 'I'm so glad you have come here, Mr Kanturk,' she went on. 'I can't have struck you as very grateful the last time we met, but I have long wanted to be able to express my gratitude to you both.'

Joel smiled wryly. 'No, gratitude was not the sentiment you displayed on that occasion. In fact, you caused us no end of trouble one way and another, you know.'

Whatever response Tezzie had expected, this was not it. Any shyness, any diffidence, vanished and her green eyes flashed. 'And if I did, you have only yourselves to blame. I don't recall asking for your assistance!'

Joel's eyes gleamed. 'Are you now saying you didn't want it?'

'I most certainly didn't—though that is not to say I didn't need it nor that I don't now realise how much I owe you! But at the time . . . No, I didn't want your assistance—or anyone else's. Besides, how was I to know you only meant me well?'

'Would it have done any good to have explained that?'

'Maybe not. You certainly didn't try! A rope was your only explanation.'

'Tell me something: would you have stayed to listen if I had tried to explain?'

Tezzie flushed. 'I'd have taken to my heels.'

'Precisely. So I used a rope—quick, efficient and effective. Tell me—how long do you fondly imagine you'd have been able to stay free?'

'Not long, perhaps—and I acknowledge that another captor would not have taken me to the convent! But none of this is to the point. You complain that I caused you trouble. I merely seek to point out that you brought it on yourself.'

Joel's voice softened, and he allowed himself a warmer smile. 'We both know there were no other means by which I could get you to the convent. Will you accept my word that I should infinitely have preferred to handle it in a more civilised manner?'

She looked at him in serious silence for a few moments. 'Yes,' she said. 'I do accept that. I'll go further: I accept that you were right to do what you did, and the fact that I did not appreciate it at the time in no way diminishes my gratitude.'

The gleam returned to his smile. 'Then come here.' He reached out round the end of the counter and caught her wrist. After a moment's hesitation, when Joel half thought she might pull away from his grasp, she obeyed it instead and stood before him in front of the barrels of corn-meal. 'Are you truly grateful?' he asked.

The question was perfectly serious, but there was something in the tone that roused her suspicions so, although her gratitude was unqualified, she replied with some caution.

'I have just said as much.'

'Then you can have no objection to demonstrating it in a more tangible way.'

Tezzie opened her mouth, but before she could ask him what he meant, she found the words stifled as his mouth descended upon hers, crushing her lips and forcing her head back. Hernando Vigil was about to protest, but he saw the way Tezzie's hand instinctively found a resting-place on the broad shoulders that towered above her, and decided that no protest was necessary.

When Joel released her, she drew back, as uncertain of what he expected of her as she was of the feelings he had engendered. To disguise her confusion, she took refuge in anger.

'That was unwarranted, Mr Kanturk! You take

advantage of my trust.'

'Joel,' he corrected her. 'Such intimacy permits us to ignore formalities, I think! As for its being unwarranted, I regard it as a small price to pay to indicate the degree of gratitude you say you feel. In fact, the more I consider the matter, the more I think it was too low a price.'

As Tezzie backed away from the purposeful gleam in Joel's eye, another voice intruded itself.

'The lady has made it clear your advances are not welcome, sir. A gentleman would now accept her rebuff and leave. Or must I force you to do the right thing?'

No one had seen James Garway enter, and no one knew how long he had been there, but everyone could see he was very angry indeed. Joel, however, did not seem unduly perturbed either by the younger man's anger or by the hand now resting on a regimental sword.

'I doubt very much if you could, Lieutenant,' he said good-humouredly. 'And I'm not at all sure you read the lady right, but then, my acquaintance with her is slight. I bow to your superior understanding.'

'I have been acquainted with Miss Milagro for several months,' the lieutenant informed him stiffly. 'She is not the sort of woman you have taken her for. Quite the contrary, in fact!'

'Not encouraging you, I take it?'

Lieutenant Garway flushed at this all-too-accurate assessment, and Joel turned back to Tezzie. 'Miss Milagro, is it? An unusual name, but not inappropriate. Don't worry, Lieutenant, I shan't queer your pitch—if you have one—but you'll likely see me around. I'll be in Santa Fe a while yet: I've an aunt to see who's about due for a visit. Miss Milagro, your servant. May I convey a message from you to my aunt?'

'Yes, indeed,' Tezzie assured him warmly. 'Please tell her how comfortably I am situated and how kind the Vigils have been—and convey my love to her as well, of course.'

'I thought you said your acquaintance with Miss Milagro was slight?' Lieutenant Garway asked suspiciously.

'Oh, it is,' Joel assured him. 'My aunt, on the other hand, knows her well.'

'So that's where you met?' the lieutenant persisted.

'I suppose you could say that,' Joel replied, and turned to Tezzie. 'Would you agree, Miss Milagro?'

Tezzie coloured. She had no desire to explain to the young officer the precise circumstances in which she had met Joel Kanturk. 'I would not dispute it,' she said.

'Yet you did not apparently know Miss Milagro's name?' The lieutenant had the uncomfortable feeling that some crucial aspect of their relationship was evading him, and he did not miss the fleeting glance of alarm Tezzie shot at this tall stranger.

'My aunt is a trifle unconventional—out of this world, one might say,' Joel told him. 'As far as I can remember, she called Miss Milagro "Tezzie", and said it was short for Theresa.'

'I was a great deal younger then,' Tezzie explained.

'Three years, to be precise, and I feel bound to say that I have never before observed so great a change in anyone as you have achieved in that time. Don't you agree, Pete?'

Pete grinned. 'You've grown up quite a bit, Tezzie,' he said.

Hernando Vigil thought it was high time he brought the whole conversation to an end. 'She was of an age when one would have expected great changes,' he said. 'And now, gentlemen, we have a store to run. Was there something you were wanting?' He glanced from Joel to Pete and back again.

'There was,' Joel said. 'But after seeing Miss Milagro, I'll be hanged if I can remember what it was! We'll be back.'

As the two men left the store and the jingling clatter of their spurred boots reverberated on the raised board-walk immediately outside the building, they did not notice the short, squat, unshaven Mexican who was tying his mule to a hitching-rail.

Pedro Valdez noticed them, though—and recognised them, too. There was no mistaking the taller of the two men, and he remembered the story he had heard from those miners who had returned from Frijoles canyon. He had heard a faint whisper of two such men down in the Sandias, where the hunting was rich. Why had they returned to Santa Fe? And what had happened to the girl—his girl, Valdez thought savagely—whom they had abducted? He went up the steps and into the store.

Tezzie was talking to Lieutenant Garway when the Mexican entered, but she was facing the door and recognised him instantly. The colour drained from her face. Could it be coincidence that Valdez was so close behind Joel and Pete? Had he been following them in expectation that they would lead him to her?

The lieutenant saw her sudden pallor, and was immediately concerned. 'Are you all right, Tezzie? Can I get you some water? Should you sit down, perhaps?'

She shook her head. 'It's nothing,' she said. 'Please ignore it.' Inwardly she fought hard to regain her self-possession. If she behaved entirely normally and betrayed no particular awareness of Valdez or interest in his activities, she would surely escape his recognition. After all, she looked very different now from the way she had looked when she had been in his possession. There was no reason at all why he should recognise her.

Had Valdez not recognised Joel and Pete, it is entirely likely that the girl in Vigils' store would have attracted his attention no more than any other attractive woman might be expected to do. Seeing the other two men had, however, both jogged his memory and aroused his suspicions. It was initially hard to reconcile the smoothly coiled golden hair with the unkempt, lack-lustre mane of the wolf girl, and he would not have expected her to have been able to stand upright as well as this woman did. But once he mentally unpinned her hair, made her crouch and covered her with grime, he had no doubt at all that this was she. He also had no doubt at all that she would have much less difficulty in recognising her erstwhile owner than he had had in recognising his former chattel. Until he decided what to do about her, it would be better to slip away before she spotted him.

Accordingly, he gave every appearance of a man who could not find what he sought, and left the store.

Tezzie heaved a sigh of relief. Thank God he had not got close enough to recognise her!

CHAPTER SEVEN

LUZ VIGIL had persuaded Tezzie away from a bronze satin for her ball-gown in favour of a green as dark as the junipers in the deserts around them.

'The bronze becomes you very well, Tezzie,' she had said, 'but no one has ever seen you in anything but brown, and this green is the most flattering colour. Not only that, but it brings out the green in your eyes.'

The Vigils were insistent that Tezzie's ball-gown was to be a present from them, and they spared no expense to be sure that her appearance at her first ball should be all she could wish.

Some fashion-plates had come in from the East with the mule-train bringing supplies, and Mrs Vigil drew Tezzie's attention to the fact that the full skirts and tiny pointed waists could have been designed with her in mind, while her sloping shoulders and the mature curve of her bosom would set off the currently fashionable shallow V of the neckline to perfection. The colour was not, perhaps, one that was usually worn by an unmarried woman, but Mrs Vigil thought Tezzie was old enough and sufficiently beautiful for that to be excused.

The gown with its complexity of cunningly pleated fabric in the bodice and its ruched trimming was not easy to make, and the skirt was of such a fullness that they were obliged to make several equally full petticoats which, starched, would hold it out. Mrs Vigil cut out the gown and fitted it, but most of the sewing fell to Tezzie, and that was a task which left her plenty of time to think.

She had had reservations about going to the ball because she had not wished Lieutenant Garway to read

too much into her presence there at his invitation. The
Vigils had cleverly overcome that problem by taking
her themselves, and she had consequently been looking
forward to an uncomplicated evening of novelty and
pleasure. Now, in one day, the calm surface of her life
had been disturbed by the unexpected appearance in
Santa Fe of Joel Kanturk and Pedro Valdez. Neither
gentleman was likely to be at the ball for the men of
the garrison, of course, and Valdez she must put out of
her mind: he had certainly not recognised her and could
not conceivably cause her any problems. Joel Kanturk
was another matter.

Tezzie acknowledged that she had very good cause
indeed to be grateful to Joel, but there was something
about him she found disturbing, and she did not like it.
The very first time she had seen him, he had had the
same effect, making her desperately aware of her nakedness. If James Garway—or any other man—learnt her
story or knew that other men had seen her as no man
other than a husband had a right to do, he would be
justifiably disgusted. Joel Kanturk cared little for
conventions or for what others thought—his behaviour
in the store vouched for that—yet at least he had not
given Garway any hint that they had met other than in
accordance with convention, and for that she must also
be grateful.

In the brief period between his capturing her and
giving her to the nuns, she had never been able to guess
his intentions, and she was no better able to do so now.
The sardonic smile, the serious words uttered in a
bantering tone—which was she to believe? The words
or the voice? There had been occasions during their
conversation in the store when she had thought him to
be deliberately setting out to provoke her, yet why
should he? And to what else, other than provocation,
could she attribute that quite unjustified kiss? She had
never quite forgotten his gentle, farewell kiss at the
convent. She supposed, in the present circumstances,
something like that might have been in order. But to

kiss her as he had . . .! In the solitude of her room, she blushed. It was not only her recollection of his kiss that caused her colour to rise, but also the recollection of her reaction to it. For a few brief moments she had wanted it to last for ever, to feel herself crushed against him as her lips had been crushed against his.

Yet he had regarded it lightly—his whole manner said so. Besides, though he gave no indication of the disgust most men would feel on learning her history, she reminded herself that even Joel did not know everything about her past, and there was one thing hidden so deeply that she had almost persuaded herself she had forgotten it. Even Joel Kanturk would not be able to stomach learning that part of her story.

Forget Joel Kanturk, she told herself. He was clearly intending to stay in the area of Santa Fe for a while, and though she might well see him from time to time, there was no reason to expect him to linger unnecessarily; once he was gone, life could return to normal. At least he was as unlikely to attend the ball as was Valdez.

Luz Vigil's black hair and ample figure were admirably served by a gown of crimson, and a black lace mantilla worn without the high Spanish comb but in other respects in the Spanish style. Tezzie's golden hair and her softly rounded creamy shoulders rising from the wide neck of her dark green satin gown were a total contrast, and the two women were perfect foils for each other. Luz looked Tezzie up and down and patted her hand affectionately.

'We set each other off to perfection,' she said. 'Perhaps we should spend the whole evening side by side so as not to spoil the picture.'

Tezzie laughed. 'I may use that as an excuse not to dance with Lieutenant Garway!' she warned.

'Nonsense, my dear! You will dance with whoever asks you—but not too often with any particular man, of course. There is very little point in going to a ball if you are going to make excuses like that! Besides, that

dress is made for dancing, and I haven't been teaching
you the steps every evening just to see you keeping the
wall warm!'

The Governor's Palace was decorated for the occasion
with thousands of the *luminarias* usually reserved for
Christmas. Each *luminaria* was a paper bag containing
sand, both to weigh it down and to prevent fire breaking
out, and a lighted candle. The effect of thousands of
these flickering little lanterns arranged along the edges
of the roof of the single-storey building was magical,
especially as one approached from a distance. The
palace itself was built to the same design as the convent
and the Vigils' house, the same design as every other
house of any size or importance in the Territory. It was
simply much larger. Designed for easy fortification, its
thick adobe walls formed a quadrangle, the rooms of
which opened on to the central patio and into each
other, corridor-fashion. *Luminarias* lined the patio edge
of the roof, and the jutting *vigas* held their share of the
ubiquitous *ristras* . Only the public rooms were being
used, of course, but they were large and numerous and,
with every communicating door opened, the space
seemed unlimited. There was a small orchestra, and
Tezzie saw nothing strange in an ensemble that included
violins and bugles, maracas and drums. Johann Strauss
might have been surprised at the transformation of his
music thus engendered, but to Tezzie Milagro, at the
first ball of her life, it was perfection.

The Vigils had been adamant that, no matter what
time the ball was due to open, they would not be the
first there.

'Far better to make an entrance,' Mrs Vigil told
Tezzie, who was anxious not to miss one minute of the
excitement.

Tezzie was not at all sure she wanted to 'make an
entrance', as Mrs Vigil put it, but her employer was
firm on the subject, and she was forced to admit that
there was something rather pleasant, if a little daunting,
in having so many people turn to watch one's arrival.

No one thought it at all strange that the Vigils should
have brought their assistant with them and, in a garrison
town, the preponderance of young men was such that
few young women felt unduly threatened by the presence
of even so outstanding a beauty as Tezzie Milagro.

James Garway had been at the palace from the
moment the doors were opened, anxious not to miss
Tezzie's arrival or to be deprived of one minute of her
company. By the time the Vigil party arrived, he had
mentally buried them a hundred times as a result of
Apache attacks or their buckboard meeting a carelessly
placed rock in the trail. The fact that it was less than a
mile from the Vigil house to the palace in no way
lessened his fears, and when they did eventually arrive
after their short and totally uneventful journey, his relief
was so extreme as to border on the comical. He was at
the forefront of the group that surged forward to greet
them, each man anxious to claim Tezzie's hand for at
least one dance. There was little danger of her being
obliged to keep the wall warm!

Every man present acknowledged that the young
lieutenant had the best claim to Tezzie's first dance,
though that did not prevent them all from trying to
persuade her otherwise. The matter had almost been
settled when someone else pushed their way through the
press. Not that Colonel Whipton, the garrison's
commanding officer, needed to do much pushing, a tap
here and a nod there being all that was necessary to
bring him to the front.

Of medium height and stocky, he was rumoured to
have a wife back east who refused to move further west
than Philadelphia, and more than one young army wife
who did follow the drum found herself in an invidious
position when her husband was out on patrol. What
woman, after all, would wish to jeopardise her husband's
career?

The colonel had, like everyone else on the garrison,
visited the Vigils' store from time to time and shared
the generally held opinion of the young assistant's

promise, though he did not voice it. Nor, while she was so very evidently under the careful eye of Hernando Vigil, did the colonel betray any overt interest at all. When the girl came into the ballroom, however, one glance was enough to tell him he had underestimated her charms, so he now took full advantage of his rank and insisted she bestow the first dance on the commanding officer. Garway had little choice but to lay claim to the second, and to take consolation in the fact that at least the second dance would be a waltz.

Tezzie did not enjoy dancing with Colonel Whipton, and was very glad that the movements of the dance kept them apart for most of each figure. He kept his eyes on her, no matter where they were in the dance, and she had the uncomfortable feeling that he was undressing her in his imagination. She began to wonder whether it had been unwise of Mrs Vigil to suggest a gown which revealed her shoulders, but a quick glance round the room was enough to assure her that she would have looked more out of place if her shoulders had been covered. When the final chords were played, she was very happy to drop the obligatory curtsy, and only regretted that customary politeness required her to be returned to her chaperon on the colonel's arm.

The only qualms she experienced when dancing with James Garway concerned her ability to execute the steps without stumbling, and so much of her attention was initially given to this that she had no time to be embarrassed by the close proximity in which this dance obliged the couple to be. The lieutenant was an accomplished dancer, light on his feet and with the natural good manners to allow her to become more confident before engaging her in conversation.

'Mrs Vigil has taught you well,' he said, when he judged her to be able to divert a part of her attention.

'She has certainly tried!' Tezzie's eyes were sparkling, and he thought she had never looked more beautiful. 'It doesn't seem to be quite the same thing, though, to be dancing here. It was much easier in the Vigil's parlour.'

He laughed. 'I'm sure it was! Never mind, you do very well. I should never have guessed this was your first waltz.'

Tezzie smiled ruefully. 'It's very kind of you to say so, but I think you would have! Still, I gain confidence by the minute, and that is in no small part due to you.'

'Then we must have several dances, and by the end of the evening you will be thoroughly accomplished in the art.'

'Mrs Vigil says I must on no account be seen to dance too frequently with anyone,' Tezzie told him demurely, but the sparkle in her eye belied her voice, and he laughed.

'Then we must hope Mrs Vigil is so engrossed in conversation with her friends that she won't notice,' he replied.

It was not very long before Tezzie felt confident that her feet were now able to move independently of her mind, and her enjoyment expanded with that confidence. It was severely jolted when the movement of the dance brought her facing the door and she saw Joel Kanturk enter the ballroom. She stumbled and apologised to Garway for her clumsiness.

'The fault was mine,' he said. 'I should not have tried to divert you with conversation.'

That had not been the reason, but Tezzie saw no need to disillusion him. How had Joel Kanturk been able to get an invitation to the ball? Pete Lingstrom, too. The continued whirling of the waltz gave her plenty of opportunity to catch fleeting glimpses of him, and she was more than a little surprised at what she saw.

Only the heavy tan betrayed that this was a frontiersman, and only the grey eyes betrayed his probable origins. Joel was dressed to great effect in the Mexican style. A short, close-fitting but unfastened black jacket with silver buttons topped the distinctive black trousers that flared below the knee. Silver conchos studded the seams of these, and a broad concho belt with a large turquoise at the centre of each silver medallion connected the trousers to the ruffled white shirt above. He wore the Mexican 'tie' of bootlace-thin leather, the ends capped with silver and its movable clasp a round sunburst of turquoise-inlaid silver, a piece of Zuni craftsmanship of the first order. A striking figure at any time, Joel drew the eye of every woman in the room, and not a few wished they were twenty years younger and unmarried!

When the young lieutenant led Tezzie back to the Vigils, Joel was standing beside them. He immediately took Tezzie's mittened hand and held it to his lips. 'Miss Milagro—you look charmingly.'

She wondered if she detected a note of irony in so social a remark, but decided to pretend she had not. She lowered her eyes with becoming modesty. 'You are very kind, Mr Kanturk.'

'Not at all,' he replied politely, and this time Tezzie knew she had not been mistaken. She raised her eyes to his and smiled sweetly.

'You cut a very dashing figure yourself, Mr Kanturk. I declare, you quite put the officers in their regimentals in the shade.'

'Ah . . . I take it that Mrs Vigil has not told you that while it is a gentleman's duty to compliment a lady on her appearance, no lady should pass any comment at all on a gentleman's.'

'I do not need Mrs Vigil to point out that a *gentleman* would not draw a lady's attention to that fact!' Tezzie snapped.

'A *lady* would not have needed it to be pointed out.'

Her eyes flashed, and for a moment Joel wondered whether she would succumb to the urge to strike him.

The possibility crossed James Garway's mind, too, and he was puzzled that such antipathy should apparently exist between two people whose acquaintance with each other was supposedly so slight.

'No one who had known Miss Milagro for long

would doubt her standing,' he said.

Joel inclined his head. 'I bow once again to your superior acquaintance.' He turned back to Tezzie. 'Let me have your card. I claim a dance for old times' sake.'

The sweetness of Tezzie's smile was undiminished. 'How sorry I am that you were not here earlier! I'm very much afraid I don't have so much as one unclaimed dance.'

'Let me see.'

Confidently, Tezzie handed him her dance-card and the little pencil that hung from it. The Governor prided himself on doing things in the first style of elegance, even if there were many of those he invited who could neither read the card nor sign their name. Every dance was initialled.

Joel scrutinised it and then glanced at Tezzie's assured smile. With two quick strokes he crossed off two signatures and substituted his own. Then he handed the card back to her.

Tezzie looked down at what he had done. 'You can't do that!' she exclaimed.

'I claim the privilege of a long-standing acquaintance,' he said. 'I shall have the waltz before supper, and then I shall take you in for refreshment.'

'I have given those to Lieutenant Garway,' Tezzie protested.

Joel smiled. 'The lieutenant is a very lucky man: I noticed his initials were attached to two further dances. Hasn't Mrs Vigil told you not to dance too often with one partner? Besides, with his name appearing so often, who else can as easily afford to forgo some of your company?'

The lieutenant bowed stiffly. 'I concede that I am perhaps too keen to monopolise Miss Milagro's time, sir, but I would have preferred a request to relinquish some of it to this high-handed appropriation of the lady's favours!'

'So you don't mind? Good! Take comfort in the thought that I shall not be in Santa Fe much longer.

The field will then be yours.'

'You're leaving?' The question was out before Tezzie had time to consider its wisdom.

Joel studied her for a moment as if calculating what might lie behind the spontaneity of the question. 'Do I detect regret?' he asked lightly.

'Certainly not!' she replied, too emphatically. 'I hadn't looked for such good fortune so soon, that's all.'

Joel shook his head. 'You really must learn not to say the first thing that comes into your head, Tezzie.'

Tezzie flushed at the justified reproof. 'I must apologise, Mr Kanturk. It was inexcusable,' she said with some dignity.

He laughed, and flicked her chin briefly with his forefinger. 'Don't spoil it, Tezzie! The simpering society miss doesn't suit you at all, though I suppose if you intend to marry a soldier, you would be well advised to cultivate it. I shall see you later. Your servant, ma'am, gentlemen.'

Tezzie's irritation that the taciturn frontiersman she remembered could prove to be so remarkably adept at turning a conversation to his advantage did not persist very long once she was dancing again. She hoped he could see how much she was enjoying herself with a succession of partners, and tried not to feel piqued that he seemed to have left the ballroom altogether and therefore was not in a position to learn this salutary lesson. By the time he came to claim her hand for his waltz, she had almost forgotten their exchange and was enjoying herself unreservedly. His reappearance reminded her of what had gone before, and she looked at him with a wariness to which he seemed oblivious. His own manner was courtesy itself.

'If I tell you you dance very well,' she ventured cautiously, 'will that be regarded as an unladylike remark?'

'Not at all! It is a compliment I am happy to return,' he said politely.

'I didn't think you would, you see,' she explained.

'Dare I ask why not?'

There was a smile in his tone which she mistrusted. 'Don't laugh at me,' she said, unaware of a pleading note in her voice.

'I assure you that I am not. Why did you not expect me to dance well?'

'I don't think I expected you to dance at all,' she told him. 'When . . . when we met previously, you did not seem to be the sort of man who would be at home in this sort of company.'

'Tezzie, I have no wish to distress you but, frankly, it is not the sort of company in which I would have expected to see you, either.'

To his relief, Tezzie chuckled. 'How foolish of me! And how kind of you not to point out that at the time we first met I was totally unaware that occasions such as this even existed!'

'How much of your past do the people here know, Tezzie?'

'I think Mother Superior gave the Vigils a fairly full account. No one else knows anything.'

'You don't think Mrs Vigil has gossiped?'

'I'm sure she hasn't. She and her husband have treated me like a daughter. I did once hear her tell someone I was an orphan—which is true enough. She said the convent had brought me up, but didn't think I would make a good nun.' She chuckled again. 'That was true enough, too! Why do you ask?'

Instead of answering her directly, he asked another question. 'Will you marry that besotted young lieutenant?'

'He hasn't asked me.'

'He will. What will your answer be?'

Tezzie hesitated. The question was one she had refused to face, even though she suspected that it was only a matter of time before James Garway himself expected her to answer it. 'I don't know,' she said at last.

'He's a fine young man. You could do worse.'

'Does one marry a person to avoid someone worse?'

'Some women do. Tezzie, do you love him?'

'I'm not sure I know what that means,' she said.

'Then you don't.' They danced in silence for some time before Joel spoke again. 'Whether it's James Garway or someone else, you're going to have to face one thing, Tezzie, and that is how your potential husband will feel about your past.'

'Does he have to know?'

'I suppose if you feel sure no word of it will ever leak out, then you would probably get away with it. Whether it's a good basis for marriage to have so large a secret behind it is another matter.'

Tezzie thought about that for a few moments. 'How can I gauge how a potential husband will feel if I tell him?' she asked.

'You can't. No man would be happy about it. Some could live with the knowledge, though.'

'And if I married him, and he found out later?'

Joel shook his head. 'I can only speak for myself, Tezzie. If I found my wife kept a secret of that magnitude from me, I think I would kill her.'

The face that looked down at her was suddenly harsh and unsympathetic, and Tezzie knew he meant exactly what he said. She could not repress a shudder.

'I've distressed you,' he said contritely. 'It was not my intention. Tezzie, if a man loves you, he will do so in spite of your past, but he must have the chance to decide. If he finds out for himself later, it is not the past that will destroy you both, but the deception.'

Tezzie managed to summon up a smile. 'It sounds as if I would be well advised not to fall in love!' she said.

He laughed, appreciating that the time had come to lighten the conversation. 'That's certainly one solution, though how any woman can resist attentions, such as those being lavished on you by an admiring army, is beyond my comprehension.'

They did not converse again during the brief remainder of the waltz, and Tezzie found so much pleasure in following a dancer who led with such strength and

decision as Joel did that she was genuinely sorry when
it came to an end and he led her back to Mrs Vigil to
collect her shawl before going into the supper-room.

Tezzie looked with dismay at the numbers of like-
minded people. 'Oh, dear,' she said. 'Wouldn't it be
wiser to come back later, when the crush is thinner? In
any case, I need fresh air more than sarsaparilla. Could
we walk in the patio?'

Joel put her shawl round her shoulders, and opened
the door leading out to the central quadrangle where
grasses struggled to survive in the sand that was not
their natural home. Two huge cottonwoods broke the
severe lines of the patio, and Tezzie went over to them,
laying her hands on the rough grey bark.

'I love cottonwoods,' she said. 'I love the feel of their
wood. They always look as if they have been there for
ever and will be there for ever more.'

Joel put his hand out to the gnarled trunk. 'I know
what you mean, but it is an illusion: they are as mortal
as we are.'

His fingers were but an inch from hers, and it seemed
entirely natural that they should meet and that hers be
clasped in his. Tezzie was suddenly conscious of a
change in the atmosphere between them. It became
charged with the tension of unspoken and only half
comprehended feelings. Her fingers fluttered briefly under
his clasp, but not with any desire to escape, and he
knew that and was glad. Their hands remained thus
lightly clasped, and then his hold tightened impercep-
tibly and he drew her touch from the cottonwood and
towards him until his arms could encircle her tiny waist.
Her upturned face, softly illuminated by the flickering
luminarias , was breathtakingly beautiful, and Joel gazed
down at it until the unconscious invitation proved
stronger than he had imagined. His mouth sought hers
in a kiss of lingering intensity that made her heart beat
faster and her lips plead with silent urgency that it
might never end.

Her arms reached up to draw him closer, and Joel's

heart rejoiced in her willing response. His lips explored
the slender column of her throat, pausing only to kiss
the pulse that beat there, then briefly touched her
eyelids, closed in the joy of his embrace, and when his
lips returned to hers, her mouth parted willingly at the
ardour of his kiss.

As their tongues met, Joel knew it had been a long,
long time since he had met a woman who roused him
to such a passionate intensity, allied as it was to
something more, something deeper that this was no time
to analyse. His kisses grew hungrier and his caresses
more demanding, and he exulted that her body
responded with pliant urgency.

Both were temporarily oblivious of their surround-
ings, and Tezzie's thoughts were confused in the
unfamiliar emotions his embrace aroused. She wondered
that so simple a thing as a kiss could call forth such a
sense of unidentified longing. Her body sought always
to be closer to his, and she could feel his heart beating
with the same urgency as hers. She became aware, too,
of the sudden hardening of his body as its contours
moulded to her own. The seductiveness of his caresses
had disguised what his body now told her, that it sought
what those others had taken without preamble in the
scrub beside the Rio Grande. The thought that Joel,
her rescuer, differed only in a subtler approach, disgusted
her, and she broke away from him with a little cry.

His hands were on her shoulders, gently. 'Tezzie,
what is it? What's wrong?'

He tried to turn her head towards him, but she turned
her face away. 'No,' she whispered. 'Not that, please.
Not you!'

Aghast at the implications of what she said, Joel
opened his mouth, intending to reassure her, but a new
voice broke in on them.

'You go too far, sir!'

Joel, his arm still round Tezzie's shoulders, turned
angrily to find an equally angry James Garway before
him. Tezzie, her distress heightened by the embarrass-

ment of a witness's presence, put her hands to her burning cheeks and could barely repress a sob.

'It is all right, Lieutenant,' she managed to say. 'Please go away. I . . . we . . . shall be back directly.'

'There is no need for you to protect this man,' the young officer said, 'though it is like you to wish to. You are clearly very distressed—and with good cause. Thank God I came out when I did! You are no gentleman, sir. To take advantage of a lady's innocence like this is unforgivable!'

'I assure you I regret the distress Miss Milagro feels as much as I am sure you regret the embarrassment your continued presence is causing her,' Joel said stiffly. 'She has already told you to go away. I suggest you do so.'

'And allow you to pursue your unwelcome assault? You must think me a fool, sir! Remember, I witnessed your equally unsought advance in the Vigils' store recently. You need a lesson, sir! Name your seconds.'

Joel's anger turned to amusement. 'Don't be ridiculous, Lieutenant! Miss Milagro will hardly wish to be the cause of a duel. I'm sure she would prefer to see this whole incident quietly buried. Besides, what claim have you to be her champion?'

Garway flushed. 'None—officially, but she has no family, and I am hopeful that she and I will establish a more formal bond in the near future. That, I believe, entitles me to act on her behalf.'

'Does it, indeed?' Joel's voice was enigmatic. 'Your "formal bond" will be rather difficult to establish if I kill you, don't you think?'

'You underestimate my skill,' the lieutenant told him.

'Quite possibly, but I don't underestimate my own. Go back inside, and I will undertake to bring Miss Milagro to the supper-room when she has had time to compose herself.'

'You are a coward, sir! Worse, you are a coward who seeks to take refuge behind a lady's skirts.'

Joel frowned. 'Now it is you who go too far! Very

well, since you are bent on suicide, Mr Lingstrom will doubtless act as my second.'

Tezzie could scarcely believe what she was hearing. 'There is no need for this, gentlemen,' she pleaded. 'I have suffered no harm. There was only a . . . a misunderstanding of which I'm sure Mr Kanturk is fully conscious. It's ridiculous to exchange shots over so slight a matter.'

'I fancy I am the better judge of that,' Garway told her. 'I saw how upset you were. It seemed no slight matter to me. The man is a scoundrel and must learn his lesson!'

'I wonder if you have any idea how pompous you sound!' Joel told told him. 'Tezzie, I'm sorry it has come to this. Shall we accompany you back to the supper-room now, or would you prefer Lieutenant Garway to bring Mrs Vigil to you?'

'There's no need to worry her,' Tezzie replied. 'I shall be all right now if you will take me to the ballroom. I find my appetite quite vanished.'

It needed only one glance at Tezzie's face to tell Luz Vigil that something had happened to upset her, but she wisely judged that the garrison ball was not the place to press for an explanation. She made no reference, therefore, to anything being amiss. Tezzie hoped her employer had noticed nothing, and determined to enjoy the rest of the evening. The ball had lost its sparkle, however, and was much more tiring than she had anticipated, and she was not at all sorry when Mr Vigil fetched the buckboard to take them home.

CHAPTER EIGHT

PETE LINGSTROM greeted the news that he was to be Joel's second with incredulity.

'You're crazy!' he said. 'What sort of a damn-fool thing is that to get pushed into?'

'I'm not after your opinion. Just see Garway's second—Lieutenant Baden—and fix it up.'

'The army won't allow it. They'll put a stop to it. Is that what you're banking on?'

'Are you accusing me of cowardice, too, Pete?'

'You know I'm not! It's just that I've never known anyone push you into a fight you didn't want—and I'm damned if I can see why you wanted this one!'

'I don't. Let's say I wasn't thinking straight.'

Pete looked at him thoughtfully. 'At least you're likely to be the better shot,' he said at last. 'You shouldn't have much difficulty in killing him.'

'None at all, I imagine. The problem is that I don't want to—and even less do I want him to kill me.'

Pete whistled. 'With only one shot each, you do have a problem!'

'Exactly. I can kill him outright or wound him. If I only wound him, he can take his time to aim at me. If I wait till he's had his shot, I can set out just to wound him, but I take a gamble that he won't have killed me first—and I don't underestimate him that much.'

'Maybe he doesn't intend to kill you,' Pete suggested hopefully.

'Maybe he doesn't, but he was angry enough to have killed me in the patio then and there. Maybe he'll have cooled down. Would you want to bet on it?'

Pete shook his head. 'What will you do?'

Joel shrugged. 'Who knows? Maybe some Apache will save me the trouble. Let's hope he faces me square on—that way, I can at least guarantee to get his gun-hand.'

'Are you sure he can't shoot with either hand?'

Joel clapped his hand on Pete's shoulder. 'You're a great one for inspiring confidence, my friend! Just keep any more bright ideas like that to yourself.'

A sleepless night did nothing to assuage Tezzie's exhaustion. She tossed and turned in her little room, a prey to conflicting hopes and fears. Why had James Garway pushed Joel into a duel, particularly into such an old-fashioned, formal one? And why had Joel allowed it to happen? She was sure he could have backed out of it had he wished to—except that 'backing out' was not something she imagined Joel could do lightly. Tezzie had no desire to learn of the death of either of them, and her feelings towards each were mixed.

James Garway was a good man and it seemed he loved her, yet she could not imagine him arousing in her the sorts of feelings Joel had created. This was quite possibly because he had never behaved with the same impropriety—and even as she acknowledged the probability of that guess, Tezzie knew she did not want him to. Why, then, did she not feel inclined to condemn Joel's behaviour? The truth was that, far from condemning it, she had welcomed it. Only when she suspected that his purpose was the same as that of those others, had she felt the need to pull away. Yet the disgust she had thought she felt could not be so very great, for as she tossed on her feather mattress she longed for his arms to be round her once more. She did not long for James Garway's.

She tried to come to terms with this illogical conflict. Was she really disgusted because Joel wanted what other men had taken? Or was she disgusted at herself, perhaps because she had glimpsed something in herself that had responded to his desire, a glimpse of a possibility that there might be circumstances in which there could be more pleasure than pain in what he sought?

But Joel, of course, did not know what had happened to her before, and she had been long enough in the Vigils' world to know that those nightmare times were unforgivable. She longed to forget them, but they were always there, nudging away at the back of her mind, making her pull away from a man who, whatever his desires might have been, would certainly not have sought to satisfy them in so public a place as the patio of the Governor's palace on the night of a ball!

It was fear that had made her pull away, a many-faceted fear. There was the simple fear of pain coupled with the knowledge that what was taken by force destroyed both the ability and the desire for reciprocation—and her experience taught her that force was inevitable. There was the fear that Joel would discover he was not the first, and she knew from Mrs Vigil that that mattered to a man and that they could always tell, though precisely how that was so had never been explained. Only that evening Joel had talked about deception. He had been thinking of it in relation to her marrying James Garway, but his opinion had been unequivocal. Yet if she told him everything that had happened in the past, she could guess all too clearly his reaction: the hastily disguised revulsion, the courteous but determined rejection of her. There was the fear of losing him, even though she had no reason to think he was hers to lose.

She lay suddenly still. Her thoughts had been entirely of Joel Kanturk. James Garway had scarcely entered into them. She had just admitted to herself a fear of losing Joel, but what was there to lose? A passing embrace in the Vigils' store which meant nothing, and another, tonight, which had certainly been more than just teasing?

She sat up in the darkness, staring at the lime-washed adobe walls.

She had told Joel she did not know what love meant

in the context of a man and a woman. She knew—
because the nuns had taught her—what was meant by
Divine Love, but there was something in the way the
nuns talked about it that told her the two things were
not the same. She thought about the Vigils. There was
a mixture of affection and respect in their relationship
which perhaps came closer to what was meant by love,
and yet even here Tezzie had sensed that this was not
the full picture. She had sensed, too, that to demand a
definition, an analysis, from someone would be to
demand the impossible, though she had not been at all
sure why it should be so.

Now she knew. She knew what love meant, and she
knew why it defied definition. She knew, quite suddenly
and without the slightest hint of doubt, that she loved
Joel Kanturk.

As if that decision had settled something, she lay
down again and fell instantly asleep, though so late was
it that when she woke next morning she looked as if
she had scarcely slept at all. Mrs Vigil noticed the
shadows under her eyes, but did not comment. Neither
did she ask any questions when Tezzie requested
permission to go into Santa Fe with Miguel when he
delivered corn-meal to La Fonda.

It proved less easy to find Lieutenant Garway than
Tezzie had anticipated. This was not because he was
inherently difficult to find, but because she was obliged
to feign unconsciousness of the whispered speculation
among the soldiers she had to ask. They knew who she
was, of course, and noticed that she did not appear to
have slept too well. She preferred not to ponder any
possible interpretation they might choose to put on her
presence.

Eventually the lieutenant was found and fetched and,
anxious that no clandestine purpose should be attributed to this unexpected meeting, he started to escort
her to the plaza.

When she saw where they were headed, Tezzie
protested. 'Not the plaza,' she said. 'Miguel is at La

Fonda—I would not wish him to see me and perhaps
report to Mrs Vigil.'

Garway looked puzzled. 'He will surely have used the
side entrance and be quite out of sight of the plaza?
However, if you will be happier, perhaps we should
stroll down here.'

He guided her into the shade of an arcaded sidewalk.
'I'm flattered that you should have sought me out,
Tezzie,' he said. 'You should not have done so, however.
It could give rise to gossip we both would wish to avoid.
I had planned to call on you at the Vigils' after the
duel. You can guess why I shall do so, I imagine.'

'That is precisely why I'm here, Lieutenant. The duel
cannot go ahead. It must be stopped.'

He smiled kindly and patted her hand. 'Your sentiment does you credit. Matters are too far gone for there
to be any going back now, I'm afraid.'

'Nonsense!' Tezzie exclaimed. 'All you have to do is
to send Mr Kanturk a note saying you behaved precip-
itately, or misjudged him or something—it probably
doesn't matter what—and that you wish to withdraw.
He can hardly go on with it then, can he? Especially if
you don't turn up at the appointed meeting.'

The lieutenant was horrified. 'Tezzie, you can't know
what you're saying! It's a matter of honour. A man
cannot withdraw from that!'

'Well, if it's my honour you're fighting about, let me
tell you that I hold it a great deal cheaper than a man's
life!'

The lieutenant glanced anxiously around, but no one
was within earshot. 'Tezzie, don't say such things! I
know you speak from innocence and your sentiments
are truly touching, but a woman's honour is priceless,
a man's life by comparison is nothing. In any case, I
don't intend to be killed, you know.'

It did not seem to occur to him that his final sentence
detracted somewhat from the lofty sentiments previously expressed, and Tezzie was too much concerned to
stop the duel to point this out to him.

'I don't want *any*one killed!' she protested. 'In fact, I have made a vow. You know that I was brought up by the Sisters of the Convent of the Blood of Christ?'

He nodded.

'Very well, then. I have sworn that if blood is drawn in this duel, I shall return to the convent and take my vows.'

He stared at her. She seemed perfectly serious, and there was a stubborn set to her mouth that he had never noticed before. 'You cannot really mean that,' he said doubtfully.

'Draw blood, and find out,' she replied.

'It's all very well to say that, but if I delope, it could well be my blood which is drawn!'

'My pledge will still stand,' she promised.

'Tezzie, you don't understand. I intend to survive this duel, and when it is over I shall seek your hand in marriage.'

'Nuns don't marry—surely you know that? Well, they do, of course, but that's different.'

'Are you telling me that if blood is drawn you won't marry me?'

'I shan't be able to, shall I?' Tezzie pointed out reasonably. 'Not that there's any guarantee I should have done, anyway,' she added with an honesty he took to be mere provocation and therefore chose to ignore.

He shook his head. 'You put me in a quandary, Tezzie. How can I fight a duel, much less win one, without blood being drawn?'

'By finding some excuse to withdraw. Say I pleaded with you, if you like: it would be true.'

He shuddered. 'I accused him of sheltering behind a woman's skirts. I'm certainly not going to do the same!'

'I leave it to your judgment, Lieutenant, but I'm sure you will think of something. Now perhaps I should return to La Fonda. Miguel is bound to have finished by now.'

Tezzie made no attempt to find out whether Miguel's business at the hotel was finished. Once she was sure

the lieutenant had left the plaza, she crossed the hotel
patio and slipped out of a rear door, making her way
to a smaller, much less imposing, establishment a few
streets away.

The Mexican rocking on the porch outside was not
at all surprised that a young woman should arrive
asking for one of his guests, though Tezzie did not seem
to be quite the type of woman he was accustomed to
admitting. His interest was not sufficient to induce him
to get up out of his rocking chair, however, and he
merely nodded towards the door, and said, 'Number
six, on the left.'

Pete opened the door, and his eyes widened with
surprise on seeing the visitor.

'Tezzie! What are you doing here?'

Beyond him, Joel was sprawled on the bed, but at
Pete's opening word he sat upright, staring in disbelief
for a moment before joining Pete at the door.

'For God's sake, Tezzie, you shouldn't be here!' he
exclaimed.

'If you're afraid it will cause comment, you'd better
let me in, then,' she replied defiantly, though she was
more than a little daunted by his vehemence and with
the sudden slight chill of realisation that perhaps she
had been unwise to come.

The two men stood aside to let her in, and Pete,
murmuring something about the need for some coffee,
left the room, closing the door behind him.

'Does Mrs Vigil know you're here?' Joel asked.

'Of course not! She'd be quite shocked.'

'As well she might! What on earth is so important
that you do something so imprudent?'

'This duel,' she said flatly.

He looked at her enigmatically. 'It's certainly an
important matter,' he agreed. 'In what way does it
concern you?'

'It must be stopped.'

'It can't be. Lieutenant Garway was unwise to push

matters so far, but he did so, and that's that, I'm afraid.'

'You could withdraw,' she suggested.

'Yes, I could—and have Garway's expressed opinion that I am a coward confirmed. No, thank you, Tezzie.'

'Surely it is better to be thought a coward, but alive, than to be a hero, and dead?'

Joel's hard grey eyes softened. 'Do you fear for my life, Tezzie? You need not.'

'To be absolutely truthful, I think it's much more likely that Lieutenant Garway's life will be at risk,' she said.

Tezzie had the strange feeling that Joel had in some indefinable way withdrawn from her. It was an unwelcome feeling.

'Does his life mean so much to you?' Joel asked.

'I don't want *any*one to die over such a foolish matter,' she protested.

'He was defending your honour—or thought he was,' Joel pointed out. 'Is that so foolish a matter?'

'That's exactly what he said.' Tezzie made no attempt to hide her exasperation. 'It's such a silly argument— and in any case, since it seems to be my honour under discussion, I think I should have some say in whether it is worth risking lives for.'

'You've spoken to Garway about it?'

'I've just come from him, and he is as unreasonable as you! He wouldn't withdraw, either, not even when I told him what I would do if it went ahead.'

'What will you do?'

Tezzie could have wished there was more apprehension in his voice and less amusement. 'I have told Lieutenant Garway that if blood is shed in this duel, I shall go back to the convent and take my vows.' She rather thought she had managed a nice blend of dignity and determination, and was therefore all the more disconcerted at his reaction.

Joel Kanturk threw back his head and roared with laughter.

'Lieutenant Garway didn't think it was funny!' she said indignantly.

'I don't suppose he did.' Joel paused long enough to wipe his eyes. 'You told me yourself only last night that you're not the material nuns are made of, and you were quite right, Tezzie. You've not been about in the world very much, but you enjoy it, and you could no more renounce it than swim the Atlantic. What's more, Mother Superior is far too worldly-wise to let you try.'

'I don't pretend it would be easy,' she conceded. 'Nothing worth while ever is.'

'Easy? For you, it would be impossible!'

'So you won't withdraw?'

'To keep you from a nunnery? No.'

'What would make you do so?'

His face was suddenly serious again, and there was a soft light in his eyes that made Tezzie's heart leap. For a few moments it seemed as if he might be going to admit to something that would make him change his mind.

'Nothing that you would be likely to offer,' he said at last.

Tezzie looked at him doubtfully, uncertain whether he was inviting her to pursue the matter. She decided he wasn't, and that if she did, he would only use her efforts as a means of disconcerting her.

'Very well,' she said. 'The only entirely satisfactory solution will be for each of you to kill the other!'

The door slammed behind her with gratifying force, and she ran from the little hotel back to La Fonda where Miguel was now waiting for her. *Please God*, she prayed as she ran, *don't let it be Joel who dies*!

Tezzie did not find it easy to discover where the duel was to be held or when, though she knew it must be soon. At first she thought no word of it had slipped out, unlikely as that might be, but then she caught the occasional whisper among soldiers in the store. There were no surreptitious glances in her direction, so she presumed the cause of the duel was not generally known. She knew it was highly probable that the Vigils were well informed as to its time and place: most gossip reached their ears sooner rather than later, though they rarely commented on it in front of Tezzie. Their unchanged manner towards her told her they had not so far connected her with the proposed event, but she dared not broach the matter to them in case they drew the correct inference from her enquiry.

She resorted to numerous subterfuges to find out more about it. It was quite amazing how often her work sent her to the part of the store from which she had caught a few words in order to bring back some item or other that just happened to be there. On such occasions it invariably took a considerable time to select the exactly appropriate article. She found that the exceptionally keen hearing her life in the wilderness had developed very quickly returned with the practice it was getting. Sometimes, in order to hear through the other voices in the store, she felt as if her ears must be growing out of her head on stalks.

The first thing she gleaned was the day. The duel was set for the next day but one after her visit to the adversaries, Garway's military duties precluding an earlier meeting. No time was mentioned, but Tezzie knew such things took place at or just before dawn. But where? With thousands of square miles of empty desert around Santa Fe, she needed more than an inspired guess. She had almost begun to despair of ever finding out, when, towards the end of the day before that set for the encounter, she caught a whisper.

There was an *arroyo* to the south-west of the town, a couple of miles from the Santa Fe Trail. Precisely where in it it was to be fought she did not learn, and this presented something of a problem. These dry water-courses could run for miles from the mountains to the river, having been gouged out of the sand by the sudden flash floods caused by storms up in the mountains. She must give herself plenty of time and join it as close to

the capital as possible, then follow it towards the
mountains. On one thing her mind was set. If neither
man would withdraw, then she must stop the duel.

Waking up early was easy. Slipping out of the house
called for stealth. Tezzie gave a silent prayer of gratitude
that the store was of only one storey; had it been
otherwise, someone sleeping above must surely have
heard the bolts drawn back and the removal of the
heavy wooden bar which went across the door. She
paused briefly on the porch outside to pull her cloak
more closely round her, for the early morning air was
chill, and then set out down the trail.

She was quite unaware that a figure slipped out of
the adobe-walled corral across the road and watched
her disappear before saddling up his mule and following
her.

Since Pedro Valdez had recognised Tezzie in the store,
she had done very little that he had not observed. He
had followed the buckboard to the ball and back again.
He had seen her meet Lieutenant Garway and, although
he had thought she had eluded him in La Fonda, he
had been fortunate enough to catch a glimpse of her
leaving that other, smaller, hotel. Knowing she would
recognise him if she saw him, he had taken good care
to keep well out of sight and to attract no attention, a
task greatly simplified by the fact that a Mexican dozing
on a sidewalk under his hat occasioned no comment at
all. The owner of the corral had been willing enough to
let it to Valdez for his mule, unaware that the mule's
owner slept there, too. Valdez had no idea what opportunity might offer him, but he was determined to be
there to take advantage of it when it did. It was a
vigilance that seemed to be paying off.

Tezzie walked swiftly, and the scattering of adobe
homesteads outside the city was soon left behind. When
she came to the place where the *arroyo* cut across the
trail, she hesitated before turning north up the dry,
sandy bed. She strode on, pausing only once to listen.
Had she heard a horse's hooves behind her? She decided

she had not, and went on. After about two miles, her
pace slackened and her resolution wavered. Dawn was
breaking over the mountains. The duellers must be
assembled by now, yet she had seen no hint of them.
Had she misheard? No, she was sure this was the *arroyo*
that had been meant. As she hesitated she heard, unmistakably this time, the sound of a horse behind her. She
frowned. Just one? Perhaps whichever of them it was
had come on his own. That must mean the other—and
the seconds—would not be too far behind. She had not
been mistaken, after all.

She turned to run back toward whichever man it
might be, confident that they would refuse to fight if
they knew she was watching. When she caught sight of
the mule, she stopped in her tracks. A mule! Neither
Joel nor Pete rode a mule, and no officer would be seen
on one except in an emergency. The mule had only to
come a few paces closer before she recognised its rider.

Valdez! Her stomach churned with a sickening dread,
and she picked up her skirts and ran.

Valdez put his spurs to the mule's sides and the
animal lurched into a canter. Neither fast nor
comfortable, it was nevertheless fast enough to overtake
a woman on foot, hampered by her long skirts.

Three years of civilisation had taken their toll, and
Tezzie found she had neither the speed nor the stamina
she had once possessed. Her shod feet sank into the
sandy floor of the *arroyo* in a way that bare ones had
never done. They did not sink deep, but sufficiently to
slow her down. Her lungs pleaded for more air, more
room to expand, and her heart strove painfully to
deliver what she was demanding of it.

It was no good. The mule gained on her inexorably.
She expected any moment to hear the hiss of a lariat in
the air, and swerved from side to side to make it more
difficult to aim it accurately. In doing so, she only made
it easier for the mule to catch her up, and Valdez, who
had limited faith in his skill with a lasso, drove the
animal straight at her, the impact knocking her over.

Tezzie fell face down, gasping for breath that was smothered by sand. Valdez was on her before she had time to think, lashing her hands and feet and making escape impossible. He heaved her up across the mule's withers and mounted clumsily behind her. He knew where he was taking her, but it was a long ride, made longer by the need to steer well clear of habitations, both Mexican and Anglo. With luck, he might be there before dark.

Joel and Pete rode out of Santa Fe together without speaking. Joel glanced at the sky. In less than an hour it would be dawn. Plenty of time. Pete, accustomed to his companion's long silences, made no attempt to force conversation. Quite apart from Joel's normal taciturnity, what man would feel talkative with a duel before him?

They came to the place where the arroyo swept across the trail and turned south into it. Another half-hour, and they would be there.

Joel neither dreaded nor looked forward to the forthcoming encounter. He bore James Garway no ill-will and certainly had no desire to kill him. He had even less desire to be killed. He had learnt to survive in this harsh, wild country, even to love it in a strange way, and it would be ironic if it proved to be some outmoded gesture of chivalric convention that did for him in the end.

It was not the duel that occupied his thoughts. It was Tezzie. The young woman at the Vigils' store was very different from the pathetic, cringing creature he had taken to the convent, and yet, when he thought about it, he wondered if she was so different. There had been nothing pathetic or cringing about the way she had fled from the people of Cerrillos, nor in that spontaneous gesture of freedom as she stood in the creek seconds before his rope descended round her waist. He had not believed that the wolf-girl stories were true, and still was not entirely convinced. He accepted that it was a possibility only because his aunt was prepared to believe it, and she was no fool. If he survived today, perhaps he would visit her and find out if she had discovered whether the story was true. He did not even know if it mattered any more, except in so far as he disliked unanswered questions.

And what of Tezzie? His rescue of her meant nothing: he would have done as much for a hound-dog. It had been a shock to see her at the convent before he left, looking suddenly human and vulnerable—and unexpectedly feminine in the over-large rough habit. Seeing her in the Vigils' store had been a much bigger shock. He had felt almost jealous of Hernando Vigil's position as her appointed protector, and when the same spirit that had made her flee her tormentors had made her round on him, he had taken her in his arms. But why? What impulse had prompted that? It certainly had had little to do with requiring a show of gratitude. He had been more than half teasing, offering further provocation. He would have been neither surprised nor offended if she had struck him. Instead, after her initial brief resistance, she had responded with a warmth that had been pleasantly disturbing. So disturbing, in fact, that he had obliged the Governor to invite him to the ball.

The man he was going to meet loved Tezzie, of that Joel was sure. Whether James Garway was the right man for her was another matter altogether, and he was certain the love was one-sided. On the other hand, it would be a foolish woman who lightly rejected the lieutenant. He was young, pompous, and lacked much sense of humour, but he was sincere and kind and would make a good husband if he could accept Tezzie's past.

When Joel had held Tezzie under the cottonwood tree, it had had nothing to do with teasing. He had wanted her then more than he could recall ever wanting a woman since he had left Ireland. For a few blissful moments he had thought—no, known—she felt the same, and then she had pulled away, upset, distressed.

Her words were engraved on his memory. *No. Not that, please. Not you!* What was he to read into that? His mouth set in a grim line. There was only one interpretation. He remembered what he had said to Pete when they had filed out of the side-show, and wondered how Lieutenant Garway would be able to live with that knowledge if it ever came to his notice. The fact that a girl had been brought up by wolves could be presented in a romantic light. Her existence as a side-show freak was less easily managed. Anything more was nothing other than sordid, and likely to be totally unacceptable to the James Garways of this world.

And what of Joel Kanturk? Could he accept it? The thought was uncomfortable, and he pushed it away. He certainly would not have been able to when he was younger. In any case, it was irrelevant: he was not thinking of marrying Tezzie Milagro, Garway was—always assuming that Tezzie didn't take the veil! He smiled grimly to himself. Of only one thing that might happen was he completely sure: in no circumstances would the Tezzie he now knew become a nun.

James Garway and his second were already there and, with them, a doctor of sorts. Neither soldier had dared ask the garrison doctor, who would have been failing in his duty had he not reported the forthcoming duel to his commanding officer. Joel took one look at the one they had found, and hoped any injuries incurred by either side would be either very superficial or instantly fatal.

Duelling pistols were not articles much found in New Mexico, and Pete and his fellow second had agreed that each principal might use the weapon with which he was familiar. It fell to the seconds to empty the magazines and re-load with just one bullet. Each checked that no more had been inserted and that the solitary bullet was in the firing position. The sky had lightened, but the sun had not yet reached a height of brilliance sufficient to handicap either man. Visibility was as perfect for the present purpose as it would ever be, and the seconds agreed they must waste no more time.

Their guns in their hands—for this was a duel, not a gun-fight—the frontiersman and the soldier paced away from each other and turned. Joel faced the soldier squarely; Garway stood sideways on, presenting a narrower target, but one which, Joel thought bitterly, increased the chances of a bullet hitting some vital organ. Seeing Joel present a broad front, the soldier wavered and moved so that he was neither quite one thing nor the other. The doctor lifted a grubby square of linen and, as it fluttered to the ground, Joel fired.

His opponent's gun shot out of his hand, and the force of the impact brought the lieutenant to his knees. He looked at his gun-hand in amazement. There was blood, but no pain. His fingers could still clench. He groped in the sand for his weapon and found it, apparently undamaged. He got to his feet. Under the code of honour he was entitled to his shot. Joel stood, still facing him, fully aware that the code required the soldier to have his shot, and fully aware, too, that Garway could take his time over it now.

James Garway took very careful aim. Killing the frontiersman would present no problem. Nor would it solve any. He raised his pistol towards the sky and fired. Then he slipped to the ground, unbearable pain suddenly raging through his hand, due at least in part to the pressure he had had to exert.

Joel and both seconds reached him before the doctor, and Joel whipped off his bandana to wrap round the hand.

'Get him to the garrison surgeon,' he told Lieutenant Baden. 'You can't hide what's happened, and at least he'll get good treatment. He's best not left to the mercies of this one.'

The sound of galloping hooves drew their attention from the wounded man, and they looked up to see a small contingent of soldiers bearing down on them. The

newcomers drew rein and surrounded the group in the
arroyo.

'What happened here?' Major Middleton asked.

'Target practice, sir,' Lieutenant Baden answered
swiftly. 'Accident, sir. Things went a bit wrong.'

'You've second sight, Lieutenant, have you?' the
major went on.

'Sorry, sir? Don't quite follow.'

'Perhaps you always bring a doctor when you go out
on target practice—just in case?'

Baden thought quickly. 'It pays to be careful, sir.'

Major Middleton was not amused. 'Mount up,
Lieutenant. You're under guard!' He turned to Joel and
Pete. 'You, too. Mount up and fall in.'

'We're civilians, Major,' Pete protested.

'If this were a purely civilian matter, you'd be free to
kill yourselves with my blessing. Involve the military,
and you come under military law.'

Joel and Pete had no choice but to do as they were
told, though Joel was amused to see that the doctor
was being allowed to slip off apparently unobserved;
perhaps his reward for information laid.

When the party returned to Santa Fe, Joel was locked
up in the garrison jail, and after the doctor had attended
to his hand, James Garway was put in the next cell.
Pete Lingstrom and Lieutenant Baden were dealt with
summarily by Colonel Whipton: the latter being repri-
manded, and the former being instructed not to show
his face around the garrison again.

Lieutenant Baden was waiting for Pete when he
emerged, and accompanied him to his horse.

'You won't be able to visit Kanturk,' Baden said. 'I
can get messages to him, though. Just let me know
where you're staying.'

Pete told him. 'What will he get?'

Baden shrugged. 'Who knows? If they were both
army, I'd say they'd get off with a demotion. One of
them being a civilian makes it different. He won't hang.'

'Thanks,' Pete said sarcastically. 'Keep in touch.'

When Lieutenant Baden slipped into the guard-house later, he found that the only thing on Garway's mind was Tezzie. He begged his friend to ride over to the Vigils' and let her know that neither man had been killed.

'No need to tell her I'm wounded, either,' Garway added, remembering Tezzie's stated intention. 'In fact, I don't even want it hinted at. Understand?'

Lieutenant Baden did, and duly rode out to the store. He found both the Vigils working there, and obviously worried.

'See Tezzie? I wish you could,' Mrs Vigil told him. 'When we came down this morning, the store door was open but nothing had been taken, which seemed very strange. Tezzie didn't come in for breakfast, and when I went to wake her up, she was gone. She's wearing one of her working dresses, and her cloak is gone, too, but nothing else. She's left no note, no message. We are worried to death.'

It did seem very peculiar, but women were unaccountable creatures, and, in any case, Lieutenant Baden could throw no light on her disappearance.

'I'm sure she'll soon be back,' he volunteered. 'When she does return, would you tell her Lieutenant Garway and Mr Kanturk are quite all right?'

Mrs Vigil looked at him in bewilderment. 'What on earth does that mean?'

'Just let her know. She'll understand.'

Lieutenant Baden was not unduly perturbed when he returned to the guard-house and persuaded the man on duty to look the other way.

James Garway was. 'She must have heard!' he said. 'She has gone to take her vows.' He sank his head between his hands. 'I should have done as she asked! I should have withdrawn.'

'Nonsense, man!' Joel's voice came from the next cell. 'She may well have gone to the convent, though I can't think why she should have done. It certainly isn't to take her vows.'

'You don't understand!' James Garway told him. 'You don't know how strongly she felt about the duel.'

Joel was tempted to disillusion him, to tell him about Tezzie's other visit that day, but decided it was kinder not to. 'All I know is that Tezzie Milagro will never be a nun—and Mother Superior is the last person to encourage such a wild fancy. All the same, she was brought up there, and if she's upset about something, that's very likely where she would go. Lieutenant, can you get hold of Pete?'

Baden nodded.

'Good. Tell him to ride out to the convent and see if she's there. That will put our friend's mind at rest—and the Vigils'. Tell him to let them know if he finds that's where she's gone.'

'And if it isn't?'

Joel frowned. 'I can't see what else can have happened. If she isn't with the nuns, there's no need for Pete to give the Vigils any more cause for concern. Let's face that problem when we have to.'

Mother Superior was very surprised to see Pete, and very disturbed by his question. 'Tezzie's disappeared? Why, for goodness' sake? Has she quarrelled with the Vigils?'

'I don't think so. They're as mystified as anyone. Is she here?'

'No, of course she isn't! Mind you, it's where I'd have expected her to come, but if she hasn't, I don't think you'll find her easily. If she's chosen to run away, she has all those years as a wolf to draw on. She can't have forgotten the skills of survival she learned then. If that's what's happened, you'll have to think like a wolf to find her.'

'You believe those stories, then?' Pete was momentarily diverted from his purpose.

'She was here long enough for us to learn the truth,' Mother Superior told him. 'There's not a nun here who doesn't accept her story. If you want to track her down, that's what you'll have to look for—a woman who thinks like a wolf.'

Pete left the convent in an uneasy frame of mind. If Mother Superior was right, what chance was there of finding Tezzie? Any footprints she might have left in the sand outside the store would have been long since erased by the marks of those who had passed later. He pondered the matter. If there was no chance of picking up her trail, perhaps it would be best to try to guess where she would go. Last time she had been running, she had made for Frijoles canyon. It was too late to go there now and, anyway, he had a feeling he had better let Joel know the situation before he started acting on his own initiative. All the same, there was no point in returning to Santa Fe by the most direct route, and there was one possibility that might bear fruit.

Pete swung his horse out in an arc that took him northwards round the west of the city and, once on the trail, urged it into a steady ambling gait that ate up the miles. Even so, it took him more than an hour to reach his goal, and he approached it with caution. An Indian pueblo was not the safest place to enter, although he and Joel were known in this one. Joel had brought him here when an accidental cut with a hunting-knife had failed to heal. The people had been suspicious, but the shaman had treated the wound. They had been allocated an old adobe slightly apart from the rest of the pueblo, and had lived there until it had healed. Like all Indians, the Tesuque were a reserved people, and when they found their visitors meant them no harm and took no liberties, they gave them bread from their *hornos* and once they even brought their great delicacy, fry-bread, delighted at the men's expressions of pleasure when they ate it. For these gifts of food they accepted no payment. Pete knew he would be recognised. He also knew that that would not necessarily guarantee him safe passage.

The pueblo seemed to be deserted, but Pete knew it could not be. Somewhere behind the thick mica panes in the small windows were people watching him. His horse needed water, but he could not take it without permission. So he sat there and waited.

Eventually an old man emerged. Pete had picked up a little Tewa during his enforced stay, and used it to ask if he might water his horse. The old man said nothing, but gestured towards the stream that flowed through the village. Pete dismounted and watered his horse, knowing that the man was watching him. When he had finished, he said—in Spanish because his Tewa was too limited, 'I'm trying to trace an Anglo woman—young, with golden hair. Has she been seen?'

The old man said nothing, and turned away towards the houses. Assuming there was nothing more to be achieved there, Pete gathered up his reins ready to remount. His foot was already in the stirrup when the old man returned and, with him, a boy of ten or eleven closely followed by a sad-eyed tawny hound, its coat staring and its belly swollen with worms. The old man pushed the boy forward.

His Spanish was not much better than Pete's, but he had seen such a woman, he said. He had been out on the mesa. No, she wasn't running. He allowed himself a rare grin. She was slung over a mule like a sack of pinto beans, and she was struggling.

'Are you sure this was an Anglo woman?' Pete asked, astounded. This was something for which no one had bargained.

The boy was offended that his word should be doubted, but Anglos did not always know they were impolite. 'The hair was unmistakable. It gleamed in the sun. It was a long way off, but even you would have been able to see it.'

Pete took the reproof without comment. 'Could you also see who was taking her?' he asked.

'Of course. It was a Mexican. His blanket was Mexican, too. The mule was brown.'

The boy knew no more except to indicate the general direction in which they had been travelling. It seemed quite possible that this unknown Mexican might be heading for the Frijoles caves, but it was too far to go there tonight. Pete thanked the boy, and headed back to Santa Fe.

He had no idea who the Mexican might be, but there were unlikely to be two Anglo women missing from Santa Fe at the same time. If the boy could detect the absence of the central seam that most surely distinguished a Mexican blanket from a Navajo one, he was hardly likely to be mistaken in his other observations.

It was dark when he got back to Santa Fe and sought out Lieutenant Baden. The soldier heard his story, and whistled through his teeth. 'Sounds as if we need to get Kanturk out of there, though I don't see how. Garway'll want to go too, of course.'

'Garway'll be no use without both hands,' Pete reminded him. 'What do we do? I can't visit the guard-house. It has to be up to you, and you'll be court martialled when your part in it is discovered.'

'Somehow we've got to make it look as if I was only accidentally involved. Can you have two horses standing ready?'

'Whenever you say.'

'Give it an hour. If I can get him over the roof, you'll need to be in the lane behind the palace.'

'I'll be there.'

Baden's plan, such as it was, hinged on the fact that the evening meal would be served to the prisoners in about an hour, after the rest of the garrison had eaten, and that it would arrive towards the end of the guards' shift, when they could be expected to be tired and rather less alert than they should be. He would have preferred to have had more time. A scheme like this demanded careful planning, not a few makeshift ideas thrown together with a prayer!

He finished his own meal and drifted across to the guard-house. He paused outside and lit a cigarillo. 'Red chili stew again,' he told the guard.

The guard sniffed. 'Sometimes it seems the only change they can think of round here is to make it green chili stew!'

'Tasty, though. Beef in it today, for a change. I don't much like mutton.'

'Who does? Better than starving, though.'

'True. O.K. if I go chat to Lieutenant Garway?'

The guard hesitated. 'I shouldn't, sir. It's the civilian, you see. They say he's real sneaky.'

Baden shrugged. 'I've no interest in him. Civilians! Lieutenant Garway wouldn't be in this fix if it hadn't been for him. Hope they throw the book at him!'

The guard grinned. 'I hear that's just what they plan to do! Go on, then, sir, but be careful.'

Baden stepped unhurriedly inside. 'Hi, Jim,' he said, just loudly enough to ensure that the guard heard. 'Don't get too excited about supper—it's red chili stew again.' Then, in a lower voice, he quickly recounted the story Pete had brought back.

Joel's reaction was immediate. 'Get me out,' he said.

'I'm working on it, but we've got to play it cautiously.'

'I'm going, too,' James Garway interjected.

'No, you're not,' Joel told him. 'You can use only one hand, and they'll hunt you down as a deserter a lot more determinedly than they will me—and shoot you at the end of it all. You stay here.'

'We need you as a witness, Jim,' Baden said. 'Someone's got to give a convincing account of how Kanturk got out single-handed.' He turned to Joel. 'The only chance I can see is to jump whoever brings you supper.'

Joel nodded. 'We'll have to play the cards we're dealt.'

The lieutenant, who had glimpsed the cook-house door opening, wandered out again and stood idly drawing on his cigarillo, watching a soldier carry a tray across to the guard-house. The guard unhooked his keys from his belt. Baden smiled at the boy with the tray.

'I'll take that, trooper,' he said.

The youngster was surprised, but not sorry. As soon

as he had delivered the food, he was off duty. 'If you're
sure, sir.'

'I am. After you, corporal.' The lieutenant nodded to
the guard, who followed him in, not liking to precede
an officer, and then reached round him to unlock
Lieutenant Garway's cell.

'Supper, Jim.'

The dish was delivered, the door relocked.

The guard stepped ahead of Baden to unlock the
other cell. As he did so, the door was slammed hard
back from inside, smashing him unconscious against the
wall.

Joel and Lieutenant Baden dragged him into the cell.
'You get in here, too,' Joel told the army man. 'At least
you've got something to eat!'

'Go over the roof,' Baden said. 'There are horses out
back.'

Joel locked the door and threw the keys into a corner.
At the open door of the guard-house, he paused. The
cook-house door was closed. He could see no one. This
was unexpected good fortune, but for how long could
he rely on his luck holding? Not long, of that he was
sure. There were bound to be guards on the roof, and
even if they couldn't see him in the shadows, they could
hardly miss doing so once he was on the roof. He
glanced along the walls to either side and saw a further
instance of his present luck: three barrels stood neatly
stacked, one on two, against the jutting end of a *viga*.
Perfect! Keeping half an eye on the cook-house door,
Joel slipped quietly along the few yards to the barrels,
and then, with a last glance round, climbed rapidly to
the top. From there it would be a simple matter to
swing his long legs on to the flat roof by way of the
viga, and he must do so before someone crossed the
parade-ground below—it could not remain empty much
longer. He hoisted himself up and flattened himself on
the earth-covered roof. Light flooded out below him. A
door had been opened, and he caught a pungent whiff
of tobacco-smoke. It was to be hoped the smoker would

step no further outside and would assume that any noise from above him was the guard.

A quick glance round told him he had very little time, certainly not enough to enable him to lie there until the smoker had gone. There were indeed guards on the roof—two to each side, which seemed to Joel at that moment more than a little excessive. Furthermore, so far as he could judge, his own position was almost exactly where the two soldiers on this stretch would meet and turn. By sheer good fortune once more he had reached the roof very shortly after they had marched back to return to the corners. He must be gone before they turned towards him again.

He drew himself swiftly but cautiously to his feet and, crouching as low as was conducive to speed, he covered the few feet to the outer parapet. But speed and silence are incompatible companions, and both guards heard the movement. They spun round almost simultaneously and fired, hitting the spot where he had been a split second after he had swung himself over the edge and on to the jutting *viga* outside. Pete was already hurrying the horses to the precise spot, enabling Joel to drop into the saddle, but before they could spur their mounts away, the guards had seen them and were already taking aim. The sound of shots had alerted the garrison, and men came running from all directions, small-arms at the ready.

Darkness was on the side of the fugitives, and although rifle and pistol fire followed them until they had turned a corner, their ally made accurate aim impossible, and the random shots were wasted.

Both men headed out of town. Tomorrow they would be hunted. Tonight they must move!

CHAPTER NINE

LONG BEFORE HE reached the ruined pueblo in Frijoles canyon, Valdez was beginning to have doubts as to whether it had been altogether wise to have recaptured the wolf girl. Once she had got her breath back, it proved very difficult to keep her on the mule. Despite having bound hands and feet, she wriggled and squirmed until the mule decided it had had enough and refused to go any further. Valdez was obliged to dismount and to join her wrists and ankles by a rope under the animal's belly. That at least kept her still, but it had the disadvantage of making it necessary for him to walk because, in order to make her secure, he had had to lay her across the saddle. He did try to ride behind, across the animal's loin, but the mule left him in no doubt of its feelings on that idea, so Valdez picked himself up and walked.

By the time he reached his destination, he was almost too exhausted to think. He was tempted to leave Tezzie where she was, but the mule needed a rest, so he released her from its back and then tied her hands and feet together behind her where she fell, before hobbling the mule for the night. Valdez then clambered over the crumbling walls at the base of the cliff and bedded himself down in one of the roofless rooms. He took a bottle of whisky from his saddlebag and had several long swigs. In the morning he would decide what to do with the girl.

The night was bitterly cold, and Tezzie, trussed like a turkeycock, had no blanket. Discomfort and cold kept her awake. She guessed she had probably spent colder nights outside, but three years of warm beds had decreased her ability to tolerate them with any ease at all. She soon heard Valdez snoring, and it gave her a brief burst of optimism: if he were so soundly asleep, escaping him should not be difficult—if only she could get rid of the ropes! It did not take very long for her to realise that that first hurdle was the most impossible of all. Valdez knew how to tie a rope.

Tezzie was sure now that he must have recognised her when he came into the store. What a fool she had been to underestimate him! He must have been watching her because he had acted on the only occasion she had gone somewhere unaccompanied.

Her information about the duel had been dangerously incomplete. Either she had mistaken the *arroyo* altogether, or she should have turned south instead of north when she hit it. With the benefit of hindsight, she knew that if she had wanted to stop the duel she would have been better advised to have told Colonel Whipton about it. He would most certainly have ensured that at least Lieutenant Garway did not keep the appointment.

What would the Vigils have done when they found she was missing? Tezzie guessed they would first send to the convent, but she had no idea what they would do next. No one could possibly imagine she had been captured, and tracking her would be impossible, because there would be nothing remaining in the dirt outside the Vigils' store that might lead them to her. In fact there would be no distinguishable trail to be followed until she had turned off the much-travelled Santa Fe Trail into the *arroyo*. There, if anyone knew she had gone that way, her tracks might be found. An Indian could certainly follow them from there. Joel Kanturk might also be able to, but no one could follow a trail on a moonless night like this.

Joel Kanturk. She did not know even if he was still alive. She knew it was a great deal more likely to have been James Garway who died in the duel, if anyone had, but there was still the possibility it might have been Joel. It was Joel who had rescued her, albeit in a ruthlessly unsympathetic manner, and had thereby made it possible for her to live in a civilised society among her own kind. She owed him a huge debt of gratitude. It was no wonder she did not want anything to happen to him. Nor was it to be wondered at that she might regard him as being someone likely to rescue her again. Joel Kanturk, who laughed at her threat to take the veil, and who seemed to think she should marry James Garway.

Deep in her heart, Tezzie knew it was not gratitude for Joel's past actions that made her fear he had been killed. From the time he bade her farewell at the convent, he had been the first, the only, man from whose touch she neither flinched nor froze. On the contrary, it had been so different from anything she had known, and had aroused such unexpected responses in herself, that she had welcomed it. He was not as other men—or so she had thought. But then, under the cottonwood, she had realised that he was no different, and the knowledge frightened her. Joel was harsh and cynical, but he had never been unkind, yet his body, too, had yearned to inflict on her the same pain and degradation as those others. She shivered, not entirely from the cold. Dare she hope he might be content with less? It seemed unlikely. Joel's desires were not displayed on his face, as were those of other men—Colonel Whipton, for example—but she had felt the strength of his yearning and dreaded to contemplate what might have happened had the time and the place been different.

Perhaps it would be better if he had been killed, if he were even now lying in the undertaker's back room. At least he could then never learn that she had nothing he would want if he knew the truth. The nuns had stressed the need to behave with the utmost propriety at all times. Mrs Vigil had underlined that message. Not only must a woman go to her marriage-bed a virgin, but there must be no whiff of a suspicion that circumstances might have arisen to jeopardise that desired state.

Joel had told her she should tell any intending husband

of her past, because a discovered deception would be more certain to alienate him than the truth. But Joel did not know the full extent of her past, and even he had acknowledged that not all men would be able to live with the little he knew of what she had to reveal. No man, she thought, remembering the lessons of Mrs Vigil, could live with the truth. Even Joel, who might enfold her in his arms and desire her as much as any man, would not want to take to his marriage-bed a woman whose naked body had been stared at by others. Few men would. He could probably bear to touch her at all only because he imagined nothing worse had befallen her. If he knew the truth . . . Besides, she thought suddenly, what if he did overcome any scruples? How would she feel when he had finished with her body and left it bleeding and bruised? Would she then feel anything but fear and revulsion for him? She knew she would not, and that thought was the most depressing of all.

The depression and the cold combined to induce a lethargy which a small part of her brain told her was dangerous, but which her bound body had no desire to counter. It was the succession of short, low-pitched whistles from a screech-owl that woke her and reminded her of the urgency of her present plight. There might be nothing she could do about it yet, but if she dozed off she could well lose whatever slight opportunity offered. For all practical purposes, she knew she could discount the probability of rescue from outside. Valdez must have laid some plans, and they probably involved returning to the circus side-show. Very well. Opportunities could not be entirely lacking, hopeless as her situation was just now. It could not be long till dawn. She fancied the sky was already half a shade lighter in the east.

When Valdez woke up, his head ached. It was the sort of ache brought on by cheap, rotgut whisky, and there was only one cure he knew of. He groped for the bottle and had some more. That priority dealt with, he

staggered off to relieve himself and then staggered back.
He glanced at the girl as he passed her, and grinned
complacently. Much good running off had done her! It
had taken time, but he had got her back. He kicked
her. Not hard enough to do any damage, but hard
enough to remind her who was master again. He took
out his knife and drew considerable satisfaction from
seeing the apprehension in her eyes, but all he did with
it was to slice through the rope at her back that joined
her hands to her feet. She still could not go anywhere,
but the act would give her hope that he would later
enjoy dashing. Then he scrambled back over the
crumbling wall and reached for his bottle.

The truth was that, now that he had her back and
had time to look at her as well as to think, he was not
convinced that any of those plans he had made would
be any good at all. She had learnt to stand properly
and to speak. Nothing could take those skills away, not
even the whip. If he put her on exhibition as she was
now, one of two things would happen: either people
simply would not believe she had ever been the Wolf
Girl of the Rio Grande, or they would be outraged that
someone so obviously civilised was being exhibited like
that. In either case, it was likely to be he who was
tarred and feathered this time. Of course, he could
remove her clothes and let her get filthy again, but he
had already discovered she was unlikely to resign herself
to the sort of treatment she had put up with, however
sullenly, before. He took another gulp at the bottle. The
plain fact was that she just was no longer the investment
she had once been.

He staggered to his feet again. Perhaps so much bad
whisky on an empty stomach had not been a good idea.
Bottle in hand, he lurched unsteadily towards the wall,
and clambered over it at the third try. He stood there,
swaying slightly and staring down at his victim.

'You bitch,' he said, his voice slurred. 'You lousy,
inconsiderate, thoughtless bitch! You could almost pass
for a respectable woman now, d'you know that?' He

took another slug from the bottle and, as if it brought him enlightenment, a crafty grin spread across his unshaven face. 'You may be no good as a wolf girl any more, but at least I can do what I wanted to do before—and there's nothing you can do to stop me this time!'

Tezzie watched in horror as, after a further swig of whisky, he fumbled with the fastening of his trousers. What chance had she now of evading him, with her hands and feet tied? Then good luck—and bad whisky—gave her the opportunity she had longed for. Already unsteady on his feet, Valdez found it still more difficult to keep his balance when his trousers were around his ankles. He swayed and lurched the two or three paces towards her and, as he came within reach, Tezzie swung her bound legs round and, with as much force as she could muster, drove them against the back of his, hitting him just below the knee.

With a bellow of surprise, he overbalanced. The bottle flew out of his hand and broke in two on the adobe wall. Valdez toppled over and, as he fell, his head hit the wall as well and he lay there, crumpled and still, blood oozing on to the clay.

Tezzie sat up shaking with relief. Where was his knife? Presumably it was in his discarded belt. She began to wriggle towards it, not quite sure how she could make use of it, yet knowing she needed a cutting-tool before anything else. Then she caught sight of an alternative. By the most fortunate chance of all the broken bottom half of the whisky bottle had wedged itself, jagged side up, in the sand at the foot of the wall.

Tezzie resisted the impulse to try to cut her hands free first: it would be much easier to free her feet, thus leaving her free to run away if the need arose, and once her feet were unfettered she would be better able to manoeuvre herself into a good position to work on her hands, something she had to do 'blind', since they were behind her.

It took longer to cut her feet free than she had anticipated because, although the neck of the bottle was

conveniently wedged, jagged side uppermost, it was by
no means immovable, and Tezzie could not escape the
fear that her efforts might eventually dislodge the tool
she needed so badly. Neither could she be entirely sure
that Valdez would not prove to be in a stupor rather
than dead, and that he might therefore at any moment
come to and realise what she was doing.

This fear diminished as the minutes passed and he
lay without a perceptible flicker of life, and it was with
a great sense of relief that Tezzie felt the rope round
her ankles fall away. Freeing her hands, which necessi-
tated turning her back on the bottle and working by
feel alone, took even longer and was a great deal more
hazardous. Several times she felt the glass slice through
skin instead of rope, and each time she could only pray
that the wound was superficial.

At last her hands, too, were free, and she ran to the
stream to stanch the blood in clear, cold water. She
made a bandage of sorts from the frill of her petticoat,
and regretted that the whisky had drained away, leaving
only the water to cleanse the cuts.

Valdez still lay where he had fallen, unmoving. Tezzie
moved cautiously round him and picked up his belt. It
held a gun, but no knife. Then she suddenly remembered
he had bent down for it that morning. It must have
been in his boot. She hesitated. A gun was useful. A
knife was better. The combination was ideal. Gingerly,
unwillingly, she went back to the unnaturally slumped
figure. The thought of having to touch this man was
one that brought her stomach heaving into her mouth,
but it had to be done. She needed whatever weapons
she could find. She was going back to Santa Fe, but she
was not risking that long journey without weapons
when there were weapons to be had. She found the
knife and extracted it. The man's leg was lifeless and
heavy. She looked at his face. The blood had stopped
trickling. Perhaps he was dead. Tezzie didn't care if he
was, but she supposed she should make sure, if only for
her own peace of mind. She could not do that without

touching him again, however, and that was something
she was unable to make herself do. It was not fear of
touching a corpse—in her days as a wolf, that was how
she ate—it was fear because Valdez was who he was.
She shuddered. No, she would have to survive in
ignorance.

She fastened the gun-belt round her waist on top of
her brass-buckled belt, and jammed the knife into the
holster beside the gun, unable to think of a safer place.
She was about to set off down the canyon when she
remembered Valdez' mule. The animal had been hobbled
at a point where there was relatively good grazing beside
the creek, so it had not strayed far. Tezzie had not
saddled or bridled a horse since she left the convent,
where she had two or three times got the paint ready
for the nuns, so it took her longer than it would have
taken Valdez—or Joel. When she had finished, the mule
made it perfectly clear that it had co-operated long
enough. However, despite the animal's shaking its head,
spinning round in a circle and cow-kicking, Tezzie
persevered and eventually succeeded in scrambling on
to its back. Fully aware that it was carrying a complete
novice, it amused itself by trying to rub her off on rocks
as they passed. It would have tried to unseat her by
bucking, but some instinct warned Tezzie to keep the
reins too short to enable it to get its head down, so that
expedient was denied it. It was going to be a slow and
uncomfortable journey to Santa Fe, but at least it would
be better than walking.

Joel and Pete made what speed they could toward the
pueblo, not because they had any chance of following a
trail in this darkness but because they needed to be as
far out of reach of the Santa Fe military scouts as
possible. Even Indian scouts would have to wait till
dawn to follow them on so dark a night as this.

'I shouldn't have come back for you,' Pete said
eventually. 'I should have gone straight on after them.'

'What good would that have done? It would have

been dark before you caught them—if you caught them. Besides, he may prove to have friends. If that's so, it'll need at least two of us.

'But I might have caught them! As it is, no matter what speed we make, she'll have been with him all night.'

It was probably just as well that Pete could not see the pitying look Joel cast at him. 'Be your age, Pete! If that's what he's after, he's not going to limit the activity to the night.'

'I know that, but if she's away all night, she's compromised.'

Joel sighed. 'Pete, after all these years, you're still the conventional townsman. All right: it *looks* worse if she's gone all night. Are you concerned about what it looks like or what it actually *is* like? Do you care about what happens to her, or only about what other people think has happened?'

'Of course I care what happens! The thing is, if I could have got her back to Santa Fe before nightfall, her absence could have been more easily explained.'

'Only you couldn't. You might just have caught up with them before dark, but you could never have got back to Santa Fe. The only difference would be that it would have been you who compromised her.'

'I could at least have done the honourable thing,' Pete said stiffly.

'What—marry her?' Joel sounded more amused than impressed. 'I didn't know you wanted to marry Tezzie Milagro. Thought you had your eye on that nice girl in Española!'

'Didn't think you'd noticed her.' Pete sounded defensive.

'Could hardly fail to. Why, you even went to church to sit behind her!'

'And what's wrong with that?'

'Nothing—quite admirable, in fact. It just makes nonsense of any suggestion of marrying Tezzie.'

'At least I care!'

Joel made no answer. There was no reason why he should care. After all, he thought savagely, whatever happened to Tezzie—and Pete's guess was unlikely to be far from the mark—would be nothing new to her. What difference could it possibly make to him? Then he recalled the sudden change from a warm, willing, womanly response to his embrace, to the rigidly frightened child. *'No. Not that, please. Not you!'* Then, before he could reassure her, they had been interrupted. Yet how could he have reassured her when he remembered the feel of her in his arms, the tiny waist that his hands could span, the voluptuous curve of her breasts inviting his lips, the enticing curve of her hips? It angered him that she should so accurately read his desires—and reject them so baldly. At the same time, she had read him wrong: he wanted nothing that was not given willingly, and had never before met a woman he desired who had not been willing. If Tezzie found him repulsive, he did not want her; if she was holding out for a gold band . . . well, she much mistook her man: Joel Kanturk did not marry what others had helped themselves to. He hadn't done it before and he wasn't going to do it now.

It crossed his mind that there was an inconsistency between his opinions and his actions. If he cared so little, why was he going to these lengths to find her? He shifted uneasily in the saddle. He supposed it was because he did not like to see so much of other people's effort—the nuns', the Vigils'—going to waste. In any case, no woman deserved to be abducted. He would be doing this for anyone.

Because there was no moon, it took a long time to reach the pueblo. They stopped outside it, and unrolled their blankets beside the trail. There must be nothing covert about their being there. When they awoke, they found themselves surrounded by cautious but not overtly hostile Tesuques. Some were using old-fashioned long-guns as a prop for arms resting on the barrel. Others held rifles deceptively casually at their sides.

'We would like to speak with the boy who saw the Anglo woman,' Joel said in Tewa. 'We want to pick up her trail, if it can be done.'

The Indians gestured to the two men to follow them, and Pete observed that their horses were nowhere to be seen. This was soon explained when they entered the pueblo. The horses were being watered. It remained to be seen whether they would be given back.

The boy was fetched, and he repeated what he had told Pete the previous day.

Joel nodded. 'The woman has been stolen, and we wish to get her back. Was there anything else—anything that might help us to track them?'

The boy thought. 'The mule had a loose shoe,' he said finally.

'You're sure?'

'I heard it clink when they crossed rocks. You can't mistake the sound.'

'Nothing else? Anything to narrow the area we have to search?'

The boy considered. 'They were heading down the Cañada Ancha towards the Rio Grande. When they get there, they can turn upstream or downstream along the White Rock canyon. Or they can cross it. Hundreds of little canyons lead down on the other side.'

'Including Frijoles,' Joel commented.

'A good canyon, Frijoles,' one of the men remarked. 'It has grazing and water, and plenty of shelter.'

'I have used it,' Joel told him. 'Is there anywhere else as good?'

'If a man stole my wife, that is the first place I should look.'

'Might he not go elsewhere for that very reason?'

The man shook his head. 'There are places just as good for the guiltless to shelter, but few Mexicans—or Anglos—know them. None can be so well defended as the old caves of our people. One man can hold off an army there.'

Joel smiled 'My companion has proved it. Thank

you. We are in your debt.'

When the two men had returned with their horses to pick up their bed-rolls, they remounted and headed down the Calabasa Arroyo to the Cañada Ancha. There it took them some time to pick up the trail they wanted, but when they found it, it was unmistakable: the foot neat and round like a donkey's, but longer, one imprint slightly smudged as the loose shoe moved before it bore the mule's weight.

Several times on her ride up White Rock canyon Tezzie had cause to be glad she was riding a mule—even so cussed a mule as this one—rather than a horse. The trail was narrow at the best of times and frequently disappeared, obliging her to risk putting the animal into the stream, where it had to skirt rocks and step carefully in water which, while not deep, swirled and foamed over submerged rocks. The animal was reluctant to enter, but, having been forced to do so, proved far more sure-footed and dependable than any horse. Several times she was tempted to leave the river, but she knew it was easier to continue until the Cañada Ancha entered the Rio Grande: not only was it much wider, but it skirted the higher slopes of the mountains and led in turn to several trails that headed towards Santa Fe.

It was when she had at last turned into the Cañada that she heard the sound of approaching horses: the chink of iron on stone was magnified and funnelled towards her by the enclosing walls of rock. She looked desperately around. It was entirely possible that whoever approached might be able to help her, but it was not a possibility upon which she was inclined to place much dependence. There were plenty of places where she could hide. Hiding the mule was another matter. Then she spotted a small canyon, little more than a gully, running off to the south-west a few yards ahead. Perhaps that would provide sufficient concealment for a mule. Tezzie pressed the animal on, and for once it responded to her urgency.

Once within the narrow, rocky gully, Tezzie dismounted and led the mule behind an outcrop almost large enough to conceal it completely. She tethered it to a juniper that clung with fierce tenacity to a tiny pocket of sand in a fissure, and prayed that the animal would not uproot the small bush with a sudden jerk of the reins. Then she scuttled across the canyon, cursing the long skirts that flapped round her legs and impeded her progress. The mule might still be seen and, if it were, its owner would be sought. With luck, it would be taken for some prospector's animal and the prospector himself reckoned to be too far off to be worth the pursuit. On the other hand, a search of the vicinity might equally well be made, and the further she was from the mule, the safer she would be. At least rocks betrayed no footprints.

The horses were reined in at the entrance to the little gully.

'This don't make sense,' Pete said, his voice carefully low. 'Those prints have been as clear as written directions. Now look what's happened.'

Joel had already noticed that the line of prints heading towards the Rio Grande was now accompanied and sometimes overlaid with prints leading back again—prints that also bore the unmistakable marks of a loose shoe. Then here, at this unimportant little intersection, were the heavier imprints of an animal standing still, and a confused scrabble of sand before they cleared again and just one set went into the little ravine.

Pete was for following them, but Joel's hand on his arm held him back. 'Not yet,' he said, his voice barely a whisper in the clear air. 'That's a perfect place for an ambush. My guess is that whoever is on that mule heard us and is up there. The point is, who is it? The prints returning this way suggest that the mule is carrying a much lighter load—presumably just one person.'

Pete's face darkened. 'You mean he's left Tezzie and is coming back to Santa Fe? My God, Joel, anything could have happened to her! At least we can follow the tracks back and they'll lead us to her. I only hope she's still alive!'

Joel did not seem so perturbed. 'If the man who's in there is the one who abducted her, he can save us a lot of trouble by telling us where she is. Have you overlooked the possibility that it might be Tezzie herself who's escaped from him?'

Pete stared at his friend. 'Do you think that's likely?'

'Highly probable, I'd say. She's a resourceful girl, and I don't suppose she's any more trusting than she used to be. It depends who he was, of course, but I'd not discount the possibility that it's Tezzie who's hiding out up there somewhere.'

'Then what are we waiting for? Let's go fetch her!'

'Let's be sure first, shall we? It's still a good place for an ambush.'

Joel led the way cautiously into the little canyon, and soon stopped beside a new and different track. He dismounted and passed his reins over to Pete. There in the sand, quite clearly, was the fresh imprint of a boot, its raised heel easily visible. He raised his head and looked about him. It was a very small boot. For a man, quite exceptionally small, and the Tesuque boy had not mentioned anything unusual about the man's appearance.

Once he knew the mule was there somewhere, the search was not long. Joel made no attempt to unhitch it, however, being more concerned to find its rider. He hoped with an intensely fervent hope that his guess was right and so small a boot must belong to a woman. But if it was Tezzie who had brought the mule back this far, in what condition might she be? Whoever had abducted her and whatever might have been his purpose, he was unlikely to have resisted the temptation to satisfy his physical lusts. There were few enough women in this Territory, and fewer still who were either young or beautiful. Tezzie was a temptation indeed. Joel's greatest fear was that, while her spirit might have given her the will to escape, he might none the less find her torn and bleeding, perhaps so scarred by what had happened that she would be unable to accept help from any man, even one who had helped her in the past.

Behind the mule rose a sheer cliff-face. No one could be there. He turned round and surveyed the opposite side of the ravine. It looked more hopeful, with narrow fissures from time to time, but he rather thought whoever had hidden the mule would have put as much space between them as possible. He strode slowly into the ravine.

As far up the narrow canyon as she could get, Tezzie crouched behind an eroded outcrop of sandstone, a broad, squat pillar, the top of which would have made a perfect look-out post. She heard the faint clink of a spur-rowel as its boot touched rock. How far off was it? Nearer than the mule, her ears told her. It was amazing how quickly those old skills, honed in the wolf pack, were coming back. Yet some things were different: as a wolf, she would have lain low until the enemy had gone. As a human, she had developed a powerful curiosity to see, not so much *who* was searching, for that was of little interest to her right now, but exactly where he was and whence he was coming. If she could see him, she would know when he had given up.

Very, very cautiously she peered round the pillar. Nothing. Taking very great care that her skirts should neither rustle nor protrude, she wriggled round to look out from the other side of the pillar, a side that gave a slightly wider angle of vision into the ravine below. As she peered out, the projecting brim of a stetson appeared round a slight bend. She pulled her head back quickly and felt her heart beating rapidly.

So near!

She peered out again, even more cautiously this time. The whole man was in sight now, moving one pace at a time, each pace followed by a long, searching pause. He was exceptionally tall.

A shuddering sigh of relief flooded over her with such force that she had to lean against the column of rock, her eyes closed, for a few seconds before she was able to think with any degree of clarity. Then, the need for concealment over, she jumped to her feet, picked up her full brown skirts and ran down the rock-strewn gully like a mountain goat.

Joel spun round when he heard the clattering of loose stones that her incautious progress sent scattering in her wake. 'Tezzie?' he said, though that agile figure in its brown dress and small elastic-sided boots could be no one else.

Tezzie was too breathless to reply and, as she hurtled towards him, it seemed the most natural thing in the world that his arms should be open to halt her rush. As they closed protectively round her, she felt a fresh upsurge of relief—and not only relief, but pure happiness. She clung to him, her head nestling in the hollow of his shoulder, as if she feared he would vanish like a dream. A sob of mingled happiness and relief escaped her.

Joel's relief was no less than hers, and he cradled her in his arms without attempting to analyse why it should be so. His lips brushed her hair in a gentle caress, and when, her breath having returned, she smiled up at him, they sought her mouth in a kiss of lingering tenderness that cast from both their minds any thoughts save those of the immediate moment. The tenderness intensified as Tezzie's lips pleaded involuntarily for more, and Joel became aware with greater certainty than ever before of the latent passion that burned within her compliant, yearning body. His mouth, hard and vital, demanded and took that which hers was glad to give, and as his tongue reached into the willing cavern that opened to its demand, Tezzie's arms reached up to draw him closer still. She gave herself completely to the sensuous, questing delight, and when his strong fingers unfastened first one and then another of the buttons at her neck, she welcomed their straying warmth beneath the cloth. Joel felt the heart beating beneath the inviting globe of her breast, and knew it but echoed the pulsing of his own. Never could he recall having wanted a woman as much as he wanted this one, but as his lips caressed her breast, seeking the nipple his fingers told him was hardening with desire, a little voice echoed in his mind: *'No. Not that, please. Not you!'*

The recollection was like a douche of cold water, and he relaxed his hold with an abruptness that brought surprise to Tezzie's suddenly opened eyes.

'What is it?' she asked.

He smiled perfunctorily. 'Pete's further down the *arroyo*, by your mule. He must be wondering what's happened,' he said, seizing gratefully the excuse presented by a friend whose presence he had completely forgotten. He touched her cheek gently, almost shyly, before broaching the question he was almost afraid to ask. 'Are you all right, Tezzie?'

She laughed, her eyes shining with the memory of his embrace. 'I am now,' she said.

'When we started searching for you, we heard you had been taken by some Mexican.' Joel's face was troubled. What did 'now' signify?

'That's right. It was Valdez.' Even though she was now quite safe from him, Tezzie could not repress a shudder.

'Valdez!' Joel reached out and drew her close once more. His voice was grim. 'If he has hurt you . . .' he began.

Tezzie grimaced. 'I'm a bit bruised and very dirty—and extremely hungry—but nothing more. In any case, I think he's dead,' she added, with some satisfaction.

'You mean you weren't . . . He didn't . . .' For some reason, Joel could not find the right words.

Tezzie coloured self-consciously. 'No, he didn't—though he tried. That's why he's dead.' She explained briefly what had happened and, as she did so, the chill hand of fear clutched at her heart. Joel's relief was undisguised, but that only emphasised how important it was to him. If he knew the truth, would he feel the same concern? If he had known the truth, would he have been here now?

Joel saw the troubled look in her green-flecked eyes, and misread it. 'If he is dead, it's only what he deserves! Are you sure?'

Tezzie shook her head. 'I didn't stay to find out, but he was certainly very limp and lifeless.' She hesitated. 'Should we go and make sure?'

'I see no reason to. A meal for vultures is the most fitting end for him and, if you're mistaken, he'll eventually wake up with a sore head and no mule. I doubt if he'd dare return to Santa Fe and risk your recognising him. Come, we must get back to Pete.'

He began to guide her down the little ravine, his hand still resting, gently protective, round her waist. They had gone only a few paces when she stopped and turned, a diffident smile on her lips as if she knew she should have spoken before. 'I haven't yet thanked you for coming for me,' she said.

'Unnecessarily, it seems: you appear to have managed very well without any help.'

'It might all too easily not have been so,' she reminded him. 'I was more pleased to see you than you can imagine!'

He smiled, but said nothing, too confused by his own thoughts to risk a reply. In fact, he had been more relieved than he would have believed possible to see her at all, let alone apparently unharmed. He had naturally been additionally relieved to learn that Valdez' nastier plans had been thwarted, but that was surely just a matter of common humanity—except that common humanity did not customarily afford quite so pronounced a feeling of relief. When he had seen this woman at the convent, she had seemed a mere child and had provoked a quite unexpected tenderness in him, unexpected because it had seemed quite undeserved, given what he suspected of her past. Tenderness was still there, but there was more, much more, and Joel did not like it. It had been a great mistake to have kissed her in the Vigils' store. It had been intended as nothing more than a tease, a set-down for her flash of . . . of what? Impertinence? Spirit? Whatever name you gave it, it had needled him, but when he had held her in his arms, a subtle change had taken place and nothing that had happened since had done anything to diminish it.

When Tezzie was near he wanted only to touch, to hold. She roused him as few other women ever had—and none in recent years. He wanted to exclude her from the company of other men until such time as she had no desire for anyone's company but his own, and sometimes, when she responded as she had just now, he thought it would be both possible and easy to achieve. But then he remembered what she had unconsciously told him under the cottonwood tree in the Governor's patio. Not only would he not be the first, but as much as she welcomed and responded to his caresses, they would reach a point when she recoiled from them. Joel could bear neither the thought of that revulsion nor the thought that he might forgo the ultimate expression of his feelings in order to save her from the fear she had good reason to feel. He had no idea how to reconcile these conflicting fears.

Why it should matter so much to him was something he preferred not to dwell on. Had Tezzie been anyone else, he would have suspected he loved her, but that could not be the case: he had vowed long ago that he would never again fall into the trap of loving a woman who did not come to his bed a virgin, and therefore whatever he felt for Tezzie could not be love. There was the difference that Susannah had betrayed him and had apparently taken little coaxing to do so, whereas whatever had happened to Tezzie had occurred before he came across her, and if her reaction to the more forceful of his own advances was anything to go by, she had been a far from willing participant. One might desire such a woman, as he could not deny he did. One did not love her—and one most assuredly did not think of marrying her!

No such confused thoughts bothered Tezzie. All she
knew was that Joel had come searching for her, and his
relief at finding her had been as great as hers at
recognising him. The way he had held her, the answering
passion of his kisses, told her that he felt as she did.
She had been momentarily dismayed by the abruptness
with which he had released her, but that had been easily
explained by his concern for Pete. For the time being,
at least, those other doubts could be pushed out of her
mind. She needed only the opportunity to tell him how
she felt. Perhaps she would be able to do so to such
effect that no other considerations would matter.

Optimistic thoughts such as these radiated a happiness from her face that contrasted oddly with the unease
in Joel's, and, as they approached, Pete looked from
one to the other, trying unsuccessfully to deduce what
might have caused such disparate expressions. He bit
back the questions that arose and confined himself to
the obvious.

'So it was Tezzie, after all,' he said.

'And unharmed, but hungry!' Joel told him, a smile
banishing the cloud. 'Get her back to the Vigils as soon
as you can. Assure them that no harm came to her.' He
hesitated. 'That her honour is undamaged,' he added.

The radiance vanished from Tezzie's face, though
whether this was because of the implication of the first
instruction or the second, it would have been hard to
say.

'Aren't you coming too?' she asked, her hand involuntarily seeking his sleeve.

He removed it gently but firmly. 'Santa Fe is probably
the last place I'll be seen in for quite a while. It might
be wiser to leave the Territory completely, since I've no
desire to face a firing-squad.'

Tezzie stared at him in puzzled amazement. 'Why
should you be shot?' she asked.

It was Pete's turn to be amazed. 'Didn't he tell you?
They put him in jail because of that duel. When we
learned of your disappearance, he escaped.'

'Is this true?' Tezzie turned to Joel.

He shrugged. 'There didn't seem to be much choice at the time. Of course, if I'd known you were so capable of looking after yourself, maybe I'd not have bothered!'

Tezzie smiled fleetingly. 'I'm glad you did—things might not have turned out as well as they did, after all. But to put yourself at such a risk! Surely Pete could have found me? Or was he, too, in jail?'

Pete laughed. 'No, I was just warned off military property! Joel is the one who can follow a trail, though, not me. I can track a deer or a bear, thanks to what he's taught me, but this was too subtle a trail for me to try—especially with your life possibly at stake at the end of it.'

A sudden thought struck Tezzie. 'And Lieutenant Garway—what of him? Did you kill him?'

'Afraid you'll have to take the veil?' Joel asked savagely. Even though he knew such belated concern for the young officer meant that he was no rival, he could not quite put out the thin flame of jealousy that she was thinking about another man's welfare. 'Don't worry. He's alive—and well enough but for a wounded hand.'

'He's in jail, too,' Pete interrupted. 'He'd have come with us, even with that hand, but they'd have been much more keen to track us down if we had a deserter with us than just a civilian jail-breaker.'

'What will happen to him now?' Tezzie asked.

'He'll be demoted for duelling, I guess,' Pete told her.

'And you?' She turned to Joel. 'What would have happened to you if you'd stayed?'

'Who knows? A token seven days, I reckon.'

'But now you're likely to be shot? It doesn't make sense!'

'The seven days would be for duelling—illegal, but understandable. Escaping from jail is a different matter altogether.'

'Even if it was for a good reason?'

Both men laughed. 'If you're in jail, you stay there

till the court frees you,' Joel pointed out. 'If not, you risk the consequences. Now that I'm out, I'm putting as much distance between Santa Fe and myself as I can. Pete will take you home to the Vigils'.'

Tezzie turned to him, her eyes pleading. 'Let me come with you, Joel?'

'A life on the run is no place for a woman,' he said harshly, unwilling to admit to himself how much he longed to accept her offer.

'I'd be better at such a life than most,' Tezzie pointed out. 'After all, how else did I live as a wolf?'

He shook his head. 'The nuns and the Vigils have trained that out of you—and rightly so. What's in your past is not something I'd recommend you to think of as an asset!'

She flushed. 'I don't! It's just that in this case . . .' Her voice trailed off as she saw the unrelenting harshness of his face, and recalled that there were things in her past of which he so far knew nothing but which would disgust him utterly when he found out. 'Where will you go?' she said instead.

'Who knows? Perhaps it's best not to say. Pete's got a girl in Española, so he'll be around here still. Maybe I'll go into Arizona. Find me a good woman and settle down to raise a family.'

'I see.' Tezzie's voice was very small. She was no 'good woman', try as she might. Her right to that description had been taken away from her long ago, and Joel's use of it confirmed her suspicions concerning his priorities. Joel Kanturk could never love her, much less seek her to be mother of his children.

Joel had said what he did as much to punish himself as to hurt Tezzie. He knew that at the moment neither a good woman nor the prospect of settling down held any lure at all. Tezzie's small, rejected voice cut him to the heart. He longed to take her in his arms and tell her it was a joke, to tell her he would welcome her beside him. Yet how could he, knowing himself as he did, knowing that if he ever succeeded in coaxing her out of her fear of his intimacy, he might then feel the revulsion he had felt when he had taken Susannah that last revengeful time in the full knowledge that another had been there first and to some purpose? No. He did not love Tezzie. It was not possible for him to do so in the circumstances. But he had no need to punish her, and if she left the protection of the Vigils now, she would be entirely dependent on his good will. Better by far that she should stay behind. With a garrison the size of that in Santa Fe, she would forget Joel Kanturk.

Pete was puzzled. There were undercurrents here he did not understand, though he very much doubted whether Joel's comments about Arizona were anything more than a passing joke.

'You're right about one thing,' he said. 'If you're off to Arizona or anywhere else, I'll stay around here. I like Española. All the same, I think your view is too drastic.'

'What do you mean?'

'I'll take Tezzie back, and I'll make things right with the Vigils—that's no great problem. Why don't I also take her to the Governor? Get her to explain why you escaped? The danger she was in? Garway and Baden will back up her story. The chances are they'll believe her. No reason why they shouldn't. They might agree to let you off lightly if they know why you escaped, provided you give yourself up and save them the bother of finding you. At least then you'll be free to go to Arizona or Timbuktu—or stay right here, if you prefer! What do you say?'

'It's a brilliant idea, Pete,' Tezzie told him. 'Joel, you wouldn't have to spend the rest of your life looking over your shoulder. Please let's follow Pete's advice?'

'You'd have to explain who Valdez was—and imply that we knew he was the man who had abducted you,' Joel pointed out. 'How can you do that without telling him what the nuns and the Vigils have kept to themselves? No, that's too big a price to pay.'

'Nonsense! I'm sure I can convince them without

going into all that,' Tezzie said firmly. 'At least let me try? Stay somewhere within reach, though not too easy reach, perhaps. Let us try it, Joel—please?'

Joel hesitated uncharacteristically. He knew far better than Tezzie what she risked if her past became generally known, but she seemed confident. He could think of any number of reasons why Valdez might have taken her off, but even the admission that someone had done so would endanger her reputation perhaps irretrievably. Still, the Governor was an honourable man who would not wittingly pass on what had been told him in confidence. Perhaps it could work.

If it did, it would mean he could stay in New Mexico, and he had come to love the Territory with its broad sweeping mesas that were not as barren as they seemed, its snow-peaked mountains rich in game, the Indian pueblos and the adobe homesteads that both grew out of the landscape and nestled into it as if they were a part of it. He thought of the ghostly grey of the cottonwoods in the *bosque* along the river bottoms and the soft jade carpet that spread across the sandy soil between the junipers in spring, the summer thunderheads building up over the mountains and the cloak of whispering golden aspens that enclosed those mountains in the fall. No, this was no place to leave lightly.

Neither did he wish to put too much distance between himself and Tezzie, even though common sense suggested that it might be better for them both if he did. She had spirit and courage, and sooner or later she would find some nice young soldier and marry him. In the meantime, who knew but that she might still need help or advice? He chose to disregard the fact that help and advice were the prerogative of the Vigils or the nuns. His instincts and his heart told him he should be there in case she needed him. His common sense protested in vain.

'Just how sure are you that you can convince the Governor without damning yourself irretrievably?' he asked at last.

'Quite sure,' she told him. 'A modest blush, fluttering eyelashes—they can speak volumes, properly used, you know.'

'I have observed it to be so,' he said drily. 'Though I hadn't realised they were skills you had mastered.'

'I haven't precisely mastered them,' Tezzie confided, 'because, to tell the truth, I've never needed to use them before. But I have watched other women do so, and I'm sure I can do just as well.' As she finished speaking, she glanced sideways up at him under her lashes and then dropped her gaze as if embarrassed that he had seen her, fluttering her lashes as she did so.

Joel laughed with genuine amusement. 'If that's what you manage without mastery, heaven help the hearts of Santa Fe when you are fully proficient!' he said. 'All right, you can try Pete's scheme. I'll go out beyond the Rito de los Frijoles. That'll be safe enough for a few days, but I want a promise from you, Tezzie.' His voice was suddenly very serious, and she sensed that whatever the promise he sought, it mattered to him very much.

'What is it?' she asked.

'You must promise me that in no circumstances at all will you tell the Governor of your past, and that you will concoct a story which, while keeping as closely as possible to the truth, does not leave him room to conclude that you might have been compromised. If you can't do this, I'd rather you left matters as they are.'

Tezzie looked up into his grey eyes for a long time without speaking. How much it all mattered to him! Too much to hold out hope for any future happiness. She sighed. 'I promise,' she whispered.

He said nothing more, but swung himself up into the saddle. He stared down at her in enigmatic silence for a second and then, tipping his finger to the brim of his hat in farewell salute, rode off down the Cañada towards the Rio Grande.

Pete helped Tezzie back on to her mule and led the way up the Cañada towards the Calabasa Arroyo that

would eventually bring them to the pueblo and thence
to the capital.

It was a lonely ride, despite the company. Lonely
because of the deep empty hole somewhere inside her,
a hole so empty that it ached with a physical pain. How
could Joel ride off without a word, without a touch,
without a kiss—without even a backward look? She
longed to feel his arms around her once more and,
because it was a longing impossible to fulfil, she tried
to content herself with remembering how it had been.
How she had welcomed his caresses, how she had
luxuriated in the touch of his lips on her mouth, her
neck, her breasts! Was it wrong to welcome such intima-
cies? No, nothing so pleasurable could possibly be
wrong!

Her mind went back to that fateful ball, and the
closeness of an embrace which hinted at even closer
intimacy. She had pulled away from him then, partly in
fear of what his body portended but partly, she now
knew, because something in her had almost welcomed
that portent even though she knew it led to brutal,
agonising pain. Was it possible that one might find a
man who could induce such a longing that it overcame
fear? Married women bore children year after year, and
Luz Vigil certainly didn't fear her husband's touch.
Perhaps, if you loved a man, the pain was less? Perhaps.
But what happened when that man found out—or
guessed—that he was not the first? She had pondered
this before, and was no nearer an answer. She knew it
mattered because of the tremendous importance placed
on never being alone with a man.

It certainly mattered to Joel. Everything he said, the
promise he had just exacted, told her that. Could she
bear the look of disgust on his face if she told him the
truth? And which would be worse: to tell him and lose
him, or to have him find out? What was it he had said
at the ball? If he found his wife had kept a secret of
that magnitude from him, he would kill her. He had
been referring to her time in the side-show. The secret

she held was far greater than that. What hope was there in loving a man who would only reject her if he knew her full story? The answer was 'None', but she found that knowing the answer did nothing to change either the love or the longing. Both were doomed, but at least she knew that. All she could do for Joel was to ensure that at least he was free, even if that meant he would be free to love someone else.

CHAPTER TEN

SINCE THE Vigils knew so much of Tezzie's background, they had to be told precisely what had happened. Hernando looked grave, and Luz tut-tutted and shook her head.

'Your absence from the store has been remarked upon,' she said. 'We have given it out that you were ill. It will be best if we keep to that story, which at least will occasion no comment. Let us hope no one saw you return with Mr Lingstrom—and let it be a lesson to you, Tezzie, *never* to go out without a chaperon. Had you remembered that, none of this would have happened.'

There was no denying the truth of Mrs Vigil's remarks, Tezzie thought ruefully, but the incident could not be so easily obliterated as her employer hoped.

'I shall have to give the Governor some idea of what happened,' Tezzie told her.

'The Governor? Why on earth does he have to know anything at all?' Luz was clearly displeased as well as uncomprehending.

'Joel Kanturk would have been released very quickly if he'd stayed in jail,' Tezzie said. 'As it is, he escaped and is now a hunted man who will very likely be shot if he's caught. If I can explain to the Governor why he escaped, it's likely he can be dealt with quite leniently—provided he gives himself up—and then he would be free and not obliged to leave the Territory.'

'It would be foolish in the extreme to let anyone outside these four walls know what has happened, Tezzie. As for Joel Kanturk, I do not know him well, but he strikes me as a man well able to look after himself!'

'I'm sure the Governor will be discreet,' Tezzie insisted.

'Are you? In general I would agree with you, my dear, but this case is a little different. It is, after all, a story that can only gain in the re-telling, and even if the Governor is discreet, who knows who's listening at keyholes in a place such as the palace? No, Tezzie. It is a generous idea and does you credit, but it is an extremely foolish one, which you would be well advised to forget.'

'I can't,' Tezzie told her. 'It wasn't so much an idea as a promise. I promised Joel I would try, and he will be waiting to learn the outcome. So he remains at risk until he hears from me.'

Mrs Vigil sighed. 'A promise is a promise, alas. It is always *much* better not to commit oneself! Still, it's too late to do anything about that now. Perhaps it's as well that matters are out of your control.'

'What do you mean?'

'The Governor was due to leave Santa Fe this morning for the east. Goodness knows when he will be back.' She turned to Pete. 'Perhaps the best thing for you to do is to find Mr Kanturk and advise him to leave the Territory for the time being.'

'No!' Tezzie exclaimed. 'If the Governor has gone, we will see the Lieutenant-Governor. I'm not leaving this hanging in the air indefinitely!'

Mrs Vigil shook her head as if she were renouncing responsibility for Tezzie's actions. 'Very well,' she said, 'since you are determined on it. But, please, Tezzie, don't go like that! You can at least afford time to wash and change into something clean—and I should think you could do with a good meal.'

Tezzie was happy to agree that all these things were not only possible but eminently desirable, and when she and Pete rose from the generous hospitality of the Vigil's table, they both felt as if it would be impossible to feel hungry again.

While Tezzie and Pete had been eating, the Vigils had given much thought to who should escort Tezzie to the palace. They accepted that Pete would be going with her, but, as an unrelated man, that only made it more essential that she should have a duenna with her. Somewhat to Tezzie's surprise, Pete concurred entirely with this decision, though his reason had little to do with considerations of Tezzie's honour, it seemed.

'Mrs Vigil is quite right,' he told her. 'It would be wrong for you to have only me for an escort. Besides, word might get back to Rufina in Española, and how could I explain it if there was no chaperon?'

Neither Luz nor Hernando could be spared from their work, so they decided to send Estefana with Tezzie and Pete. Estefana was an elderly Indian who spoke some Spanish but no English. She had come to the Vigils of Cundiyo as part of their *encomienda* when she was a child, long before Hernando was born, and although the system of *encomienda* —the granting of land and its resident Indians as slaves—had long been illegal, she had remained with 'her' family and had accompanied the newly-married Hernando to Santa Fe to organise his household for him. She was none too pleased to be going into the city, which she regarded as unnecessarily large and crowded with too many of the 'wrong' sort of people, a category which appeared to include all Mexicans and Anglos, without whom there would have been virtually no Santa Fe. She sat in the back of the buckboard muttering to herself in Tewa until they drew up in the plaza, where she clambered down and refused point-blank to enter the palace. She was perfectly prepared to sit down by the entrance under the arcade which stretched the length of the building, where she would await their return. They need be in no particular hurry, because she enjoyed being with 'the people', by which she meant the Indians who squatted in the shade of the arcade selling their wares to passers-by.

'There's nothing we can do about it,' Tezzie told Pete.

'Once Estefana's mind is made up it stays made. I dare say no one will tell Rufina we went in without her.'

'I hope not!' was Pete's heartfelt reply.

Luz Vigil's information was almost correct: the Governor was away, though he had left the previous day. Unfortunately the Lieutenant-Governor had been taken ill during the night and was quite unable to perform his gubernatorial duties, nor had the duty officer any idea when he might be expected to have recovered.

'Then who is running the Territory?' Tezzie demanded. 'Someone must be in charge. Otherwise what happens to us all if the Comanches or the Apaches get wind of the fact that we have no leaders?'

The officer smiled. 'It's not as bad as that. The Lieutenant-Governor has appointed the garrison's commanding officer, Colonel Whipton, to take his place for the time being.'

Tezzie shifted uneasily. 'Colonel Whipton? I see.' She hesitated, and then tugged at Pete's sleeve. 'Come over here,' she whispered, pulling him out of earshot of the man behind the desk. 'What do we do now?'

'I don't see that we have much choice. We talk to the colonel.'

Tezzie looked doubtful. 'I don't like it. I don't like him, and I don't trust him.'

'He's the only person with the authority we need, Tezzie. In some ways he's better than the Governor, since he must be very familiar with the circumstances surrounding that duel.'

This was very true, and it was a consideration not lightly to be dismissed, but Tezzie was still unhappy about him. 'Perhaps we'd better find out what has been done about Lieutenant Garway,' she suggested. 'At least that will give us some indication of how seriously the colonel views duelling.'

Tezzie returned to the duty officer. 'Have you any idea what happened to Lieutenant Garway?' she asked. 'I heard he was injured in a duel.'

'That's right—not badly, though. The colonel had him on the carpet, I believe, and he's now a humble trooper.'

'A trooper! Isn't that rather drastic?' she exclaimed.

'It looked at first as if he'd be court-martialled and drummed out of the army: there was a suspicion he'd helped in the escape of another prisoner, the man who wounded him.'

'Surely that would be the last person he'd help to escape?' Pete broke in.

'That's what they managed to convince the colonel of, but he don't hold with duelling anyway. All things considered, Garway got off lightly.'

'And what about the other man—the one who escaped?' Tezzie asked.

'Kanturk? We'll get him back. The man must be a fool to try it. You'd think he'd have realised that the punishment for escaping is a lot worse than the one for duelling. Still, he's got a head start: we've had to send substantially enlarged patrols into the Pecos wilderness following rumours of Indian trouble, so there's been no one to spare to take a party out after Kanturk. The colonel will get around to it, though. He doesn't like people evading their punishments.'

It was not a reassuring conversation. If anything, it underlined the importance of mitigating Joel's offence as soon as possible—and that meant speaking to Colonel Whipton. There was no point in trying to put it off. Tezzie took a deep breath.

'It is in that connection that we wish to see Colonel Whipton. Would you find out if it is convenient for him to see us now?'

The young man's eyes widened. 'Yes, ma'am. Who shall I say it is?'

'Theresa Milagro and Peter Lingstrom.'

He grinned suddenly. 'Of course—the Vigils' Tezzie! I didn't recognise you. No wonder you're interested in the duel!' He vanished through a door behind him.

' "The Vigil's Tezzie"!' she snorted. 'It makes me

sound like a plantation slave!'

'He's a southerner,' Pete told her. 'It probably hasn't occurred to him that you're not.'

The young man returned almost immediately with instructions that they were to be shown into the colonel's presence. He stood up as they entered, greeting them with a rather unpleasantly speculative smile that did not quite reach his eyes.

'Miss Milagro, Mr Lingstrom, won't you be seated?' He indicated chairs immediately facing his desk and, when Tezzie had sat down, resumed his own seat. 'I understand you wish to see me concerning the escaped prisoner, Kanturk?'

Tezzie nodded, and then hesitated. 'We believe . . . I mean, there are circumstances in which he might be persuaded to give himself up.'

'Indeed?' The colonel leant back in his chair, his fingertips pressed together and a very thoughtful expression on his face.

'He wasn't trying to evade justice,' Pete broke in. 'He had a good reason for needing to escape.'

'Who should know that better than you, Mr Lingstrom? After all, you must have arranged it.'

Pete flushed. 'I played no part in planning his escape.'

'No? Then yours was not one of the horses waiting in the street for him?'

'I was passing at the time, it's true.'

'How coincidental! I don't know how it was arranged, Mr Lingstrom, but I do not believe your presence with two horses was fortuitous, and therefore I cannot believe Kanturk's escape was a spur-of-the-moment thing, which it might otherwise have seemed. I recall you were warned away from the garrison after that duel?'

Pete nodded.

'Very well. Obviously you chose to ignore that warning, so I offer you another. As acting Governor, I warn you away from Santa Fe. I give you five minutes to get out of the palace and an hour to put yourself outside the city limits. If you return, you will be jailed.'

Pete and Tezzie exchanged glances. 'The Vigils expect me to protect Miss Milagro,' Pete said, feeling entirely justified in stretching the truth again.

'Then you have time to return to them and tell them she is here—where she is quite safe, I promise you. Mr Vigil may wish to come and escort her home.'

'Go, Pete,' Tezzie said with a firmness she was far from feeling. 'Tell Estefana what has happened—and tell me where I can contact you if I need you.'

He hesitated. 'I shall be with Rufina's people, I think. It's not too far. Tezzie, I don't like this, and I don't think I should be leaving you here.'

'I don't like it either, but we have no choice, have we? Just make sure you tell Estefana.'

When the door had closed behind Pete, Colonel Whipton's smile broadened. 'Now, Miss Milagro. You think Kanturk can be persuaded to give himself up?'

'I'm sure of it, Colonel—provided that he is not charged with the escape but only with his part in the duel.'

'No small proviso! And is there any reason why he should not be charged with the escape?'

'I think so.' Tezzie hesitated. 'Colonel Whipton, can I depend upon your discretion? What I tell you must remain within these walls.'

The colonel's smile grew broader still. 'I assure you that my discretion is absolute, Miss Milagro. Do, pray, continue.'

'Mr Kanturk escaped for only one reason, colonel. He had heard that I had been abducted, and he knew that he was probably the person best fitted to find me and rescue me.'

'Better than any of our Indian scouts? You surprise me.'

Tezzie flushed 'He was anxious that the rest of Santa Fe should not get to hear of it.'

'How very thoughtful of him! Yet someone brought the news to him. I wonder what made them think he was the person?'

'He had helped me once before.'

'So you had met before the garrison ball?'

Tezzie nodded.

'My dear, this becomes more and more intriguing. Do I take it there is some sort of . . . understanding . . . between you?'

'Certainly not! Nothing of that sort, I assure you,' Tezzie protested truthfully enough, though the sudden colour that flooded her cheeks spoke volumes.

'Very confusing, Miss Milagro! Someone who knew you had been abducted went immediately to Mr Kanturk, despite the fact that he was under guard, because he had helped you before. Tell me, Miss Milagro, do you make a habit of being abducted?'

'Of course I don't! That is . . . no, of course not!'

' "That is . . ."? Come, you cannot leave so tantalising a half-sentence without further explanation.'

Tezzie remembered her promise to Joel. It had seemed such an easy one to keep, and here she was, struggling in a morass of words. To tell herself that the promise had referred only to what she told the Governor was to take refuge in semantics. Tezzie knew it should apply even more strongly to the colonel. She flushed. 'Forgive me, Colonel. I have said too much already.'

'Then it is for you to forgive me, Miss Milagro. I am certainly not prepared to offer Mr Kanturk any sort of deal while I am kept in ignorance of what may be very relevant information.' His voice was smooth, his smile bland, but he left Tezzie in no doubt that he meant what he said.

She was faced with a dilemma: if she kept her promise, she condemned Joel to a life on the run and the certainty that he could never return to New Mexico; if she broke her promise, there was a chance he would be free. The price of his freedom would be her reputation, a price that mattered to her only because Joel held it dear. His freedom was more important.

She took a deep breath. 'Have you heard of the Wolf Girl of the Rio Grande, colonel?' she asked.

He nodded. 'I saw her once. In Texas, I think. It must have been three or four years ago.'

'That was me. It was Mr Kanturk who saved me from that life and placed me with the nuns at the Convent of the Blood of Christ. The man who abducted me was the side-show owner at the circus. That is why Mr Kanturk escaped.'

Tezzie had studied her hands, clenching and unclenching in her lap, as she spoke, unable to bring herself to look at the colonel's face. She therefore did not see the more sharply speculative gleam in his eye, nor the nature of his smile as her tale unfolded.

When she had finished, he rose and went to the window. 'I quite realise why my discretion was important to you. I assure you, you may depend upon it.'

'Thank you, Colonel.'

He turned and looked at her. 'Stand up, Miss Milagro.' It was a voice accustomed to command obedience. Tezzie stood up.

Colonel Whipton's eyes raked her body, and she knew he was trying to visualise her as she had been in the side-show. It was a bold stare that expunged any confidence his earlier assurance had given her.

'A remarkable transformation, Miss Milagro! I should not have recognised you. Please sit down.'

Tezzie did so, relieved. Perhaps she had judged him unfairly.

'So Kanturk rescued you once again. You are no doubt very grateful?'

'Naturally.' This did not seem the time to reveal that his escape had in fact proved unnecessary.

'And what makes you imagine I might be prepared to waive the charges if he returns?'

'Colonel, no man in his right mind would deliberately escape from jail and thereby lay himself open to execution, when remaining there would be likely to result in no more than a week's incarceration. Surely, if the reason for his escape is shown to be sufficiently pressing and if he returns of his own free will, discretion could be exercised in respect of the escape?'

'It is certainly possible. Do I infer that he is prepared to serve the few days' punishment for duelling?'

She nodded.

'And if I agree to this, how will you let him know?'

'He can be found,' Tezzie said cautiously.

'I'm sure he can.' Colonel Whipton moved away from the window and stood behind her chair, his hand on her shoulders, feeling her tense under his touch. Slowly, deliberately, his hands explored her her neck, hesitated at the buttons of her bodice and then passed on until they cupped her breasts. 'I confess to a curiosity, Miss Milagro,' he said softly. 'There was a certain savage allure in the Wolf Girl—no doubt the reason the side-show was so successful—and you cannot be so naïve as to be unaware of the more civilised charms you now exhibit. I am curious as to how the two extremes complement one another in one woman. Miss Milagro, I offer you a deal.'

How Tezzie longed to be able to leap to her feet, to strike him, to call for help and discredit him once and for all, but, while Joel's freedom was at stake, she dared not. Ignoring as best she could his wandering hands, she said bluntly, 'What deal?'

'If you can persuade Mr Kanturk to come in, I promise I will undertake to discount his escape and to deal with him only for the duelling—and to deal leniently with that.' He paused.

'You offered a deal,' Tezzie pointed out. 'What do you want in return?'

'In return, Miss Milagro, you satisfy my curiosity. You show me those erotic tricks you learned as the Wolf Girl.'

'I learned no tricks!'

'Oh, come on, Miss Milagro. Don't take me for a fool! I heard that the side-show owner sold your services dear when the show was over, but word had it that it was worth the expense.'

'You heard lies, then!'

'I think not. Why else should he want you back? You'll be protesting your virginity next!' He paused, and her silence brought a sly smile to his lips. 'In short, Miss Milagro, I want you in my bed. A small price for one such as you to pay to gain Kanturk his freedom, don't you think?'

Tezzie was thinking fast, searching for the places where he could go back on his word—a word upon which she now knew she could place no dependence.

'What guarantee have I that you will keep your side of the bargain?' she asked.

'You need not keep yours until he rides out free.'

She thought about that, and could find no flaw. 'How do you know I'll stick to my side of it, if Joel has gone?' she asked suspiciously.

'I have an army here to prevent you following him or to keep you here until your side of the bargain is kept. It will occasion less comment if you do not make their use necessary, of course. I did promise discretion, did I not?'

'I could leave here now to find him, and simply never return,' Tezzie pointed out.

He shook his head. 'You will have soldiers with you.'

It was Tezzie's turn to shake her head. 'That won't work. He'd just think I'd betrayed him. He'll vanish—and he's a better frontiersman than any of your soldiers. If he goes into the mountains, you'll never catch him.'

The colonel hesitated. What she said was absolutely true. His eyes narrowed. 'It seems I shall have to trust you, doesn't it? Up to a point, at least. All right: you go alone—and I mean alone. You'll not join forces with the man who brought you here, and a scout will keep you within tracking distance. If you double-cross me, I'll have every man in the garrison hunting the two of you. Do we have a deal?'

Tezzie was pale but determined. 'If you would be kind enough to remove your hands, Colonel, I think we might.'

He let go of her immediately, and laughed. 'Plenty of

time for that later! Believe me, I shall look forward to
your return. I like a woman who is a realist.'

It fell to Tezzie to drive the buckboard back to the
store because Estefana vigorously denied any ability to
do so, and when they got back, she had the difficult
task of telling the Vigils that she had undertaken to find
Joel herself and let him know the good news.

'This is ridiculous!' Mrs Vigil exclaimed. 'Hernando,
tell her it is impossible, out of the question. Let that
young man—who, I see, has not accompanied you
home—let him go.'

'He's no longer in Santa Fe,' Tezzie told them.
'Colonel Whipton has banished him for his part in the
escape. He has gone to Española.'

'Then Hernando will ride over and tell him to go and
find his friend,' Mrs Vigil said with some satisfaction.
'Española is not so very far.'

'The colonel insists that I fetch him,' Tezzie said, and
added, 'He said an Indian scout would see that no harm
came to me.' She felt justified in manipulating the
colonel's words.

'An Indian! What sort of protection is an Indian?'
Luz exclaimed.

'You made Estefana come with me for just that
purpose,' Tezzie pointed out.

'That is quite different. In any case, Estefana is a
woman.'

'Luz is right, Tezzie,' Hernando broke in. 'We should
be failing in our duty if we let you go.'

'But you can't *not* let me go,' Tezzie pleaded. 'Joel
Kanturk risked his life and his freedom for me. The
very least I can do is to let him know he can have them
back.'

Hernando Vigil looked perplexed. 'That is certainly
the honourable thing to do, but it should not be left to
you to go alone into the desert to find him.'

'The colonel insisted. He did suggest a full military
escort but, of course, that would look more like a

military posse, which is why he substituted an Indian
scout.'

Luz Vigil snorted. 'Anglos!' she exclaimed derisively.
'I sometimes think they have no sense of honour! How
could an honourable man suggest such a thing!'

Tezzie knew that no useful purpose would be served
by telling the Vigil's that Colonel Whipton was far from
honourable, and held her tongue. It was Hernando Vigil
who settled the argument.

'It is the Anglos who rule us now,' he reminded his
wife. 'They have always had different standards, and we
are going to have to learn to adapt to them. Perhaps
we should be grateful that he is at least sending a scout
with her.'

'Remember, too, it is not as if I were totally inexperienced at living in the wilderness,' Tezzie reminded
them. 'It would be quite different if I had never had
any life other than here in Santa Fe.'

'But the colonel doesn't know that, does he? For all
he knows, you could perish with cold on the first night
in the open!'

Tezzie said nothing. It was best to leave the Vigils
with some of their illusions intact.

Hernando Vigil put his arm round her shoulders.
'Tezzie, we cannot like this scheme of the colonel's.
You could be wandering round for days—weeks—before
you pick up even a hint of his trail. He is no greenhorn.
If he doesn't want to be found, you'll not find him.'

'I know where to start looking—and he will be
expecting someone, though I think he will be surprised
that it's me, and not Pete. It's not as chancy an
expedition as you think. I'd like to leave at first light
tomorrow—the fewer people who see me go, the better.'

This was a statement with which the Vigils could only
concur vehemently, and although they continued to try
to persuade Tezzie to abandon the plan, they did not
feel they could compel her to do so partly because of
the debt she undoubtedly owed Joel Kanturk and partly
because, as they reminded each other, she was an Anglo

herself and the conventions need not be applied quite
so rigorously.

Having accepted the inevitability of her mission, the
Vigils saw to it that she was as well equipped as they
could make her. They refused to concede that she would
travel more comfortably in trousers, but a skirt and a
boy's shirt would be easier than her usual close-fitting
dress. Hernando suggested that moccasins would be
much more satisfactory than the tight elastic-sided boots
she usually wore, and he threaded a good hunting-knife
in its sheath on to the belt from which she was never
parted. A sheepskin coat against the cold mountain
nights and a man's broad-brimmed hat completed the
wardrobe. Nor did she lack for food: *horno*-baked
bread, pinto beans and dried meat were packed into the
saddlebags, while a good warm Navajo blanket was
strapped on behind, it having been taken for granted
that Tezzie should use Valdez' mule.

The distant sky was only just beginning to lighten
when Tezzie set out, the concerned farewells of the
Vigils in her ears. Knowing that Colonel Whipton
would have kept her under observation, she was alert
for any sign of being followed. There was none. Only,
after two or three miles, that faint prickling at the back
of her neck that told her as clearly as any hoofbeat that
she was not alone. It was a return to the instincts she
had developed with the wolves and had taken for
granted. She was both relieved and delighted that such
instincts had not disappeared altogether with the civilising process.

The first part of her journey must be to retrace the
path of her escape from Valdez, for the area Joel had
mentioned lay over the rim of the mountains in which
rose the little stream—the Rito de los Frijoles—that
tumbled past the abandoned cave-dwellings and pueblo
of its canyon. Since she knew this first stage well and
had no need to read a trail until she reached the
headwaters of the stream, she could make as good time
as the terrain allowed, and reckoned that two days'

steady riding should bring her there. Her only unease
was at the prospect of spending a night in the Frijoles
canyon. It was the ideal place for the purpose: she
would reach it in the evening, it had water and grazing
for the mule, and the abandoned dwellings offered
perfect sanctuary for anyone travelling alone. Despite
its perfections, Tezzie shivered. Events on the two most
recent occasions when she had been there gave her no
cause to love the place or trust it. It was true that when
Joel had captured her it had been for her own good,
but the fact that he had been able to do so proved that
the canyon provided excellent cover for an ambush.

When she reached the canyon, she paused at the
entrance. The pricking of her neck told her she was still
not alone, but she was not afraid of attack from that
quarter: the scout who was somewhere behind her and,
she sensed, slightly to her left, was there only to ensure
she kept her word. The light was beginning to leach out
of the sky and she must make camp soon. Common
sense told her to use the old caves. Past experience told
her not to, yet the entrance to the canyon was too wide,
too exposed. She decided to press on further upstream
and not make camp until she was some distance above
the old Indian dwellings.

She pressed the tired mule onwards and upwards, not
intending to pause until she had reached a suitable place
to spend the night. As she approached that section of
the canyon where the caves were most plentiful and the
ruined adobe nestled at their foot, she involuntarily
slowed down, her eyes drawn in dreadful fascination to
the place where Valdez' body should have been.

It would not look as it had when she fled the scene,
of course. The vultures and the coyotes would have had
their share already. Doubtless the ravens and mountain
lions had joined them, as well as dozens of lesser
scavengers. It would not be a pretty sight. Nevertheless,
she needed to see it.

There was no body. No torn clothes, no scattered
bones. Nothing. For a fleeting moment Tezzie thought

she must have mistaken the place, but the possibility had no sooner slipped into her mind than she knew it was ridiculous. This was the right place. Valdez had disappeared.

Had someone found him and given him a decent burial? It was possible. An army patrol would certainly have buried him if they had found him, but they would also have brought word of his death back to Santa Fe. Only Indians made much use of this canyon, and they certainly would not have buried a Mexican. Then she remembered the man she now sought. Joel must have come through here. Would a man on the run stop to bury someone? It seemed unlikely, but one never knew with Joel. It was a more acceptable explanation than its alternative. The idea that Valdez might not have been dead at all was not one upon which Tezzie cared to ponder. She dug her heels into the mule's flanks and hurried up the canyon.

She found a suitable place to make camp, but she built no fire and slept little. The thought that Valdez might be near at hand kept intruding, and it was not a reassuring one. She strained her eyes down the canyon and raked the sides. Whoever was following her had not built a fire, either.

Tezzie was up again at first light, glad to observe that at least the mule looked rested and refreshed. She refilled her waterbottle with the fresh, cold water of the stream and breakfasted off bread as she rode.

At last she stood on the ridge that looked down on the vast caldera called the 'Great Valley' by the Mexicans. The crater of a volcano, it must have been all of ten miles across, maybe more, and the ridge on which Tezzie stood was the volcano's rim. Grass covered the surface, still brown up here where pockets of snow still lay in the north-facing gullies. Near the centre of the plain rose the hard plug, eroded over the millenia to a rounded, tree-covered hump some three thousand feet higher. All size was deceptive from this distance in the clear mountain air, but Tezzie knew that if she had

to look for Joel among the pines on that peak, she
would have a difficult task indeed.

She had one advantage in her search: there was no
need for concealment. Her best chance of finding Joel
was, in fact, to be as visible as possible and hope that
it would be he who would contact her. She hoped he
would not catch sight of her escort, but she guessed
that Colonel Whipton's scout would probably be content
to watch her progress across the caldera floor from a
vantage-point among the trees of the mountain rim.

The mule picked its way down to the grassy floor
with sure-footed care and Tezzie pointed it towards the
plug which, now that she was obliged to look up at it,
assumed the awe-inspiring proportions she knew it must
possess. Three ravens squabbling over a jack-rabbit
carcass barely glanced at her as she passed, clear evidence
of how rarely humans invaded this land. A small group
of mule deer laid back their large ears and put a safer
distance between themselves and the visitor, but they
did not feel it necessary to take flight. As she drew
nearer the tree-covered plug, Tezzie kept her gaze on
the ground, searching for hoof-marks. She looked back
once at the rim. There was no sign of life, no evidence
of the watcher she knew must be there. Surely Joel must
have stayed on this side, knowing that whether the first
arrival here was friend or enemy, they must come over
from Frijoles canyon? Then, at last, she found what she
sought. A faint imprint of a hoof where pine-needles
had not quite covered the ground. She turned into the
trees, searching for another, and found instead a broken
twig with a coarse hair caught in its split end. Too
coarse for a person, the wrong colour for a deer. The
signs were few, and her progress was correspondingly
slow.

It was the mule who told her they were no longer
alone. It threw up its head and blew down its nostrils
in unmistakable warning, but as the horseman came
down out of the trees, Tezzie gave a sigh of relief.

'I thought I'd never find you,' she said.

'I've been waiting for you for some time,' Joel told her. 'I wanted to see if you were being followed.'

'Am I?'

'I haven't seen anything, but I've a feeling there's someone out there. Not a patrol, though.' He dismounted and caught hold of the mule's bridle. 'Give the animal a rest,' he said, reaching up to lift her down.

As his hands fastened round her waist, Tezzie felt her heart beating faster. He did not release her when her feet touched the ground but stood looking down, a warmth in his grey eyes that she had never dared hope to see there. She was suddenly aware how small was the distance between them and of an impulse to eliminate it altogether. But when she felt the first hint of his hold tightening, she recalled her agreement with Colonel Whipton and swiftly twisted out of his clasp. Joel looked surprised, but he made no comment.

'You saw the Governor?'

'Not exactly. He had gone east, and the Lieutenant-Governor is ill. I had to see Colonel Whipton.'

Joel frowned. 'I don't like the sound of that. I don't trust the man. What did he say?'

'If you go back of your own accord, no more will be said of your escape, and the matter of the duel will be leniently dealt with.'

'That doesn't sound like the Whipton I've heard about. Do you believe he means it? And where's Pete? Why hasn't he come to tell me?'

'He's in Española. Colonel Whipton has ordered him to stay away from Santa Fe because he helped you to escape. I was told to come.'

'He sent a woman on her own? Is the man mad?'

'I don't think so. He wanted a patrol to come with me. I told him you wouldn't let them find you.'

Joel laughed shortly. 'That's true enough. Can he be trusted?'

Tezzie could not stop a hint of colour rising in her cheeks. 'I think so,' and then, as an explanation seemed to be required, she added, 'There is talk of trouble from the Pecos area. I know much enlarged patrols are going out there with greater frequency. I think he will be quite glad to get the relatively minor matter of your escape settled without the fuss of sending men out for you.'

'Maybe. I'll watch my back, all the same.' He smiled an unexpectedly boyish smile with a glint in his eyes. 'You shouldn't have come, Tezzie, but I'm glad you did.' He reached out for her then, quickly, giving her no time to evade him, and she found herself locked in an embrace as urgent and demanding as any she had known. She longed to respond, part of her sensing that this, the only occasion when they had been quite alone, was a time when perhaps her body might find the answers it sought. Another part of her remembered the man who was waiting for her in Santa Fe, and the thought that he had now obtained the right to caress her as Joel was doing, and more, sent a shudder through her, a shudder of revulsion that halted Joel in his tracks.

'What is it, Tezzie?' His voice was gentle, disguising the shock her reaction had been to him, so different from the way she had responded before.

Tezzie looked up at him pleadingly. The only thing she dared not tell him was the truth. 'You should not,' she whispered. 'I have no chaperon.'

She expected him to laugh at the incongruity of her excuse, but he seemed simply perplexed. 'I thought you regarded a chaperon as an unnecessary encumbrance,' he said. 'You've certainly got into enough trouble without one in the past.'

'Perhaps I have learned my lesson,' she retorted, regaining her composure now that he no longer held her. 'You have made it perfectly clear that I should not allow myself to be compromised.'

'The lesson you've learned didn't stop you coming here alone, and what is that if it is not risking your reputation?'

'I had no choice,' Tezzie told him stiffly. 'And you should not take advantage of it!'

'You have never before indicated that you were averse

to my advances.'

'That was when we were not alone,' she pointed out. 'The situation is different now.'

'It certainly seems to be.' He looked at her, frowning, until she dropped her eyes. 'I don't think your excuses are the real reason. There was a moment—a brief moment—when I lifted you down from that mule, and you did not flinch from my touch. On the contrary: I got the impression that it was welcome. Then you had second thoughts.'

'The Vigils were not at all happy at my coming here,' Tezzie said defensively. 'I have no desire to justify their fears.'

'I'm surprised they let you come at all,' Joel commented. 'And I don't think you care very much what they believe!'

'They let me come because they know the debt I owe you—and that is why I came. Once this little misunderstanding with the army is settled, I shall no longer be beholden to you.'

Joel's frown deepened. 'Is that how you have seen it? I don't regard it in that light, and I didn't think you did. Tezzie, if it will make you happier, I promise not to come near you again—at least not until I'm out of this mess—but I have the unpleasant feeling something has happened that you are not telling me about.'

With a great effort, Tezzie looked him straight in the eye. 'Nonsense!' she said briskly. 'You've too big an imagination, Joel Kanturk.'

It was a reply that convinced him he was right, but he kept that conviction to himself and looked up instead at the sky. 'Very well, Miss Propriety! Which would you prefer to do: set off now and ride through the night, which would bring you back to Santa Fe at nightfall tomorrow, allowing you cover of darkness to return to the store, or shall we set out in an hour or so with the intention of spending two nights under the stars, which will bring you home in the full glare of mid-day?'

'Will the animals take that sort of punishment?' she asked doubtfully.

'We can reach the volcano rim by nightfall and rest them there until the moon is up,' he said. 'They'll have another rest before dawn. Yes, they'll make it. What about you? Do you have the stamina you used to have?'

Tezzie lifted her chin. 'I've as much stamina as any mule.'

He laughed. 'Not the only characteristic you share with that beast.'

They spoke little on the way back, only when necessary. Joel's thoughts were divided between the possibility of betrayal—not by Tezzie, but by Colonel Whipton, who seemed to be behaving with unusual magnanimity—and concern over Tezzie's changed attitude towards him. He kept his ears open for sounds of pursuit and his eyes open for possible advance hints of ambush, but he heard and saw neither. If Colonel Whipton were going to renege on his word—which would be entirely in character—Joel would not find out till he got back to Santa Fe. Then he would have to deal with it as best he could. Tezzie was a different problem. When he had seen her coming through the trees, he had experienced a joy he had never felt before, and when he held her in his arms he had suddenly realised that what might have happened before he knew her no longer mattered. It made the rejection demonstrated by her almost total lack of response all the harder to bear. It was as if she had suddenly reminded herself of something. He was absolutely certain that something must have happened in the last two days. Yet he could think of only one thing that could account for her so suddenly switching herself off from him. She must have decided to marry Garway. That would explain her declaration that her present action paid off any obligation to himself. It also explained her rejection of his advances. He should have killed that young man while he had the chance, he thought savagely.

Tezzie's thoughts, too, gave her no comfort. She

sensed that the warmth in Joel's eyes when he lifted her
down from the mule betokened far more than mere
physical desire, and she knew that, having seen it, she
would have dared at last to tell him the full story of her
past, had the future not been standing in the way. It
was just possible, given that warmth, that he might be
able to forgive something that had been done to her
against her will. No man could forgive what she had
agreed with Colonel Whipton. She had not considered
that she had a choice, but in truth she had: she could
have condemned Joel to a life on the run and thereby
have saved her honour, if indeed she still possessed any.
She knew that her decision had been influenced by not
only the debt she owed Joel and the love she bore him
but also the certainty she had had at that time that she
was doomed to lose him once he knew the truth. Now
that she suspected that might not necessarily be the
case, it was too late. Her decision had been made, and
she could see it through only by distancing herself from
Joel, by refusing to allow her emotions to be aroused.
If she could convince herself that he meant nothing to
her, perhaps her forthcoming encounter with the colonel
would be endurable.

When it was over, perhaps she would be wise to get
as far away from New Mexico and its associations as
she could!

CHAPTER ELEVEN

THE VIGILS were relieved to have Tezzie back safely, and even more relieved that she did not ride up in broad daylight for all to see. They insisted that Joel should join them for a meal, and left him in no doubt about their concern over Tezzie's recent behaviour.

'Had it not been for the great debt she owes you, Luz and I would have forbidden her to come,' Hernando told him. 'It is not right for an unmarried woman to be galloping about the countryside alone—and even worse to be doing so with a man who is no kin of hers.'

'I think you will find Tezzie is fully conscious of that,' Joel told him. 'If it is any comfort to you, I can assure you her behaviour has been beyond reproach.'

'I am sure it has,' Hernando said stiffly. 'It is not her behaviour that is really in question, it is what others will say—and she has certainly been laying herself open to the most scandalous gossip if it ever gets about.'

'We are very fond of you, Tezzie,' Luz said, reaching across the table and patting her hand, 'But we have been talking about it while you were away, and Hernando and I are agreed that this must be the last occasion on which you flout convention while you are under our roof. I know that sounds drastic, but we do have your best interests at heart.'

'I know that,' Tezzie said, miserably aware that the immediate future held an impropriety calculated to put any others in the shade.

'It isn't only your own reputation we have to consider,' Luz went on. 'There are our children: to a very great extent you have had charge of them. What opinion will people form of the children, if they know they have been brought up by someone with so little regard for the conventions?'

When the meal was over and Joel was ready to leave, Tezzie was uncertain whether she should go with him. He and the Vigils were unanimous: she stayed where she was. The Vigils' reasons were predictably the conventional ones.

'How can you suggest it, Tezzie, when you know what we have been saying at dinner?' Luz exclaimed.

Joel's reasons were different, though he concurred with the validity of the Vigils'. 'There's no need, Tezzie. I'm giving myself up. That is all that's needed, and since I still do not entirely trust the colonel, it's far better that you are out of the way. If I have to fight my way out of his office, I should prefer not to have to consider your welfare as well.' He turned to Luz. 'Thank you for your hospitality, Mrs Vigil.' He glanced at Tezzie before turning back to her employer. 'I should like permission to visit you when this matter is settled.'

Luz beamed. 'We shall be happy to welcome you, Mr Kanturk.'

Colonel Whipton was not in his office when Joel arrived but he was soon fetched, having given orders earlier in the evening, on receipt of his scout's report, that he was to be informed if Mr Kanturk presented himself.

'So you got the message?' he said.

'As you see.'

'Precisely what was the wording you received?'

Joel glanced from the colonel to his aide-de-camp standing behind him. Was it chance that the name of the messenger had not been mentioned, or was the colonel considering Tezzie's good name? 'I don't recall the precise wording, but in general terms it was that if I came in voluntarily, there would be no charges laid relating to my escape, and the duelling matter would be leniently dealt with.'

The colonel nodded. 'You were not told you would be absolved of the latter?'

'No.'

The colonel turned to his aide-de-camp. 'This may seem strange to you, Lieutenant, but as you know we have potential trouble brewing in the east of the Territory and, while escaping custody is a serious matter, it would be bad tactics to tie up men and scouts in hunting one fugitive whose original offence was relatively minor. Kanturk, the Lieutenant here will escort you back to the cells. You'll spend the rest of the night there in completion of the punishment you would have incurred for duelling. In the morning you will be released.'

Since the colonel had made this statement in front of his aide, it could only imply that he meant it, though Joel knew, if the Lieutenant did not, that the reasons given were specious at best. He had reached the door, when the colonel spoke again.

'You dined with the Vigils, I believe.'

Joel permitted himself a grim smile. 'So there was a scout on my trail!'

'Naturally! I would not wish to be double-crossed. How did you leave Miss Milagro?'

Joel frowned. 'She is well.'

'Good. A most attractive woman. One would not wish any harm to befall her.'

Joel's frown did not lessen as he was led to the guard-house. Why should the colonel suddenly bring Tezzie into the conversation after having left her out of it with such apparent ease? And what was the double-cross to which he referred? He was quite sure now that there were ulterior motives behind his clemency, and was reasonably sure they had something to do with Tezzie.

When the door had closed behind Joel, Colonel Whipton sat down and wrote a short letter which he sealed and left on his desk, with strict instructions that it was to be delivered to the Vigils' store first thing in the morning. It would not do for Miss Milagro to forget her obligations!

The arrival of the colonel's note did nothing to enhance

Tezzie's day. Any hope, however faint, that he might not hold her to their agreement was dashed. Mr Kanturk would be released that morning; Miss Milagro would be expected at the colonel's quarters after dark. She did not even have the dubious consolation of being able to read and re-read it at her leisure, because she was working in the store, and the last thing she wanted was to provoke questions about what she was reading and who had sent it. She was obliged to snatch glimpses at it to refresh her memory of its very explicit message and then try to guess whether something less obvious and more hopeful might lie behind the words. Every time someone came into the store she jumped, her mind being elsewhere, and when Joel ducked under the lintel she blenched and then flushed, pushing the piece of paper into the pocket in the side-seam of her skirt. She was too flustered to do it properly, however, and she failed to notice that instead of being firmly stowed away, it fluttered to the floor beside the pile of blankets.

Joel noticed it, and he noticed her sudden changes of complexion, so he forbore to draw her attention to the dropped note, contenting himself with observing that the draught from the open door had blown it under an overhanging blanket.

'Colonel Whipton kept his word,' he said.

'So I see. I'm glad.'

'Is that all you can say? I've come to thank you.'

'There's no need. It was no more than I felt obliged to do.'

'Obliged! Was there no reason beyond obligation?' Joel exclaimed. He grinned. 'Come, Tezzie. You once thanked me in a more demonstrative way. I'd like to return the compliment.'

Tezzie flushed. 'If I remember correctly, it wasn't a form of thanks that I offered so much as one which was demanded!'

'That's right—and now I'm demanding the right to return it.'

'It's not necessary. Your spoken thanks are enough.'

'I think not.' He advanced on her as he spoke, a purposeful gleam in his eye, and Tezzie retreated towards the counter until she could retreat no more. 'Will you deny me one small kiss?' he asked, half teasingly, half seriously.

Recovering a little of her composure from that tell-tale gleam, Tezzie said sharply, 'On past experience, it won't be one and it won't be small, will it?'

'Is that an invitation, Tezzie?'

'No, it isn't.'

His arms were round her now, and she fought the desire to melt into them. 'You have a short memory, Joel Kanturk. Have you forgotten already the Vigils' expressed concern for my behaviour?'

'There's nothing wrong with my memory, but I am concerned that the Vigils' demands for conformity will prove more than you can accept for very long. I'm here to suggest a very simple solution.'

She looked at him suspiciously, unconsciously relaxing a little in his hold. 'What solution is that?' she asked.

'It's time I moved on, and Pete will settle in Española with Rufina, I'm sure. I'll need a travelling companion. Why don't you come with me?'

Her heart leapt, and for a fleeting moment he saw it echoed in her eyes, but the flame died almost as soon as it was kindled and suddenly he could read nothing her her face.

'I hardly think the Vigils would approve of that solution,' she said coldly. 'Neither would Mother Superior, I imagine.'

'I am not inviting the Vigils or Mother Superior,' he pointed out. 'They don't even have to be told.'

'You cannot surely mean that I just disappear again? No, thank you, Mr Kanturk. I have a good life here, and I have no intention of relinquishing it just to traipse across the Territory after you.'

He looked searchingly into her eyes. 'I don't believe you mean that, Tezzie.'

'Of course I mean it!'

Instead of answering, he bent down and kissed her. Her lips parted in involuntary welcome for a few brief seconds before she snatched her head away from him and twisted out of his hold. Her blush might have been embarrassment, but they were alone in the store and there was no reason why she should feel any.

'What is it, Tezzie?'

She tossed her head. 'I have no wish to upset the Vigils.'

'They're not here. Why should they be upset?'

It was impossible to argue with him, especially when every part of her longed not to, so she took refuge in petulance. If she could annoy him enough, perhaps he would leave. She certainly had no desire to risk encountering him on the streets of Santa Fe when she was either going to or from her assignation with the colonel. 'Someone would be sure to tell them,' she said, ignoring the fact that there was no one to do so. 'Go away, Joel! You've got your freedom. Use it. I was perfectly happy until you arrived.'

'You thought you were, perhaps.'

'I was! Life was smooth and uncomplicated, and somehow you managed to change all that.'

' "Smooth and uncomplicated" doesn't necessarily mean happy. Are you going to marry Garway?' he added suddenly.

'Good heavens, no! What made you think that?' Her amazement was unfeigned. That was not the reason for her deliberately assumed coldness.

'I'm glad. He wouldn't suit you at all.' He reached out for her, but she whisked herself neatly behind the counter. 'Tezzie—come with me.'

'No.' The determination faltered then. 'I can't, Joel. You wouldn't really want me to if . . . No, it's not possible!'

'If . . . what?'

She shook her head, tears beginning to gather, though she fought them back. 'You pick me up on the slightest thing—just because I get a few words muddled. If . . .

Nothing! Go away!'

'Is that what you really want me to do?'

'Of course it is! You've the whole of New Mexico to choose from. Just keep away from Santa Fe.'

Knowing she had exhausted such arguments as she possessed, and afraid he would continue to push her, Tezzie opened the door into the house and closed it firmly behind her, listening to the silence that ensued, followed by the sound of spurred boots on the wooden floor. There was a brief pause before they continued to the door, then the hollower sound as he crossed the porch and descended the wooden steps. Finally she heard the thud of a horse's hooves. When she peeped round the door, the store was empty.

Several customers came and went before Tezzie was sufficiently composed to reach into her pocket for that fateful note. To her horror it was not there, and as thorough a search of the store as she could manage between customers failed to reveal any sign of it.

After supper, Tezzie pleaded a headache and went to her room. Mrs Vigil had noticed that she looked pale and tired and had no hesitation in recommending her to lie down.

'You've had a very exhausting few days,' she said. 'I should be extremely surprised if you didn't have a headache, to say nothing of the sleep you need to catch up on. No, you go to bed right away, and sleep on as long as you need to in the morning.'

Tezzie sat on the edge of her bed, waiting for the house to be silent, only too much aware of how desperately she needed the sleep recommended by Luz Vigil. It was a good thing the need to be thrifty with kerosene would send the household to bed soon, because the danger of her falling asleep while she waited was very real.

At last the lights were all out, and Tezzie felt she could safely venture forth. Picking up her shawl, she opened her door cautiously, thankful that the thick adobe walls prevented the sound from travelling. She

slipped out into the patio, closing the door behind her
as carefully as she had opened it. She stepped lightly
across the sand and into the lobby that separated the
house from the office behind the store. The earth floor
of this lobby had been recently tiled—a refinement the
Vigils hoped to extend to the rest of the house—so
Tezzie had to take more care not to be heard there. The
fragrance of the orange blossom Mrs Vigil grew in a
tub enveloped her as she passed it and followed her into
the office, but once the door into the store had closed
behind her, the scent was effectively banished. It was
just as easy to get out of the store as it had been on
that other occasion, and Tezzie was soon making her
way along the Santa Fe Trail into the city, her dark
shawl over her head as if she were an Indian woman
going to market.

The sentry on duty at the garrison had obviously
been given instructions to admit her and to direct her
to Colonel Whipton's quarters. Tezzie took the precaution of holding the corner of her shawl Indian-fashion
across the lower part of her face, but the man evinced
little interest and no sign of recognition.

Colonel Whipton had been expecting her with some
impatience. 'You're late,' was his welcome as he closed
the door behind her.

'I had to wait till everyone was in bed,' she said.

'Very appropriate.' He took her shawl and, as he did
so, his hands glided down her body, a superficial,
cursory exploration at at which Tezzie involuntarily
stiffened.

He made no comment, but went over to a small table
and poured an amber liquid into a glass. 'Brandy,' he
said. 'You'll find it relaxes you.'

Tezzie obediently sipped. She had come to keep her
bargain, and anything which made a dreaded duty easier
was not to be lightly rejected. The taste made her
grimace and shudder, but there was no doubt that the
warmth filtering down inside her made her marginally
less anxious.

The colonel stood behind her and slid his hand round her waist, sinking his mouth into her neck as he did so. 'There's no great hurry,' he said. 'We have the night before us. All the same, I intend to get full value.'

He undid her belt and threw it on the floor. Then he began to unfasten the buttons on her high-necked bodice. His hands moved beneath the cloth, fondling and stroking and finding their purposeful way downwards until she caught her breath in a spontaneous gasp of shock.

As if that had been the signal he was waiting for, he pulled her bodice down, ripping the sleeves when they resisted, and when the dress lay round her feet, he took her wrist in a clasp she could not escape and led her to the bed behind its screening partition. 'Undress,' he said curtly, removing his jacket and then his boots as he spoke.

Slowly, reluctantly, Tezzie did as he told her. When he placed his belt with its side-arm carefully on a chair, she noted it, and noted, too, that it was well out of reach. She had assumed that his taking of her, while it would be painful, would also be swift. She had not bargained for this slow torment. Even now he seemed more interested in watching her divest herself of her remaining garments than in immediately pursuing his goal.

When she finally stood before him, naked, he smiled. 'Yes,' he said. 'You're cleaner, of course, and you've rounded out most pleasingly, but you're still the wolf girl. Let your hair down.'

The sight of the golden coils of hair tumbling one after another over her shoulders as each pin was removed seemed both to gratify and to excite him, and he reached out to stroke them. As if their touch galvanised him further, he twisted his hand in her hair and pulled her towards him. The exploration of his other hand now was urgent, insistent and of an intimacy that made her feel sick. Tezzie pulled away as far as her hair permitted.

'Oh, no, you'll not escape,' he whispered. 'Do you

think I don't realise how much this revolts you? Did
you look for a speedy release? You misjudged your
man, my dear! Your revulsion but adds to my pleasure,
and I have much more for you than you can dream of
yet.'

As he spoke, he pushed her irrevocably on to the
bed, his hands still in her hair so that there was no
escape. He let go of her hair and ran his finger slowly
down her spine. Tezzie turned her face away from him
on the pillows. She was tense with fear, yet that
unexpected touch made her whole body tingle. She was
momentarily mesmerised by the sensation he induced,
but then, horribly aware that part of his attention was
now given to removing the last material object to stand
in the way of his ultimate gratification, the full extent
of her revulsion for this man, for his present conduct
and the principles—or lack of them—that allowed him
to resort to the measures he had used, struck her. The
sudden, brutal rape she had experienced before and had
expected now seemed almost preferable to this sophis-
ticated sexual torture. At least it was explicable.

With an impulsive movement, she rolled over the bed
and off the other side. She crouched there, wolf-like.
'No,' she hissed. 'No. I'll not be taken by you. Not
now. Not ever!'

The colonel paused, aware that a man with his trousers
neither on nor off is at a disadvantage. 'Oh, yes, you
will, my dear! We had a deal.'

'Then I'm going back on it,' she said flatly.

'I'll ruin you if you do,' he said. 'Once word gets
round about tonight, you'll be finished in Santa Fe.'

'Your reputation will hardly be enhanced,' she
retorted.

'On the contrary, in some quarters it will be regarded
as something of a joke, and I shall be quite envied. You
forget: men are expected to seek such gratifications;
ladies are not expected to lend themselves to it. If, on
the other hand, we bring this to a satisfactory conclusion, no one but us will know about it.' He had pulled

his trousers up by now and was moving stealthily round the bed towards her.

'I shall know about it,' Tezzie said. 'And I suspect you will use it to blackmail me into further visits.'

'I think not. Once my curiosity is satisfied, I shall have no further interest.' He was near enough now to touch her, and he reached out.

Tezzie, pinned against the wall, snatched up the lamp beside the bed and threw it at him. He ducked, and it hit the wall opposite, the glass containing the kerosene smashing and a burst of flame rushing up the wooden partition towards the curtains.

At the same time another burst of flame from the door sent the colonel reeling back, blood pouring from his head. As he slumped to the floor, Tezzie's stunned silence broke, and she stared down at the body and screamed.

Joel Kanturk, his gun still smoking, strode across the room and snatched the coverlet off the bed, throwing it round Tezzie's shoulders.

'Come on, quickly, before the place is crawling with soldiers!'

She went with him, obedient and unthinking, only glad there was someone to take decisive action.

So swiftly did Joel act that only one person saw him leave the colonel's quarters. Trooper Garway, crossing the central parade-ground, had heard the shot and the scream, and was still undecided as to their direction when he saw Joel bundling someone out of the door and on to a horse. The glow from the room illuminated Tezzie's golden hair, and Garway instinctively guessed at least something of the situation. He ran to the room, where the flames now had a firm hold on the curtains and some of the furniture. The adobe walls and the earth floor would not burn, but if the colonel, whose body was clearly visible, was still alive, he must be rescued. He rushed in, and although one glance at the shattered skull was enough to tell him the colonel was dead, he nevertheless dragged the body outside.

By this time the whole garrison was alerted and desperately using precious water to put out the fire, directed by Major Middleton, who thus unexpectedly found himself promoted by chance to commanding officer.

Joel put distance between himself and Santa Fe with all the speed of which a horse bearing a double load was capable. He had seen a solitary soldier on the parade-ground as he left, and knew that any description that mentioned his height would identify him. In any case, the sentry must have recognised him, since he had entered the garrison quite openly.

It was not feasible to wake the Vigils and leave Tezzie with them. There would be the delay before they woke up, and a further delay while he attempted some sort of explanation. On the other hand, his own escape would be hindered by the extra weight his horse was carrying. Tezzie must be left somewhere where she would be quite safe.

The nuns were not accustomed to someone hammering on their gates in the middle of the night, and the sister who peered out of the little shuttered peep-hole was not only still half asleep but also understandably suspicious, and not until someone had fetched Mother Superior were the nuns prepared to let Joel in.

Mother Superior was very far from half asleep. 'I suppose this couldn't have waited till morning, Joel Kanturk,' she said as he rode into the *placita*. Then she recognised his passenger. 'Tezzie!' she exclaimed.

With a sob, Tezzie half climbed, half fell from the horse into the nun's arms.

'My poor child, what on earth has happened?' Then, since Tezzie was clearly in no position to tell her, she turned back to her nephew. 'Get off that horse. Sister Maria—feed and water it: I fancy he'll want it again shortly. Come inside and tell me what has happened.'

'I can't stay, Reverend Mother. I've killed a man, and I need to get well away before dawn.'

'You can spare an hour: the horse needs it, if you don't. Sister Josepha, take Tezzie and find some clothes for her. I suppose we should be grateful there's no tar and feathers this time! Then bring her back to me. Get someone to bring bread and coffee over for Mr Kanturk as soon as she can.'

By the time Tezzie, dressed once more in a novice's habit, was shown into Mother Superior's office, Joel had finished his makeshift meal and had told his aunt what had happened.

'It that's the case, why not stay and give the army your reasons? They sound good enough to me,' she said, when he had finished.

'I couldn't do that without bringing Tezzie into it, could I? Surely you can see she mustn't be known to be involved!'

'Hm—very laudable, I'm sure, but hardly realistic!' She turned, as Tezzie came in. 'Now, Tezzie, I realise that this has been a somewhat . . . *eventful* night, but perhaps you'd be kind enough to explain to me and to Joel—who seems to have gone to rather extreme lengths on your behalf—precisely why you permitted yourself to get into so compromising a situation.'

The brisk, matter-of-fact tone had its desired effect, destroying, at least temporarily, any desire Tezzie had to burst into tears. Even so, she found she could not look Joel in the eye, and cast him instead only a fleeting glance before she spoke.

'I owe you my thanks once again, Mr Kanturk. I don't know how you came to be there, but I'm glad you were.'

'You dropped a note and, being curious—and unprincipled when it suits me—I picked it up and read it.'

She looked at him then. '*You* had that note! Why did you wait so long before acting, then?'

'It wasn't possible to tell from the note whether you were a willing participant,' Joel said grimly. 'Until I heard your voice, I couldn't be sure you wanted to be rescued.'

'You couldn't be sure? You don't imagine I *welcomed* that dreadful man's advances?'

'You went to his quarters entirely voluntarily,' Joel pointed out reasonably. 'No soldiers dragged you in there, did they?'

'Why did you go, Tezzie?' Mother Superior asked gently.

Tezzie looked at her, mute appeal in her eyes. 'I went,' she said. 'I can't see that the reason matters now.' She must be sunk beyond redemption in Joel's eyes. To give her reasons could not retrieve her reputation, and might sound all too much like a plausible pretext dreamed up after the event to evoke pity.

'Nevertheless, I wish to know,' the nun insisted.

Tezzie still hesitated. 'It was . . . it was a sort of . . . bargain,' she began.

'What do you mean? A bargain?' Joel broke in.

'With Colonel Whipton,' Tezzie told him miserably. 'It was the price he required.'

'Price for what?' Joel demanded harshly, a suspicion of the truth beginning to dawn.

'For your freedom,' she said, her voice barely audible. 'If I would . . . would go to him, the charges against you would effectively be dropped.'

Joel sprang to his feet, knocking over the sturdy pine stool as he did so. 'How dare you offer to pay such a price for something so paltry!' His fury gave an icy cutting edge to his voice.

'Don't twist my words, Joel! I offered nothing. The suggestion was his. I know how much your freedom matters to you. Oh, I know you could have left the Territory, but I know, too, that wherever the army went, sooner or later you would be at risk. It didn't seem so very dreadful at the time,' she went on mendaciously. 'It wasn't until I got there that I began to realise the full extent of what I was doing.'

'So we now know Tezzie's reasons,' Mother Superior said smoothly. 'They may have been ill advised but at least they were well meant, and recriminations are pointless. Tezzie will stay here, and if the army finds out about her I will offer her what protection I can. You, Joel, will get as far away from here as you can. I cannot approve of what you have done, but at least your motives were good. I suggest you go a lot further away than Frijoles or the local pueblos.'

'You know more of my activities than I gave you credit for,' he said wryly. He glanced towards Tezzie as he spoke, and his glance was troubled. 'I'll head south this time. The Sandias, maybe, then perhaps into Mexico.'

The nun nodded. 'You'll be well hidden there. Tezzie, it's unlikely you'll ever see Joel again. You've done all you can for him. Now the best you can do is to say goodbye to him and let him be on his way.'

Mother Superior's words struck a chill into Tezzie's heart. She knew—she supposed she had always known— he was not for her. Common sense had been telling her for a long time that her past had decided that before she had even met him, and nothing that had happened since could have done anything but make any other possibility even more remote. She choked back the tears and forced her voice to sound normal.

'I can only repeat my thanks, and . . . and wish you a safe journey, Mr Kanturk,' she said, hoping the stiff formality would disguise the tremor she knew was in danger of becoming manifest.

It did, but it could not disguise the tears that lent an unnatural brilliance to her green-flecked eyes. Joel saw them, and was moved. He longed to take her in his arms—but to what purpose? She was safer here than with him, and if he took her with him, they were the more likely to be caught. So he put what he saw from his mind, and referred only to her words.

'Joel,' he corrected her. 'You only ever remember to say 'Mr Kanturk' in front of other people, you know, and I really think it's a formality we can dispense with!'

'What is the point of dispensing with formality?' she asked, entreaty mingling with bitterness in her voice. 'It seems that the occasion isn't likely to arise again.'

He looked at her then, a warmth in his eyes as if, even at this late stage, he would throw discretion and safety to the winds.

Mother Superior, seeing it, said, 'No, Joel.'

He bowed, an irony in the gesture that did not escape his aunt. 'You read my thoughts, Aunt. As you wish. I bow to your superior judgment. Tezzie, it seems we must indeed say goodbye, and I wish it were not so. I fear you will have a difficult time ahead if anyone saw you tonight, and if I had to leave you with anyone else, I doubt if I could do it. You could not be in better hands than Mother Superior's. Be advised by her in all matters.' He hesitated. 'I hope things turn out well for you.' He sounded awkward, knowing the words were inadequate.

'Goodbye, Joel,' Tezzie whispered, no longer able to trust her voice.

He hesitated briefly, then nodded brusquely and strode out of the room. Tezzie would have followed him, not wishing to lose sight of him one second before she had to, but Mother Superior laid a restraining hand on her arm. 'Best to stay here, Tezzie. No man wants to carry the memory of tears with him.'

The last sound Tezzie heard was the sand-deadened thud of hooves as he rode out of the *placita*. Then, oblivious of the nun's presence, she sank into Mother Superior's chair and burst into tears, her head on her arms on the table before her. Exhausted physically and mentally, but above all overwhelmed by her sense of loss, the sobs racked her small frame.

Mother Superior, knowing that Tezzie could never come to terms with the rest of her life until she had mourned what was past, let her cry her fill before leading her gently to a room where she could sleep undisturbed.

CHAPTER TWELVE

HALF-WAY THROUGH the following morning, Tezzie was still asleep when a sequence of imperiously demanding thuds on the doors announced a visitor.

Sister Josepha peered out at the soldier standing there and his companions behind.

'Major Middleton presents his compliments to Mother Superior, and requests her to allow him to take the fugitives we have reason to believe are sheltering here,' he said, his tone belying the courtesy of his words.

Sister Josepha's only answer was to close the shutter over the peep-hole and to go as quickly as decorum permitted to her superior.

'Reverend Mother, the cavalry's come for Tezzie,' she said.

'The cavalry? All of it? Dear me! A trifle excessive, I feel.'

Sister Josepha flushed, and smiled a little sheepishly. 'My apologies, Reverend Mother. I have overstated the case. I dare say it's only a patrol, but I was so surprised to see it at all that it looked like the whole Santa Fe garrison.'

'Unlikely, Sister. Did they ask for Tezzie by name?'

'No, Reverend Mother. They asked to be permitted to take the fugitives that were sheltering here.'

'Fugitives? You are sure the word was in the plural?'

Sister Josepha nodded. 'And what did you reply, Sister?'

'Nothing. I shut the peep-hole and came straight here.'

'Very sensible.' Mother Superior rose from her chair, settled her habit more comfortably, tucked each hand inside the opposite sleeve and nodded to Sister Josepha.

'After you, Sister.'

Only one door was opened, and as the soldier in the van raised his hand to signal an advance, the opening was blocked by the determined figure of the old nun. 'Stay where you are, young man! This is a convent, not an insurgent pueblo. Who is in command here?'

Major Middleton pressed his horse forward and dismounted, handing the reins to the young lieutenant who had originally conveyed the message. 'Major Middleton, ma'am. Commanding officer of the Santa Fe garrison. We have reason to believe you may be sheltering fugitives from justice, and merely wish to relieve you of their company.'

'There are no fugitives here, Major,' Mother Superior said with finality.

'They may not have told you the true circumstances,' he replied. 'They would doubtless have sought to pull the wool over your eyes with some concocted but plausible tale.'

'Tell me, Major,' Mother Superior said drily. 'Do I strike you as a foolish woman?'

Major Middleton permitted himself the ghost of a smile. 'No, ma'am. That you do not.'

'Good. Then I shall be obliged if you will stop talking to me as if I were! If you would like to hand your weapons over to one of your men and follow me, I think we may usefully converse.'

The major hesitated. The invitation was clearly not extended to his men, and had this been anything but a convent he would have suspected a trap. Then, the decision taken, he unbuckled his gun-belt, handed it to the lieutenant, and followed the nun into the *placita,* hearing the door close behind him.

Mother Superior paused at the door of her office and stood aside. 'In here, Major. Sister Josepha, bring the major some goats' milk. I'm sure he would welcome some refreshment. Sit down, Major.'

Major Middleton did as he was told, and accepted the beaker of warmly frothing milk with every appearance of pleasure. He thought he detected a faint aroma of roasted coffee. Perhaps Mother Superior thought to disconcert him by offering so unsoldierly a drink. A far from foolish woman! He had not anticipated any difficulty in dealing with the nuns, who were known to be mostly Mexican, the daughters, for the most part, of simple peasant families. The fact that their Mother Superior was neither Mexican nor a simple peasant might make his task less easy, but the result could not be in doubt. His approach might have to be more oblique, that was all.

Mother Superior had a shrewd idea what was passing through his head, and decided to press home any advantage she might have.

'I thought the commanding officer was still Colonel Whipton,' she said. 'It seems that, for once, the local grapevine has failed me.'

'Colonel Whipton was murdered last night,' he said bluntly. 'As the most senior ranking officer, I have taken his place for the time being.'

'Dear me, such a responsibility—and for one who has been so short a time in the Territory.'

'Six months,' he said, unable to keep a hint of defensiveness out of his voice.'

'Precisely.' She smiled blandly. 'I'm sorry to learn of Colonel Whipton's murder. It is not something one would wish on anyone. You *are* quite sure it was murder, I take it?'

'Quite sure. He had been shot in the head, and an attempt had been made to destroy the evidence by setting fire to his quarters.'

'That would appear to be conclusive. I have observed, however, that things are very often not what they would seem.'

Major Middleton smiled grimly. 'I'm at a loss to think of any other construction that can be put on the situation we found.'

'I'm sure you are. Do I infer that you believe the person responsible is here?'

'Not one person, Reverend Mother—two. We believe they may have sought sanctuary here.'

'An outmoded medieval concept, Major, which would apply only to a church, in any case. You are quite free to look in our chapel. I take it you have already searched the churches in the capital?'

'No, Reverend Mother. Both fugitives have good reason to come here. One is your nephew, Joel Kanturk. The other is the orphan, Theresa Milagro, who, I believe, grew up here.'

'You seem very positive about their identities.'

'We are. Kanturk was seen entering the garrison, and leaving at some speed with a passenger. As for Miss Milagro . . .' He hesitated, and seemed embarrassed. 'Forgive me if this causes you distress, Reverend Mother, but a dress very like the sort Miss Milagro usually wore was found on the floor, and also a very distinctive belt with a brass horse-shoe buckle which I'm told she was never seen without, except at the recent garrison ball.'

Mother Superior looked him straight in the eye. 'Are you implying, Major, that Tezzie was in your colonel's quarters in a state of undress?'

He flushed. 'Yes, ma'am. I should perhaps add that . . . that female undergarments were also found, though they have not yet been positively identified as hers.'

'I should hope not, indeed! And what interpretation do you put on this evidence, Major?'

He shifted uncomfortably. She certainly was not making it easy for him. Did she really intend to make him spell it out? Her expression was inscrutable. He had no desire to shock a nun, but there seemed little choice.

'We presume that Miss Milagro was visiting Colonel Whipton on a matter of an amorous nature; that Kanturk knew of it and, fired by jealousy, came to stop it—which he did most effectively by killing the colonel and setting fire to the place.'

'How very dramatic!' Mother Superior commented.

'I understood Colonel Whipton was a married man?'

'I believe so,' Major Middleton said stiffly.

'Tell me, was he in the habit of seducing young women?'

The major's unease deepened. 'If our sentry is to be believed, Miss Milagro arrived of her own accord by prior arrangement.'

'I said "seduce", Major, not "rape". Do you not care to answer the question?'

'As you have pointed out, ma'am, I have not been here very long. However, I must admit—between these four walls, you understand—that Colonel Whipton's reputation where the ladies are concerned leaves much to be desired.'

'Very tactfully worded, Major. I had heard that he was a rampant womaniser, with a particular penchant for young and inexperienced army wives.'

Major Middleton flushed. 'That is the generally held view,' he conceded.

'Joel Kanturk is not here,' Mother Superior told him. 'He stopped only to leave Tezzie here, where he knew she would be safe. It will be distressing for both of you, but I think Tezzie had better tell you her story. I'll send for her.'

'Where is Kanturk now?'

'Do you think he would have been foolish enough to tell anyone? I believe that in the past he has used Frijoles canyon.'

'It's a likely place to take refuge—very easily defended and plenty of water and game, though rather too close to Santa Fe, I'd have thought. Thank you, Reverend Mother.'

Mother Superior smiled. As she had suspected, Major Middleton's education had not been in the hands of Jesuits. He took words at their face value. 'I'll send for Tezzie,' she said.

When Tezzie came, her face was pale with exhaustion and her eyes red-rimmed and swollen from crying. She stopped short on the threshold, startled at the sight of the uniform.

Mother Superior drew her firmly into the room. 'This is Major Middleton, Tezzie. He is looking into Colonel Whipton's death. I'm afraid they found your dress and your belt on the floor, so they know you were there. I have told the major you will tell him why you were there, and what happened.'

Tezzie glanced desperately round the room like a trapped animal seeking escape. 'Must I?' she whispered.

'You would be foolish not to, my dear. At the moment, they are hunting you for your part in his death.'

Haltingly and as briefly as she could, Tezzie explained her presence in the colonel's quarters and the events leading up to his death. Major Middleton listened in silence. What she told him of the colonel only served to reinforce the opinion he already held of his late superior.

'So the fire was started before the colonel died, and had nothing to do with an attempt to cover up the evidence?' he asked at last.

Tezzie nodded.

'Can you explain why Mr Kanturk should have come to your rescue?' he asked.

'He had read the colonel's note. Perhaps he knew his reputation, and guessed what had happened.'

'Does Joel Kanturk love you, Miss Milagro?'

Tezzie felt the colour flame in her cheeks. 'No,' she said. 'No, there's no question of that.'

Mother Superior broke in. 'Wouldn't you feel obliged to go to the rescue of any young woman similarly placed, Major?' she asked.

The Major rose. 'I certainly hope I would, Reverend Mother. Miss Milagro, what you have told me puts a very different complexion on the case and I have no doubt at all that, once the truth is known, all charges will be dropped. However, there is only one way by which the truth can become known. There will be an inquest into the colonel's death. As the person who saw him die, your evidence is crucial. You must attend the inquest.'

Mother Superior drew Tezzie to her protectively. 'Major, Tezzie cannot testify at the inquest without damning herself irretrievably!'

'I know that, but if she doesn't, it will continue to be regarded as murder and, when she is charged with complicity in that, she will be equally thoroughly damned. At least, this way, no charge of murder will ever be made.'

'If I give evidence, will Mr Kanturk be absolved as well?' Tezzie asked.

'I should imagine so.'

'Then I must testify.'

'I can't pretend it will be a pleasant experience, Miss Milagro, but it should be brief. It can be little more than a formality, and I'm sure the military will be as discreet as circumstances permit.'

'You will have no objection to my coming with her?' Mother Superior asked. 'She will need whatever support and comfort she can get.'

'Of course not. The Lieutenant-Governor is expected to be back on duty tomorrow. He will set the date. I will send an escort for you.'

'No,' Mother Superior said firmly. 'It would create a thoroughly undesirable impression if it appeared that it took a military escort to persuade Tezzie to attend. I will undertake to see she is there.'

Any hope Mother Superior might have had that the inquest would be held in a day or two was soon dashed. The dead man's widow was unable to get to Santa Fe for the funeral, but as soon as she learned on the highly efficient army grapevine that there were certain scandalous implications in her husband's death, she insisted that the inquest be delayed until an attorney could be brought from the east to safeguard the colonel's good name. Therefore, in deference to the widow's wishes, the Lieutenant-Governor put back the inquest until Cyrus B Zugendorfer had arrived, and had had a few days in Santa Fe in which to 'get the feel of the case', as he vaguely termed it.

An inquest, even a routine one, presented an interesting break in the monotony of life in any remote community, and Santa Fe was no exception. Because this particular inquest bade fair to being far from routine, the room set aside in the palace for it was soon overflowing with expectant onlookers. The widow was heavily veiled, as was only to be expected, and supported by her son—which was interesting, because no one had realised the colonel had one. Tezzie's arrival accompanied by Mother Superior excited a small buzz of comment. In a very plain and ordinary dress of indigo homespun wool, she looked perfectly respectable. Who, looking at her, would guess . . . In the days before the inquest, rumour had had plenty of time to feed and grow.

Evidence of identification was soon given, and there was no dispute about the cause of death. The Lieutenant-Governor then addressed the court.

'On the face of it this looks like straightforward murder by someone as yet unnamed. However, there is a witness to Colonel Whipton's death who, I understand, may be able to put another complexion on it. We're going to hear that witness, because it's my belief we can save the Territory a lot of time and trouble in the future if we do. Call Theresa Milagro.'

Mother Superior pressed Tezzie's hand reassuringly as the girl rose and went to the stand to take the oath.

'You are Theresa Milagro?' The questioner was a major brought in from a Texas garrison.

'I am.'

'Where do you live?'

'At present, at the Convent of the Sisters of the Blood of Christ. Formerly at the Vigil house on the Santa Fe Trail.'

'Where were you when Colonel Whipton died?'

'In his quarters.'

'What happened?'

Tezzie hesitated. Where should she begin? 'Colonel
Whipton was trying . . . to . . . to seduce me,' she
said, her voice so low that the audience had to strain
their ears to hear her. 'I was trying to get away from
him. I threw the lamp at him and missed—that's what
started the fire. Almost at the same time, the door burst
open and J— . . . someone came in and shot him.'

'Did you know this newcomer?'

'Yes.'

'The name, please.'

'Joel Kanturk.'

'Why should this Joel Kanturk burst in at that precise
moment?'

'I don't know. I wish he had come earlier, but at least
he came no later.'

'Was he there by chance?'

'No.'

'How did he know you were there?'

'He had found a note from the colonel.'

The audience gasped with pleasure. This was more
like it!

'You had made an assignation with Colonel Whipton?'

'I suppose you could call it that.'

'Why should Mr Kanturk have acted on that note?'

'I think it was because he was concerned for me.'

'He loved you?'

Tezzie flushed. 'No! He had taken me to the convent
as an orphan, and although I hadn't seen him for some
years, I think he felt in some way responsible for me.'

'Very praiseworthy! In your opinion, at the moment
Mr Kanturk burst in, was there any other practicable
way of stopping the colonel's assault on you?'

'I don't think so.'

'Thank you, Miss Milagro. That will be all.'

'Not so fast, young man!' A sleek, well-fed, expen-
sively suited man of slightly less than middle age stood
up. 'Cyrus Zugendorfer, Your Excellency,' he told the
Lieutenant-Governor. 'I represent the Colonel's family.

I have more questions for the witness, with your permission.'

'The facts of the case have been established,' the Texan major broke in. 'Do you contend you have fresh evidence?'

'I think I can show that this was murder in a fit of jealous rage rather than the justifiable killing of a seducer of innocent women.'

'Very well. Continue.'

'Miss Milagro, were you physically compelled to visit Colonel Whipton that night?'

'I wasn't dragged there, no.'

'You went entirely of your own volition.'

'No. The colonel had agreed to drop some charges against Mr Kanturk if I went.'

'Why should you pay so great a price for Mr Kanturk's freedom?'

'He had helped me in the past. I felt I owed it to him.'

'How noble! Tell me, Miss Milagro, at the precise moment when Mr Kanturk burst in, exactly what were you wearing?'

There was a long pause before the whispered answer, 'Nothing.'

'We can't hear you, Miss Milagro. You were wearing . . .?'

'Nothing.'

'Nothing.' He repeated the information flatly, but loudly enough to ensure no one in the room missed it. 'You are very much in the habit of appearing naked before the male sex, aren't you, Miss Milagro?'

'No!'

'Permit me to jog your memory. Were you not at one time better known as the Wolf Girl of the Rio Grande?'

The flush that covered Tezzie's face told the assembled people the answer before the barely audible 'Yes', and Mother Superior buried her face in her hands.

'In that capacity—correct me if I'm wrong, Miss Milagro: I wouldn't like to discredit you unjustly—did

you not habitually appear naked in a circus side-show
to an audience composed exclusively of men?'

'Yes.'

'So although to any decent man it might seem you
were paying a very high price for Mr Kanturk's freedom,
in fact it was no more than you were accustomed to?'

'That's not so,' she protested weakly.

'Did Mr Kanturk know of your past?'

'He rescued me from it.'

'And no doubt you were suitably grateful?'

'I told you, that was why I agreed to the colonel's
proposition. It was because I owed Mr Kanturk so
much.'

'Do you really expect this inquest to believe that you
had not already repaid Mr Kanturk with your favours—
small enough a payment though that would now appear
to be? Come, Miss Milagro. Colonel Whipton was an
officer in the United States cavalry, a man of honour
and repute. Perhaps he took you at the same face value
others in this city seems to have done; perhaps he was
a lonely man and sought some companionship, not
knowing the woman he sought it with was a whore?
You flaunted the assignation in Kanturk's face, didn't
you? That was why he came back. That was how he
knew exactly when to burst in.'

'No, no! You're wrong!' Tezzie protested. 'It was the
note. That referred to the agreement we had made
concerning J— . . . Mr Kanturk.'

'Can you produce that note, Miss Milagro?'

'You know I can't. Mr Kanturk picked it up.'

'Of course—the only evidence (if I dare use the word)
to support your vile contentions concerning the colonel!
How convenient that it should no longer exist—if, of
course, it ever did. We have only your word for that.'
He turned to the Lieutenant-Governor. 'Your Excellency, I have shown this woman to be far different from
what she had been thought to be. I am satisfied—as I
am sure you are—that Kanturk, who must have known
she had no honour to defend, can have been motivated

only by jealousy. I leave it in your hands.'

The Lieutenant-Governor shifted uneasily. He had heard Middleton's report and, knowing Whipton's reputation, had considered the whole case unpleasant, but cut and dried. Now this smooth lawyer from the east had succeeded not only in throwing a lot of dirt, but in opening the way for what would prove a very messy murder trial. The Lieutenant-Governor wasted no time on sympathy for Tezzie, now totally discredited in the eyes of any decent person. Besides, she was of no possible future use to his own political aspirations; a nasty murder trial involving the army could prove a strong handicap. What's more, the deal she had referred to with such conviction was just the sort of proposition Whipton might have made. At least she had not admitted intimate knowledge of Kanturk. That gave him the loop-hole he wanted.

'You've certainly produced a lot of new information, Mr Zugendorfer,' he said, giving due consideration to his wording. 'I know we all regret any distress caused to Mrs Whipton, an innocent party in all this. However, you haven't produced any evidence at all to prove that Mr Kanturk had reason to know—and I stress the word "know"—that Miss Milagro might not have a shred of reputation to defend: you certainly haven't produced evidence that she might not be a virgin. Nor have you proved that he intended to kill Colonel Whipton. After all, a flesh-wound would have been equally effective in frustrating his purpose. In view of the doubt that must imply, I have no choice but to bring in a verdict of death by misadventure.'

The gasp that went up suggested that the only person with any doubts at all was the Lieutenant-Governor. Tezzie stood shaking on the stand until Mother Superior came and took her in her arms. The court emptied slowly, the audience's curiosity in Tezzie, whom it now saw with newly opened eyes, preventing any rapid egress. It seemed an eternity before the room was empty of everyone except Tezzie, the old nun and Major Middleton.

The major was clearly both upset and embarrassed. He came forward hesitatingly. 'What can I say?' he began. 'I can only apologise, and that is hardly adequate.'

'A formality!' Mother Superior said bitterly. 'You told us the inquest would be a formality! We were prepared for some awkwardness, but this . . .!'

'I believed it would be a formality. We all did,' Major Middleton protested. 'We had no idea that Zugendorfer's brief was to whitewash the colonel. There's not a man in the garrison—or in the Governor's palace, if it comes to that—who doesn't know what sort of a man he was. Our main concern was to play it down as far as possible in order not to damage too much the army's reputation—and our Texan friend did his best to ensure that result. I hope Whipton's family is paying Zugendorfer handsomely: he's certainly earned it! He's turned the colonel into nothing more than an errant husband who strayed from loneliness.'

'He has destroyed Tezzie,' Mother Superior pointed out. 'Even if she goes away from New Mexico, this will follow her. Not at once, perhaps; but sooner or later, probably just when she's made a new life for herself, it will surface again.'

'I know that. Reverend Mother, if there is anything I can do—anything any of us can do—you have only to say the word.'

'You've done quite enough for the time being,' Mother Superior snorted, but she did not reject the offer of a closed carriage in which to take Tezzie back to the convent.

CHAPTER THIRTEEN

SO DEEP WAS Tezzie's distress that it was many days before she was aware of the passing of time, and even then she remained so stunned that she seemed to be living in a different world. Only once did she say something which betrayed that part of her mind was grappling with what had happened.

'Will they make sure Joel knows he's not wanted for murder?' she asked Mother Superior suddenly, one day.

'They'll not waste time hunting him down for that,' the nun replied. 'He'll get to hear about it sooner or later, I dare say.'

'Will he come back when he hears?'

'Probably not. It would all depend on what sort of a life he's made for himself by then.' Mother Superior could see no reason to raise hopes that were unlikely to be fulfilled, cruel though it might be to dash them so positively. Tezzie did not refer to the matter again.

The months passed and the summer sun blazed down from the cloudless sky, its effects only partly mitigated by the altitude. The rivers shrank as their waters were diverted to irrigate the corn, beans and chilis that provided the staple diet for everyone from the richest Anglo to the poorest Indian. At the convent, Tezzie did her share of the work because it was expected of her. She was more biddable than she had been before but silent and withdrawn, very different from the forthright girl they had known in the past. Mother Superior told herself it was a passing phase, but as it seemed increasingly disinclined to pass, she became more and more worried. Her relief when Tezzie asked if she could consult her about her future was boundless, and for the better part of a day she felt as if a massive weight had been lifted from her spirits.

'I conclude this is something to which you have been giving a great deal of thought,' she said, when Tezzie sat before her that evening.

'I know I can't go on as I am,' Tezzie said. 'So I have made the decision. Reverend Mother, I wish to take the veil.'

Carefully, Mother Superior eliminated any indication of approval or censure from her voice. 'It is a very big step, Tezzie. What makes you so sure?'

'What else is there for me?' Tezzie asked simply. 'The peaceful life here suits me, and I fit in well, you know that. I'm not afraid of hard work, and the peace of mind the nuns have is much to be prized.'

'One does not become a nun because there is nothing else,' Mother Superior said gently. 'Nor is there any guarantee you would stay at this convent—in fact, it is highly unlikely that you would be allowed to do so. As for peace of mind, I'm not sure the sisters would necessarily agree that they have found it. Tezzie, you have not produced one single valid reason for becoming a nun and, since you're consulting me, I feel bound to say I don't think you are at all suitable.'

'Because of my past, I suppose.'

'No, that has nothing to do with it. Your normal temperament is impulsive and direct: not disqualifying factors, by any means, but they would make the life very difficult for you to accept. However, women have overcome such characteristics. You are still suffering from the effects of the events of this spring, and that clouds your judgement. Finally—and most important of all—you have no vocation, and without it, such a life would prove impossible.'

'You can't know whether I have a vocation or not,' Tezzie protested.

'I think I have more experience than you on which to base such a judgment,' the nun told her gently. 'No, Tezzie, whatever the solution to your problems is, it does not lie in becoming a nun.'

Tezzie's initial reaction to Mother Superior's words was anger, and for the next few days she threw herself into her work with a vigour calculated to dissipate that anger, there being no other way to do so. Gradually her fury subsided and, as a calmer mood prevailed, a small, persistent voice told her that Mother Superior was right. She looked at the nuns with a more observant eye, and began to appreciate for the first time that her own life at the convent was a great deal less restricted than theirs, bound as they were by their vows, particularly the vow of obedience. Not that Tezzie was disobedient to Mother Superior's wishes—it was simply that she was under no specific obligation in that respect, and she now began to perceive that this very fundamental difference was not nearly as insignificant as she had allowed herself to believe.

However, if she could not be a nun, what was she to do with the rest of her life? Surely she could not continue to live at the convent indefinitely? It occurred to her for the first time that she had never regarded it as anything other than a temporary home, and she was fairly sure that was Mother Superior's opinion, too, though the nun had never referred to it.

After the revelations of the inquest, it was unthinkable to expect the Vigils to give her a home once more, and no one else in Santa Fe was likely to for precisely the same reason. She could change her name and go somewhere else, she supposed. The more she thought about it, the more this seemed to be the only feasible course of action—and the more her spirits sank. California was the place, they said. It was true the great Gold Rush was largely over, but people still flocked there. If she could but put together a small stake, she could open a store and in no time build up a thriving business. How she was to accumulate that essential stake was a detail with which she did not bother herself. In any case, the brilliant prospect only depressed her more. It was a long time before she could bring herself to admit why this should be so and, when she did acknowledge it, she knew it had been at the back of her mind all along. The further from New Mexico she went, the further she went from Joel Kanturk.

Once more she sought out Mother Superior, and this time as she broached the subject, her eyes shone in happy anticipation.

'You were right, Reverend Mother,' she said. 'I would never make a good nun, but I can't stay here indefinitely—you must be as a aware of that as I am—and I have been thinking about little else since we last spoke on the subject. Reverend Mother, I have at last realised what I must do.'

'That can only be a good thing,' Mother Superior said cautiously. 'At least, it should be. With you, I am never quite sure!'

'I'm going to look for Joel Kanturk,' Tezzie told her.

'Do you really think that's a good idea?'

'Probably not, but I have no choice. Reverend Mother, I must find out whether there is any hope of a future with him. I'm very much afraid there will prove not to be, but at least then I shall know, and that will leave me free to decide what to do without always having the reservation in my mind that one day . . . perhaps. Do you understand?'

'Yes, I do.' It crossed Mother Superior's mind that there was a chance Tezzie was wrong, but she had no intention of telling her so: it would be a cruelty to build up her hope when there was still the possibility it would eventually be dashed. There were practical considerations to be taken into account, too. 'Do you intend to go hunting for him on your own?' she went on.

'I think I have to. There's no one to come with me.' Tezzie looked doubtfully at the older woman. 'Will you let me, Reverend Mother?'

'Could I stop you?' the nun said wryly. 'I can't think of an alternative either, though I would be lying if I said I was happy about it. Where will you look?'

'He said he'd head down to the Sandias, so that's

where I start, I suppose. He could have gone on into Mexico by now, but I hope not. At all events, I've a long walk in front of me.' She hesitated. 'I don't suppose you've still got the clothes I arrived in?'

'Those totally unsuitable men's clothes? Yes, we still have them. There were occasions when they were nearly given to the poor, but I had a feeling in my bones that you would be back for them. I don't think you'll have to go to Mexico, though. My information suggests that Joel is still in the Sandias.'

Tezzie stared at her in astonishment. 'Your information? You mean he keeps you informed?'

'Not at all. This is a huge Territory, Tezzie, but the population is small and the Mexican majority are all related to one another. They're Catholic, too, so one way or another I usually find out what I want to know. Joel is my nephew and, although that is something which should no longer weigh with me, I must confess I have always kept an ear open for news of his whereabouts. As for your walking, that won't be necessary: take the paint.'

'But the nuns need him for collecting the firewood and a hundred other tasks!' Tezzie protested.

'They managed without him before—but regard it as a loan: we would like him back some time. You won't find him a comfortable ride, but it will be quicker and less tiring than walking.'

Tezzie threw her arms round the nun. 'Reverend Mother, you're an amazing woman! I was so sure I'd have to use all my powers of persuasion to get your permission to go! Instead, you're doing everything to make it easy for me!'

'It will be difficult enough without my putting further obstacles in your way,' the nun told her. 'I'm not at all happy about it. I know you are putting yourself in some danger just by travelling alone.'

'I know that, Reverend Mother, but at least my childhood, so undesirable as it was from some points of

view, equipped me to have a better chance of survival
than most!'

Tezzie set off the next day. The nuns had no saddle,
but a blanket slung Indian-style across the paint's back
was an adequate substitute. They found a homespun
woollen jacket for her and a Mexican hat of rough
straw. The jacket was rough, too, but warm, and the
nights would be very cold up in the mountains. The
trousers Pete had bought were still far too large for her,
and Tezzie regretted for practical, as well as sentimental,
reasons, the loss of her beloved belt. She had to make
do with a narrow strip of woven webbing that did the
job equally efficiently but somehow wasn't the same.
Moccasins were the only suitable footwear—soft and
comfortable and calculated to make it possible to walk
quite soundlessly. The real surprise came when Mother
Superior gave her a large and lethally honed hunting-
knife. Tezzie had seen it before. The nuns used it to
skin the carcass of any sheep they had to slaughter.
    'You need some kind of protection,' Mother Superior
told her. 'We have other knives we can use. Though,
like the paint, if you can return this to us one day, we
shall be grateful.'
    Thus equipped, Tezzie headed the scrubby, tough
little horse towards the Santa Fe River and followed its
course as closely as possible until she reached the
channels of the Rio Grande not far from the Santo
Domingo pueblo. The Indians saw her and took note
of her passage, as they took note of the eagle or the
mountain lion.
    The river here had emerged from the confines of its
White Rock canyon and flowed expansively across a
valley broad enough to allow it to divide and roam at
will while still falling gently southward. Many of its
alternative channels were dry now it was summer,
waiting for the flash-floods that the next few weeks
would bring. The cottonwoods and the willows, their
roots deep in the water-table, provided shade from the

ᴴeat of the day, but the accumulation of dead branches
ᴬnd spiny undergrowth made progress through this
ᵇosque both difficult and slow.

On the second day of her journey out she was hailed
ᵇy a small army patrol which had just reached the limit
ᵒf its range. When Lieutenant Baden realised that the
ᵖerson on the Indian pony was not only a woman but
ᵃ singularly notorious one, he reddened with embarrass-
ᵐent.

'Miss Milagro,' he said awkwardly. 'We thought you
ᵥere an Indian or a Mexican, and were going to ask if
ʸou had seen anything we should know about.'

'Nothing at all, Lieutenant.'

He hesitated before continuing. 'May I ask where
ʸou're going?' he said. 'It's more than idle curiosity.'

'South,' Tezzie said cautiously, stating the obvious.
Mexico, probably.'

He smiled. 'Out of the Territory? Good.' He moved
ʰis horse slightly closer to hers, and dropped his voice.
Miss Milagro, you know a Pedro Valdez, I believe?'

Tezzie stiffened. 'I've heard of him,' she conceded.

'It seems that he heard something of your part in
ᶜolonel Whipton's death, and came back to Santa Fe
ᶠrom Texas. He sought an audience of the Governor,
ᵃnd claims you tried to murder him. Governor Bent
ᵈoes not entirely believe him. In fact, he was heard to
ᵐutter that it would be a service to the community if
ᵒmeone would, though he'd never admit to having said
ᵗt, of course! Still, he can't ignore it. By all that's right,
ᴵ should take you back with us. Fortunately,' he added
ʰastily, observing Tezzie's sudden pallor, 'I wasn't
ᵒfficially informed—I just heard the gossip—but get out
ᵒf the Territory as soon as you can, before you meet
ᵒmeone who has been told officially.'

'How long ago was this?' Tezzie asked.

'He rode in during the evening of the day before
ʸesterday.' He hesitated again. 'I also heard he was told
ʸou were at the convent, and had said he'd bring you

in himself. If that's true, he must know by now you're
not there.'

'Thank you, Lieutenant. I'm grateful for the information. I hope you don't get into trouble.'

The young man grinned. 'No fear of that: orders is
orders, but I wasn't given any relating to this, and the
army doesn't really like men who use their own initiative. Colonel Middleton may rail on a bit if he hears,
but that will be all.'

'*Colonel* Middleton?'

'Yes, ma'am. He's been promoted.'

'Then if he takes you to task for not bringing me in,
at least offer him my congratulations.'

'He'll appreciate that,' the lieutenant said without
irony. 'He hated the way things turned out for you.'

Tezzie rode on, knowing now that she must avoid
settlements. She had never intended to ride into them,
but in future she must avoid even being seen. Damn
Valdez! she thought savagely. Why hadn't she made
sure he was dead?'

Her original intention had been to travel on south
past the thriving city of Albuquerque—now said, with
its population of fifteen hundred, to rival Santa Fe in
size—in order to take an easier, if longer route into
Sandias. Lieutenant Baden's information changed her
mind. It was unlikely that news of the charge against
her had reached this far yet, but if Valdez was on her
trail, as he was likely to be within a few days, any
glimpse of her might reach his ears. It was safer to head
straight into the Sandias and lose herself from view as
quickly as possible among the *piñons* and ponderosa
pines of the lower slopes.

So she turned west towards the mountains some miles
before she reached Albuquerque, and as she left the
bosque and came into the wide semi-arid plain that led
to the Sandias, she caught a glimpse of the twin adobe
towers of the church of San Felipe de Neri that marked
the centre of the fast-growing town. The skies over the
mountains were a clear, cloudless blue, and she felt she

could safely use the smooth, sandy stream-beds whose sides offered cover from casual observation. She made what speed she could. The paint, with his straight shoulders and upright pasterns, was an uncomfortable ride, but he was sure-footed and tough, able to keep going when better blood would have been exhausted. Tezzie began to realise that she could reasonably expect to be able to make camp that night within the shelter of the trees.

She lit no fire. Even a small one might be spotted from the town below, for she was not so very far into the mountains yet and, while no one from Albuquerque would investigate, they would recall it if a stranger started asking questions. She hobbled the paint, wrapped herself in the blanket that had done duty as a saddle and finished the last of the bread and cheese the nuns had given her. From now on she must live off the land.

For the first time since she left the convent, she felt free to think. Until now she had been concerned only with reaching the Sandias as soon as possible and, since her meeting with the army patrol, with trying to ensure she was not being followed. The former goal was achieved. As for the latter, she seemed safe enough so far, and even as her thoughts now roamed, one small part of her mind was still alert for the slightest hint of anything untoward.

One thing that gave her great satisfaction was the speed with which the old skills and instincts she had learned as a wolf were returning. Fending for herself would present no problems, and she wasted no time in thinking about it. Finding Joel now that she had reached the mountains was quite another matter. To search thoroughly one relatively small, lone, tree-covered mountain, such as the Redondo Peak had been, was a daunting enough prospect, but the Sandias were neither relatively small nor lone, and even someone who knew the best hunting-grounds, the best cover and the springs of fresh water would be hard put to it to find any single

individual, especially if that individual had no wish to
be found.

Nor was Tezzie's task even that simple: Joel was quite
likely to have crossed Tijeras canyon into the Manzano
Mountains which, despite their separate designation,
were really an extension of the higher range. Her only
confidence lay in her good knowledge of these
mountains, and even though it might take her weeks or
months, she knew the places to search. Even so, her
best hope of finding Joel lay in his hearing about her
and coming forward. She knew that there would be
occasional hunting-parties of Indians, who might or
might not wish to be seen, but who would certainly see
her. Sooner or later word would reach Joel, and any
description would be enough to identify her. If he
wished to be found, he might then make it possible. If
he did not, he would be far away before she learnt any
hint of his whereabouts.

Tezzie rather thought he might be willing to be
encountered, if only to learn whether he was wanted for
Colonel Whipton's murder, but would he then want to
go his own way?

She loved him. Once she had admitted that to herself
the strength of her love surged forth in a way that
frightened her. When she thought about him, his absence
left her with an aching void, an almost physical pain
somewhere deep inside, which she neither understood
nor could ease. Nothing would ever ease it save the feel
of his arms round her. Her love was such that even
though he might demand the one thing she least wanted
to give any man, she would give it to him because it
would be what he wanted.

Tezzie did not expect Joel to love her. She knew that
was not possible. She would try to be content with
whatever he might offer, knowing that he might offer
nothing. Marriage was not something she dared even
contemplate. Joel already knew too much about her.
No man who had seen what he had seen in Colonel
Whipton's quarters would be likely to consider marriage

to the woman involved. And that was only part of it: Joel did not know that men had already taken her before she fell into Valdez' hands, and he had made it quite clear, when he had been advising her what to tell Lieutenant Garway, that she should have no secrets from the man she married. Even if there had been some remote possibility of marriage, what she would be obliged to tell him before the ceremony would be certain to kill that possibility beyond hope of redemption.

Her duty was to let him know that he was a free man. Her heart told her that if there was anything beyond that information that he wanted, she would not deny him. She would do anything to be with him again, and the longer it was before he sent her on her way, the better.

It was perhaps strange that, having reached so eminently sensible a compromise between what she wanted and what she could reasonably expect, she should sleep so badly.

The next day was well advanced when she became gradually aware of that strange prickling sensation on the back of her neck that indicated that she was being watched, and, by definition, followed. There was the possibility that it might be Joel. It was a possibility she dismissed. That sort of luck did not seem to come her way. It was much more likely to be an Indian. It might also be Valdez. Her progress into the mountains was loud enough to attract attention—the horse ensured that. Tezzie toyed briefly with the idea of turning it loose and decided against it. The animal was too useful and, besides, she had promised the nuns she would bring it back some time. If her pursuer was an Indian, he would probably vanish once his curiosity was satisfied, but somehow she thought he was not. As her awareness of being under observation increased, more and more of her attention became devoted to identifying from where it came and whether it was gaining on her. Had it been an Indian, she knew she would have heard nothing at all. There would have been only that instinctive sensation. This pursuer, however, was making small but definite noises. He was clever. There was nothing so blatant as a snapping twig, but just the occasional faint swish as something brushed past a spray of leaves, the brief cessation of bird-song. She thought her follower was behind her and as far to one side as the terrain permitted, which was not very far. Could it be Valdez? He seemed to be the most likely candidate, all things considered.

Tezzie dismissed any idea of catching some supper. It would do her no harm to go without food for a day or two, and successful hunting demanded one's full concentration, something she could not give it while her pursuer remained on her tail.

She selected a camp site with great care that night. A small clearing surrounded by ponderosas and backed by a rocky outcrop with a substantial overhang seemed as good a place as she was likely to find in which to build a small fire, though she was obliged to hobble the paint at some distance off where there was some passable grazing to be scratched. Then she built her fire, small and discreetly placed, but by no means invisible. The trees ensured that one would have to be very close indeed to have an uninterrupted view of it, and she took care to stay behind the fire so that anyone among the trees would keep well back to avoid being illuminated by the flames. She passed ostentatiously backwards and forwards between the fire and the rocky outcrop so that no one should have any doubt as to her identity. Then, when the flames had died down to a ruddy, much warmer glow, she sat down far enough from it to be visible only to someone who thought they knew what they were looking at. Very slowly and cautiously she arranged her blanket loosely round her warm jacket, and placed the resulting roughly cylindrical bundle on the ground where she had been sitting. A large rock wore her old sombrero, pulled down far enough to disguise its lack of features. Then she slipped quietly back on softly moccasined feet until she felt the rocky wall behind her. She was well out of the fire's glow now, and well away from its heat, too. She shivered. It was going to be a cold night at this altitude, with neither jacket nor blanket. Still, that meant it would be easier to stay awake.

Time passed, and Tezzie crouched against the rock, determinedly preventing her teeth from chattering. The waxing moon rose and cast its weak and pallid light down through trees, the rock-face under the overhang remaining in deep shadow. The fire still glowed, but it was dying now, and Tezzie felt a momentary panic. She needed the firelight's glow to identify her pursuer if he ventured into her camp. A faint rustle banished her anxiety, and her hand closed round the hilt of her hunting-knife.

A short, dark figure halted just inside the line of trees opposite. The size and the shape were right, but the features were as yet undistinguishable. The visitor stood where he was for a long time, but there was no sign of movement from the sleeping blanket. He moved stealthily forward, and a helpful, unexpected whisper of a breeze fanned a half-burned branch into a brief flare of life. Brief, but sufficient to tell Tezzie all she needed to know. Not only did that short-lived flame illuminate Valdez' features, it also glinted evilly on the blade of the knife he was holding.

He was only two paces from the shape by the fire, and his attention was concentrated on that to the exclusion of any other possibility—so that he was unaware of any change in the density of the shadows under the rock.

His knife rose in the air, then plunged into the softly yielding form before him. Before he had had time to do more than note that whatever he had stabbed, it was certainly not a body, it was too late. Something cold sliced between his ribs. He felt no pain until it was as swiftly withdrawn and, as the blood and air escaped from his lungs, he turned, gasping and gurgling, to face this unexpected assault. He recognised his assailant and lunged towards her, his knife still in his hand. Tezzie recoiled, nauseated. She had killed for food without a second thought, but this was different. It was a man. Even though she knew him to be all that was despicable, as well as perfectly prepared to kill her, the fact that he was human made it different. Had he not still clung to his own weapon and had she not been unsure how much strength he could summon, she might have overcome her repugnance sufficiently to put a swift end to his suffering, but as he stumbled towards her, her only thought was to keep out of his reach.

The end was not long in coming. After only two unsteady paces, Valdez plunged forward on to his face. Blood gurgled from his mouth, and he lay still.

Tezzie hesitated. Once before, she had left him for dead without taking the basic precaution of checking. This time she dared not do so, even though she could not see how he could possibly be alive. Mastering her nausea, she bent down and sought the pulse that beats in the little depression just in front of the ear. It was still. Valdez was dead.

Wiping her knife hurriedly in the earth, she plunged it back in its sheath, snatched up her blanket, jacket and hat, and fled as quickly as she dared in the dim light to the place where she had left the paint. Of the little horse himself there was no sign, but she could hear him tearing at some of the mountain's sparse grass not very far off, so she squatted down at the base of a tall pine, wrapped herself in her blanket and sank into a succession of uneasy, nightmare-ridden dozes that lasted until dawn took its interminable time to arrive.

The horse had wandered some way by then, but the short-spaced tracks of his hobbled hooves were easy enough to follow and Tezzie was very soon ready to be on her way. She hesitated briefly, wondering whether she should return to check again that Valdez was indeed dead, but she knew it was unnecessary. She supposed that, had she had the right equipment, she should have buried him, and decided she was not at all sorry that she had no spade. The animals of the forest would soon pick the carcass clean. It was to be hoped that, in the unlikely event of a patrol stumbling on the body, no identification would by then be possible, far less any guess as to who might be responsible.

Tezzie shuddered at these thoughts—which were by no means as consoling as they ought to have been—and swung herself up on the paint's back. At least now she was free to concentrate on the hunt for Joel. She would soon be in bear country, and that meant there would be water and fish, as well as berries and small game. It would be likely country in which to find him, and a good place in which to satisfy her own hunger that now, other concerns eliminated, pushed itself to the forefront of her mind.

Ten days later she was holding a cut-throat trout skewered on a stick over a low fire, when she was aware once more that she was being watched, this time from the other side of the little stream by which she was camped. It was the first time in all these days of searching that she received any hint of the presence of other human beings. The fish was soon cooked, and as she removed pieces of the succulent flesh from the bones she reflected upon how much more delicious was cooked trout than raw, and how wise Mother Superior had been to obtain for the nuns a stock of the new striking matches that made starting a fire so easy. She had given Tezzie a flint, as well as some of the precious hoard, but for the time being Tezzie had matches enough for another week if she was careful with them.

As she ate, the man whose presence she had sensed let himself be seen. He was an Indian, sturdy and not very tall. He carried a Kentucky rifle negligently in one hand as if he knew he had no need to use it. He stared at Tezzie, and she gazed back at him briefly, pausing just long enough in her meal for him to be quite sure she had seen him. Then he faded back among the trees and soon was gone from sight. Tezzie's instincts told her he had not remained to watch her from the seclusion

of the forest, and she wondered when she would
encounter him again. She did not doubt that she would:
he had quite deliberately allowed himself to be seen. He
had wanted her to know he was there.

After another two days, he and three companions
stepped from the underbrush onto the trail in front of
her.

'Good day,' she said in Spanish, knowing they were
more likely to have a few words of that language than
of English. She had picked up a very little Tewa, the
language spoken by most Indians in the pueblos around
Santa Fe, but local men here would speak either Tiwa
or Keres, and she knew neither.

'You hunt?' one of them, an older man, asked.

'For food,' Tezzie told him. 'Fish, rabbits. No big
game.' She patted the knife at her waist. 'I have no
weapon but this.'

'Why?'

Tezzie knew the man referred, not to her lack of
weapons, but to the presence of a lone Anglo woman
in the mountains. 'I seek a man I believe to be here,'
she said. 'An Anglo. Very tall, with dark hair and light
eyes.'

Indians exchanged no glances, but a subtle, almost
imperceptible change in their bearing told her that she
had struck a chord.

'The mountains are vast,' the Indian remarked. 'What
hope have you of success?'

'Very little, it seems, unless someone can guide me in
the right direction.'

'Where have you come from?'

'From Santa Fe, between the lands of the Tesuque
and the Nambe.'

'You have come far. Why do you seek this Anglo?'

Tezzie hesitated. 'Do you know where he can be
found?' she asked.

The Indian said nothing, but stood silent and impas-
sive. Tezzie realised then that he knew well enough
where Joel was, but was prepared neither to lie nor to

tell her, so he said nothing.

'He left Santa Fe believing he was accused of the murder of an Anglo soldier,' she said. 'I seek him to tell him that he is free of that accusation and may return to Santa Fe if he wishes.'

'What sort of soldiers are the Anglos that they send a woman with such a message?'

'They did not send me. I owe this Anglo my life. I seek to repay the debt.'

The Indian nodded. 'That is good. It is as it should be. Consider the debt repaid.'

'I would rather tell him myself. Will you not take me to him?'

The Indian shrugged. 'He will have moved on by now, but we shall meet him again. He will be told. You can return to your people.'

'I have no people,' Tezzie said.

'In Santa Fe you have people, I think. I will tell the Anglo that you have returned there.'

'I should prefer to speak to him myself,' Tezzie insisted.

She might as well not have spoken, for the Indian said no more but raised his arm in salute, and he and his companions vanished into the forest shadows.

Tezzie watched the space where they had been for a long time. The temptation to follow them in the hope that they would lead her straight to Joel was almost overwhelming, but she knew it was useless. On horseback it would be quite impossible. On foot it was possible only if the Indians wished her to succeed, and they had made it quite clear that they expected her to go away now. It would be a very foolish person who ignored their instruction. In any case, following them would mean leaving the paint, and the little horse was not hers to leave.

The Indians were going to tell Joel she had returned to Santa Fe. If she did so, she was leaving it entirely up to him to decide whether to come looking for her—and why should he? To say 'Thank you'? That was not quite

his style. So far as she knew, he was not even in the
habit of spending much time in the area of the capital
anyway: he had gone there when he had taken her to
the convent and on this last occasion, and that seemed
to have been all. Why should he go back there now?
He would, if he loved me, a little voice inside her
whispered, and a stronger, more robust one replied:
Perhaps, but there is no reason to believe he does.

If she returned to Santa Fe, she returned to danger.
Valdez had accused her of attempted murder. Valdez
was in no position now to give evidence against her,
but that was hardly much help—and would be a distinct
handicap if his body were ever found. She could say
what had happened in Frijoles canyon, and perhaps
Pete would come from Española and speak for her, but
she shuddered at the thought of facing another public
trial. Almost anything was better than that! On the
other hand, if she continued to search here in the
Sandias, she might never find him, especially if he did
decide to go back to Santa Fe.

No. She would do as the Indian had said, but slowly.
She would take her time in getting back to the convent.
Once there, she would return the horse, seek Mother
Superior's advice, and follow it. Then, if Joel ever
turned up at the convent and perhaps wanted to find
her, Mother Superior would be able to give him some
idea where she had gone.

She looked about her. She had crossed the ridge of
the mountains days ago. Her easiest route—and certainly
the one the Indians would expect her to take—was into
Tijeras canyon and then cling to the foothills of the
Sandias until Albuquerque lay far enough away for her
to be able to risk crossing the desert plain to the *bosque*
along the Rio Grande.

Tezzie made no attempt to put the paint into any
pace faster than a walk. As she threaded her way down
the canyon trail, it seemed as if her spirits sank with
the altitude. She had spent the better part of two weeks
in the mountains and was now no nearer finding Joel

than she had been at the beginning, and she knew that
the same was just as likely to be true of the next two
weeks, and of the two weeks after that. Yet, while she
searched, she had been able to hope. Now that she was
turning her back on the Sandias, she had the miserable
feeling she was abandoning hope altogether, even though
her common sense told her there was very little point in
doing anything else.

She made camp that night far enough away from the
mouth of the canyon to avoid being spotted by any
traveller heading perhaps for the turquoise-deposits in
the north. Her next camp was among the lowest trees
and in sight once more of the towers of Albuquerque's
church. When at last she felt she could safely swing to
the west and head for the river, she made use once more
of the network of dry watercourses, because the high
banks gouged out of the sand by the occasional rushing
torrents provided a cover that was quite lacking on the
broad sandy plain where sagebrush and chamiso, rabbit-
brush and stunted little junipers were the only ground-
cover.

She set off while the sun still rose and headed into a
cloudless sky of a blue that deepened and intensified as
the day wore on. By noon it was too hot to allow the
paint to continue, and she found some shade where a
juniper, more successful than most, had struggled to a
height of two feet. She tethered the paint to the shrub
and lay down in the small pool of shade. The Mexican
habit of sleeping during the heat of the day was a good
one! When the sun moved round and her head was no
longer in shadow, the heat would wake her up. If
anyone came near, her horse's whicker would disturb
her. With luck, they could expect an hour's rest.

It was the hot sun that finally woke her. She knew
she must be rested, although she did not feel as if she
were, and she almost envied the paint. He had obviously
benefited from the siesta: he had something closely akin
to a spring in his step. That might be because he already
smelt the water of the river somewhere beyond the

distant dark line of the *bosque*, but whatever the reason, he had become uncharacteristically skittish. Had Tezzie been better acquainted with horses, she would have been less easily satisfied with this explanation of his behaviour.

The sun still blazed down on the desert, but its warmth did nothing to lift the depression that settled more firmly on her spirits with every passing hour. Only the knowledge that it would be unwise to return to the Indians' hunting-grounds and the suspicion that to do so would be fruitless prevented her from retracing her steps.

The combination of her downcast spirits and the need to keep more of her attention on the horse than she was accustomed to doing, resulted in her pressing on resolutely westwards with never a backward glance. As a consequence, she saw only the blue skies ahead and above and was totally unaware of the thunderheads massing behind her over the mountain peaks. The huge, towering clouds the Indians called 'male rains' grew larger and higher, and turned from white to ever-darkening grey until the mountains themselves changed from green and grey to purple, and it was sometimes difficult to tell where mountains ended and clouds began. When the storm burst, the tops of the mountains were invisible to anyone looking at them.

Tezzie was not. Lost in her own thoughts, she and the paint pursued their steady way down the *arroyo*, Tezzie, at least, oblivious of the flash-floods that were even now gouging their way down the thousands of watercourses towards the plain on which not a single drop of rain had fallen. Only the horse was aware that, for some reason he did not understand, things were not as they should be, and he grew still more restive and difficult for his inexperienced rider to control.

She heard the roar of the torrent only seconds before she saw it, and frantically put the paint at the bank. But the bank was higher here and slightly overhung. The surging, sand-filled yellow deluge was upon them before the paint had done more than scrabble for a foothold. It knocked his legs from under him, and as he fell sideways into the tumbling waters, Tezzie found herself struggling alone for a brief second until the flood closed over her head and bore her downstream.

CHAPTER FOURTEEN

TEZZIE SURFACED once and gasped, filling her lungs with precious air before she was submerged once more. She had no control over her direction and could feel her arms and legs flailing in the water, not with the deliberation of one seeking to reach the bank but with the involuntary confusion of one controlled by a far superior force.

Only when she surfaced a second time was she conscious of any change, of a power to resist the intense force that held her in its turbulent grasp. A tight band pinned one arm to her side, though the other remained free, and she felt herself dragged against the current to the bank which here, several hundred yards further downstream than the place where she had first gone under, was only two or three feet high, and the stream-bed broader, so that the waters were marginally less deep.

The band bit painfully into her chest but at least she could breathe, and her free hand clutched at the top of the bank, pulling handfuls of sand down and gaining no purchase. Then her free hand was grasped firmly from above and she was hauled, coughing and spluttering, on to the safe, dry land beside the stream-bed. The worst of the torrent was already well on its way towards the Rio Grande, and all that was left just here was a swiftly moving yellow stream that would be gone by the morrow.

'At least you're alive,' said a deep, familiar voice. 'What sort of a damn-fool thing were you doing, riding down an *arroyo* at this time of year?'

She shook her head as if to clear a cloud from her

brain. Her mouth found the word, 'Joel?' but only a cough spluttered out.

'Don't waste time trying to talk. You can't, not yet.' As he spoke, he swiftly untied the lariat with which he had pulled her from the water. Then he wrapped her in a blanket. Neither cold nor shock had reached her yet, but both would do so before long.

He picked her up and carried her to his horse. 'Bear up a bit longer, Tezzie,' he said. 'The open desert is no place to spend the night if it can be avoided. There's an empty adobe on the edge of the *bosque*. I'm taking you there. Let's hope the cold doesn't eat into your bones before we reach it.' He swung himself up behind her and pushed his horse into a comfortable, mile-consuming amble, only pausing to collect the paint which had scrambled ashore as soon as the bank was low enough and, having shaken the water out of his coat, was now browsing contentedly among the scattered sagebrush. He had trodden on and broken one rein, but the other was soon fastened round Joel's saddle-horn, and the paint exhibited no resentment at being obliged to accompany the other horse.

Tezzie was conscious of nothing except that she was no longer being tossed and tumbled. Then, insidiously, she became aware that she was both cold and wet. Long before they reached the little adobe, her teeth were chattering and the uncontrolled shivering had begun. Joel pressed the horses on faster. A blazing fire was the first necessity.

The little homestead consisted of only one room, but its owners must have had notions of grandeur, for it had a tin roof and a pot-bellied iron stove stood in one corner, its rickety, rusting chimney poking up through the roof. Joel put Tezzie down on the earth floor before removing the saddle from the one horse and the blanket from the other, and turning both horses out in the adobe-walled corral. There was plenty of last fall's tumbleweed to start a fire, and a quick foray into the *bosque* behind the house produced enough dry cottonwood to ensure a blaze for the time being, at least. Once Tezzie was dry, warm and perhaps asleep, he would search for enough wood to see them through the night.

Both the paint's blanket and the one Joel had wrapped round Tezzie were now thoroughly saturated, and once the fire was blazing in the stove, he propped them up behind it to dry out as quickly as possible. Joel had no hesitation in stripping Tezzie's drenched clothing from her shivering body: she was in no state to do it for herself, and she must get dry as soon as possible. He had a spare shirt in his bed-roll, and he eased her into it much as a parent dresses a baby. On top of the shirt he put his warm sheepskin coat, an essential garment for anyone who habitually slept in the cold night air of the deserts and mountains. Then he sat on the floor in front of the roaring stove with Tezzie cradled in his arms. He rocked gently backwards and forwards as one rocks a child and very, very slowly, as the warmth stole gradually back into her cold and aching body, the shivering subsided into occasional spasms and finally ceased altogether as, at last, she slept.

Joel continued to hold her for a long time, reluctant to let go of something he had so nearly lost for ever. Only the need to fetch more firewood obliged him to lay her gently down by the stove and cover her with the now dry blankets. When he had gathered enough fuel to see them through the night and beyond, he sat opposite her, tailor-fashion, keeping watch through the night.

Tezzie slept the sleep of sheer exhaustion, and it was the smell of coffee brewing on the top of the pot-bellied stove that eventually wakened her. She stirred and murmured unintelligibly, before her eyes opened to see Joel looking anxiously down at her. She shook her head as if to clear the clouds of sleep.

'Joel?' she said.

'Who else? How are you?'

Tezzie thought about that. 'Stiff,' she said. 'Still tired, too, I think.' She paused as if canvassing her system. 'I ache all over as if I had been beaten black and blue,' she concluded.

'You have been—by the *arroyo*.' He picked the enamelled pot up from the stove-top and poured some black coffee into a tin mug. 'Here. This will make you feel better. In a day or two you'll be back to normal. Could you manage some breakfast?'

She suddenly knew she was hungry. 'Is there any?'

'Bacon and flapjacks. Will that do?'

She nodded, and watched him fetch the skillet and slice bacon into it from a hunk in his saddle-bag, and while that sizzled tantalisingly, he kneaded the little cornflour cakes that would fry in the bacon fat. There was only the one tin plate, just as there was only the one mug, so they shared it. When Joel had had all he needed, he stood up. 'Help yourself to coffee,' he said. 'There's bread in the saddlebag if you're still hungry. I must water the horses and find some fodder for them.'

' "Horses"?' Tezzie echoed. 'You mean the convent's paint is all right?'

Joel grinned. 'He scrambled out under his own steam with only a broken rein to show for it! He's fine.'

When he came back, Tezzie had found her own clothes, now completely dry, and had put them on. 'What is this place?' she asked.

He shrugged. 'What it appears to be, I suppose. It's been empty for over a year—only the tin roof has stopped it reverting to a heap of mud. I've stayed here quite often: it's a good place. A young couple lived here, but they decided to move into Albuquerque, or so it's said.' He looked around him. 'They must have been crazy. This place is perfect: it's got water, timber, grazing. Dig an *acequia* and some *sangrias*, and you've got fertile, irrigated land. What more could they ask?'

Tezzie laughed. 'You sound like a farmer, not a frontiersman,' she said.

'I suppose that's what I am, at heart,' Joel said, in the surprised voice of one thinking about it for the first time. 'I could certainly do things with this place.'

Tezzie nodded. 'I wonder how long they were here? It's got a long way to go before it compares with the Vigils' home, but they certainly started well, with a tin roof and an iron stove.'

'There's a *horno* outside, too, though it needs some work on it before it can be used,' he told her, and then changed the subject abruptly. 'Tezzie, why were you riding down a stream-bed at this time of year? You know better than that, surely?'

She flushed. 'I was so anxious not to be seen that I just didn't think.'

He look perplexed. 'Anxious not to be seen? Why? The Indians told me you were looking for me. They knew where you were headed, so you must have expected me to follow. Why, then, try to be concealed?'

'Not from you. From people going to or from Albuquerque. Valdez turned up and accused me of attempting to murder him. I've no desire to be taken by some bounty-hunter! Besides, I didn't expect you to follow me—I hoped, maybe, but I didn't expect. The Indians gave me the impression it might be a long time before they saw you again.'

Joel frowned. 'Valdez' charge should soon be disposed of. I doubt if he'll hang around long enough to offer evidence, anyway.'

Tezzie smiled grimly. 'Oh, he won't be giving any evidence,' she said. 'He was on my trail. He's up in the Sandias now, but he's dead. I killed him—and this time it was entirely deliberate,' she added with a hint of defiance.

He whistled. 'Is he likely to be found?'

'By the Indians, perhaps. By coyotes and mountain lions, certainly.'

'Then you've nothing to fear. If you turn yourself in, there will be no one to dispute your account and the case will be dismissed. Valdez was known and loathed in the Albuquerque area. Why not go to the *alcalde*? He'll certainly put in a word on your behalf.'

Tezzie shook her head. 'I'll not appear in another

court, and certainly not one in Santa Fe! I'd rather stay on the run.'

The deep bitterness in her voice told him that there was much he still did not know. He put a hand out to her. 'What happened, Tezzie?'

She turned away, and her voice quivered. 'I can't tell you, not yet,' she said. 'Can we leave it?'

'Sure, if that's what you want.' Joel looked at her doubtfully. Maybe the sooner she talked about things, the better. He longed to sweep her into his arms to tell her that nothing mattered except that she was alive and they were together, but he knew instinctively it was too soon for that. It would be best to let her pick her own time—for the present, at any rate. Maybe he might have to force her to face whatever it was that was bothering her, but the time was not yet.

Joel made no further reference to the matter, but busied himself instead stacking wood against the house so that they had a plentiful supply to hand. Tezzie began to help him, but she moved with obvious pain and eventually stopped, occupying herself instead with tying juniper fronds to a straight pole so that she had a rough broom with which to sweep the packed earth of the floor. The complete absence of furniture bothered neither of them: Joel slept on the ground more often than not, and Tezzie was fast forgetting the luxuries of civilisation that both the Vigils and the nuns had provided.

They dined on jack-rabbit that evening, and when the clean-picked bones were sizzling in the stove and they wrapped themselves up in their blankets for the night, Tezzie was reminded of that first night she spent with Joel in Frijoles caves. Then she had been terrified that he would take her. Now, it seemed, he had no interest. She only half remembered the preceding night when she had fallen asleep cradled in his arms. It was obvious he had no intention of repeating the exercise, and though she yearned to feel his arms round her once more, it was not something she could suggest with any decency.

When she woke next day, her muscles were miraculously eased and the bruises she had suffered were coming along nicely: that is to say, they now looked worse than they felt. Her relief at this improvement in her condition was tempered by the discovery that there was no sign of Joel, but her brief sense of panic was calmed when she realised that his horse was still in the corral. Joel's absence was immediately explained when he returned with a pair of handsome catfish for breakfast.

Food was obviously a subject which was weighing on his mind. When they had eaten, he asked her if she had any idea what she wanted to do.

'If we're going to stay here for any length of time, I'll need to go into Albuquerque for supplies,' he said. 'I've some flour, but not much—not for two of us. We need beans as well, and chilis. Some more bacon wouldn't come amiss.'

'Were you planning to see the *alcalde* as well?' Tezzie asked warily.

'Not if you don't want me to. You're going to have to trust me, Tezzie, you know.'

'I know that. I don't think there's anyone other than you and the nuns I can trust,' she said warmly. 'I think it would be a good idea to stay here awhile. Maybe I can get things straight in my mind in a day or two. If you want to go into Albuquerque today, I'll be all right here on my own.'

'You're sure?' Joel seemed doubtful.

'I'm tougher than you think,' she told him. 'Do you know, I hardly ache at all today.'

When he returned, the floor of the adobe had been swept, fresh wood was stacked outside, and a neat pile of juniper fronds in one corner would, with a blanket spread over them, make a softer bed than the hard floor. Tezzie had been busy.

So had Joel. When he had unloaded the supplies he had bought, which included more coffee and an additional blanket, he threw her something else: some

ndigo-dyed cotton. When she shook it out, she saw it
vas a triple-tiered skirt of the sort worn by Navajo
vomen.

'I thought you'd like it better than those trousers,' he
aid. 'There's this, too.' He took a concho belt out of
is saddlebag. 'You seem to have lost the one we gave
ou before. This isn't the same, I'm afraid.'

Tezzie's face glowed. 'I don't mind,' she assured him.
It will look even better. Go outside and find something
o do. I must try them on.'

Joel laughed and forbore to remind her that he had
o recently had no choice but to strip her down to her
kin. She seemed to have forgotten it, and her present
nodesty did her no disservice in his eyes.

When she appeared in the sunlit doorway and shyly
alled his name, she looked both pleased and anxious.
It feels right,' she said. 'I need you to tell me how it
ooks—I've no mirror.'

He looked at the full skirt that swirled softly round
er slim body, ending enticingly just above her ankles—
n eminently sensible length to which, when he had seen
t on Indian women, he had given no thought, but now,
n an Anglo one, seemed oddly seductive, particularly
llied to bare feet. Her waist was cinched in by the belt,
ach silver medallion inset with turquoise accentuating
ts tiny span.

Joel looked her up and down. 'It looks very well,' he
aid. 'The Indian style suits you.'

'Does it really look all right?' she insisted. 'You're
ot just being polite?'

He came over to her, laughing. 'No, I'm not just
eing polite.' He gazed down into the green-flecked eyes
hat looked anxiously up at him, the need for reassur-
nce still in their depths, and as he gazed, he knew he
vas lost. He drew her to him, and her heart sang as she
velcomed his embrace and felt his lips on hers in a
ender, caressing kiss that felt as if it might never end.
Vhen it did, and he drew his head back, he said,
Convinced?' and she laughed.

He kissed her again then, before the laugh was entirely done, and because her mouth was already open, there was an urgency in his kiss that was echoed by her response. There was no need for words when he led her back into the house and closed the door on the desert outside. She offered her face willingly then, and her body sought to be as close to his as it could contrive. As his mouth pressed hard on hers and their tongues met in erotic, silent dalliance, his fingers gently unbuttoned the man's shirt she wore and then, gently, enticingly, sought the soft, sensuous white curve of her breasts. The breathless quiver that shook her body intensified the desire he had always felt for her, and soon that shirt lay discarded on the ground. He caught his breath when he saw her then. He had seen her naked breasts before, but this was different. This was as much by her will as his, and when he lifted her into his arms and sank his lips on each rosette in turn before carrying her the few short steps to the blanket-smoothed junipers, there was no resistance, only a deep and shuddering sigh.

But when he had laid her down, there was a subtle change in her—a stiffening. He kissed her softly. 'We both know what will happen,' he told her gently. 'I love you, Tezzie. If you prefer me to stop now, you have but to say the word.'

There was agony in Tezzie's eyes, an agony he longed to kiss away. 'You can't love me,' she whispered. 'You can't. It isn't possible. You don't know.'

'Why isn't it possible, my love? What don't I know?'

She turned her head away. 'I have dreaded this moment,' she said miserably. 'Joel, I love you, too, but it isn't . . . I'm not . . . you're not the first.' The last words came out in a rush, and although her face was turned from him, he could sense the tears welling in her eyes.

'I didn't think I was,' he said gently. 'Were you a willing partner before?'

'No!' The answer came with all the vehemence of

loathing. 'No, and no, and no again! It was . . . It was
the men who captured me and sold me to Valdez. They
didn't keep me long, thank God, but while they did . . .
I was alway tied, Joel. I had no choice, I swear.' She
hesitated, recalling his words. 'You knew?'

'I guessed. Something you once said.'

'I'm sorry, Joel. I know it makes it impossible for
you to love me. I've been telling myself that for a long
time.'

'I'm sorry, too—for you. No woman deserves such
brutality, and I would be lying if I denied I would
rather be the first. But love is not impossible: I guessed
how it was with you and still fell in love with you. I
love you no less because my guess is confirmed. Will
you believe that?'

She turned to look at him then. 'You really mean
that?'

'I never meant anything more.'

She flung her arms round his shoulders then and laid
her head against his chest, sobbing with a mixture of
relief and happiness. Joel held her close to him until the
sobs subsided, and then held her face in his hands to
kiss the tears away. Only then did his strong hands
gently, lovingly caress her back, a soft intimation that
nothing had changed.

Tezzie looked up at him shyly. 'Joel,' she said
hesitantly, 'I am . . . a little frightened.'

He kissed her. 'There is no need. 'You'll find that
love makes a world of difference.' He put her belt aside
and slid his hand beneath the waistband of her skirt,
pulling her gently towards his thighs. 'Come,' he whispered. 'Return the compliment.'

Blushing involuntarily, Tezzie unfastened his shirt
and found her lips overcome with a desire to bury
themselves in the thick black curls that disguised the
muscles of his chest. Shocked at herself, she glanced
apprehensively at Joel's face, more than half expecting
to see a reflection of that shock there. Instead, there
was only gentle, understanding amusement in his eyes.

When they lay together naked, it was as if all that had happened so far were but preliminaries, and for the first time, Tezzie knew the true demanding urgency of a love whose ultimate expression could only lie in the climax of physical union. Joel trod a difficult path. He knew that her trust in him, while absolute, was a fragile thing. He must needs tactfully and skilfully bring her to their union while somehow avoiding anything that might remind her of the violent past. When she moaned and her thighs parted at the gentle stroking of his fingers, he knew the time had come, and that she would be his without reservation.

Tezzie welcomed him as she had never thought to welcome any man, seeking only to be ever closer in the thrusting, pulsing crescendo of their bodies, and when the world exploded into flower-strewn fields of ecstasy, they both knew that only the present and the future mattered. The past was finished for ever.

It was dark before they stirred in each other's arms; the fire had burned low. The room was chilly now, and Tezzie snuggled closer in the warmth of Joel's arms.

'We haven't eaten,' she said apologetically.

'We'll live,' he murmured, kissing her.

She chuckled. 'That's not all,' she went on. 'I'm still no nearer knowing what I should do. Further, in fact, because I don't seem able to think at all.'

'There's nothing to think about,' he told her, kissing her again, and there was silence once more in the little room while he convinced her that only their love was worthy of consideration.

'What should I do, Joel?' she said at last, and there was an entreaty in her voice which told him not to evade the issue. He propped himself up on one elbow and looked down at her, her pale body gleaming like marble in the shadows of the little house.

'I think perhaps you should marry me,' he said.

Tezzie was glad that it was probably too dark for him to see the colour rush to her cheeks. 'That's what anyone would advise if they knew . . . if they had just seen . . . Well, if they knew about the last few days. But nobody does, so you don't have to offer for me. I was asking for sensible suggestions!'

'I can't think of a more sensible one,' he pointed out. 'I don't intend to let you get away from me again, and whether we stay here or roam the Territory, I don't think I could face my aunt if I hadn't made an honest woman of you.'

Tezzie sat bolt upright. 'Face your aunt?' she exclaimed. 'Is that the best reason you can think of?'

'No, but it's a pretty powerful one, don't you think? he teased, and then, realising that it was unkind to tease her on something so important, his voice softened. 'The best reason—the only reason—is the one you already know. Tezzie, I love you, Can't you believe that?'

'I want to! Part of me does. Part of me isn't quite sure if it's possible.'

'It's possible. My only problem is wondering how long it has been so. I think it began the first time I saw you washed and clean in that ill-fitting habit.'

She looked at him wonderingly. 'You felt something then? So did I, though I had no idea what.'

'I had an idea, but I pushed it from me and stayed away for three years. Tezzie, all that is done. I love you. For God's sake put me out of my misery! Will you marry me?'

'Your aunt said you'd find a good woman, settle down and raise a family. Was she right?'

'Isn't that what I'm saying?' His exasperation was tinged with something very close to fear now, fear that she would refuse him for some reason not yet made clear.

'I don't think I'm a very good woman,' Tezzie said in a small voice, and Joel realised with sudden humility that the past was not as dead as he had hoped.

He put his arms round her and kissed her deeply and lovingly. 'You're the only woman I could bear to settle down with. The only woman I want to give me sons. I love you, Tezzie! There is not one ounce of my being that does not love you. You have only to say the word, and we can be married in Albuquerque tomorrow.'

'Then, yes, Joel Kanturk! I'll marry you in Albuquerque tomorrow.' She chuckled. 'After all, I wouldn't want you to be afraid to face your aunt!'